REST HOME
RUNAWAYS

What Reviewers Say About Clifford Henderson

Advance Praise for Rest Home Runaways

"A search for one last shot at freedom leads four elderly runaways on an adventure that at once touches the heart, and leaves readers rooting for the 'escapees.' This is a beautiful, heartfelt story."—Randy Peyser, author of *Crappy to Happy* as seen in the movie, *Eat Pray Love*

"Geriatric anarchy breaks out in this poignant and funny new novel by Clifford Henderson, who writes with verve and compassion about the loss of self-determination that comes to the elderly and the difficulties that descend on their children. Underlying this fast-paced story is one clear message to our older selves: *Do what you need to do. Give them hell.*"—Elizabeth McKenzie, author of *Stop That Girl*

Maye's Request

"Henderson has a way with oddball families. ...The novel's serious subject matter—shattered families, religious fundamentalism, emotional instability—is balanced nicely by Henderson's flair for lighthearted prose that carries the narrative without undercutting the serious issues she explores."—Richard Labonté, *Book Marks*

"Clifford Henderson takes the reader on a frightening journey of physical, emotional and spiritual illness to a place of love, enlightenment, healing and forgiveness. There are times in this story that will be difficult to read, but you will feel no choice but to continue because the writing gently nudges you forward to come out the other side, hopefully unscathed. *Maye's Request* is Clifford Henderson's third novel, and like the others before, she continues to excite, enthrall and entice."—*Out in Jersey*

"I truly laughed out loud at some passages and cried at others. A beautifully written and touching story of love, healing, family, and truth. Ms. Henderson has made me an instant fan!"—*Bibliophilic Book Blog*

The Middle of Somewhere

"The characters in this book are easy to relate to, I found myself caring about their struggles, and celebrating their triumphs. ...Clifford Henderson writes with depth and ease. Her writing gives you the sense that her muse was not only visiting, but had moved in."—*Out In Jersey*

"...Henderson grabs her readers in a firm grip and never lets go. *The Middle of Somewhere* is a wonderful laugh-out-loud read filled with pathos, hope, and new beginnings."—*Just About Write*

"I loved this book. I was laughing from the first paragraph all the way to the end, and in the meantime fell in love with all the characters. Although this is Henderson's first published novel her writing is replete with complex characters and a full-bodied plot, sort of like a well-rounded Merlot. I can't help but give this book a hearty two-thumbs up review and hope that you'll read it. I know you'll enjoy it just as much as I did."—*Kissed by Venus*

Spanking New

"Clifford Henderson has written a masterpiece in *Spanking New*. ... Henderson's clever exploration of her protagonists' feelings leads the reader into a world where gender and identity are fluid. *Spanking New* should be a required reading for all gender and queer study courses. While the author addresses serious issues, her book is fun, fun, fun! The playfulness, curiosity and fresh naivety as portrayed through the eyes of the story teller is refreshing and often humorous. It is pure genius on Henderson's part to write from this perspective. The protagonists are endearing and very human as you follow their struggles to navigate through life. The reader is able to sympathize with the antagonist's feelings as well, in this richly developed exploration of human being's struggles to make sense of their worlds."—Anita Kelly, LGBT Coordinator, Muhlenberg College

"*Spanking New* is a book that brings the fantasy of what happened before I was born, to life. If you have ever wondered what you were, or where you came from, Clifford Henderson gives you an interesting, oft times hilarious answer. The gender benders in this book are lovable characters, the most memorable being "Spanky" the "floating soul" that is looking to attach to his parents. When Spanky finally does manage to finagle a meeting of his soon to be parents Nina and Rick, the sparks fly, and all seems right with the world that he is about to enter, until Spanky finds out he is a girl! Other than being hilarious, this a poignant point of view, and makes for a fun and interesting read."—*Out In Jersey*

"Clifford Henderson took a warm look at people in her first novel, *The Middle of Somewhere*. She continues her warm looks in *Spanking New*. *Spanking New* is a book I found myself talking about with others, and one which I won't soon forget. This is a wise and funny book."—*Just About Write*

Visit us at www.boldstrokesbooks.com

By the Author

The Middle of Somewhere

Spanking New

Maye's Request

Rest Home Runaways

REST HOME RUNAWAYS

by

Clifford Henderson

2014

REST HOME RUNAWAYS

© 2014 By Clifford Henderson. All Rights Reserved.

ISBN 13: 978-1-62639-169-7

This Trade Paperback Original Is Published By
Bold Strokes Books, Inc.
P.O. Box 249
Valley Falls, NY 12185

First Edition: August 2014

CREDITS
Editor: Cindy Cresap
Production Design: Susan Ramundo
Cover Design By Sheri (graphicartist2020@hotmail.com)

Acknowledgments

I would like to start by acknowledging the dead. Specifically, Bob Wiggins who rarely spoke of Joy, his deceased wife of fifty-plus years and friend/mentor of mine. When I asked him why he never spoke of Joy, he looked at me quizzically and said, "Because she's with me all the time," a statement which planted the seeds for *Rest Home Runaways*. I'd also like to thank my dear friend Phil Slater, who, along with the rest of my writing group, helped midwife this novel. His words of wisdom live on in my mind.

Now, on to the living! Buckets of thanks to Dixie Cox, my partner of twenty-three years, who listens to the first draft of everything I write and braves my blustering ego to tell me what's not working; to Sallie Johnson and Gino Danna who helped me track this novel during our weekly group meetings; to my mom, a retired English teacher, who proofs for me when she isn't out bird watching; to my amigas María del Toro and Stephanie Mendoza for allowing me to be an honorary Mexican (even if I do cut my burritos in half with a knife), to the fine writers Elizabeth McKenzie and Randy Peyser who were kind enough to endorse *Rest Home Runaways*, and to Bookshop Santa Cruz for always being there for me.

And none of this would have happened without the incredible Bold Strokes Books staff. Especially the super human Len Barot; my eagle-eye editor, Cindy Cresap; and the person who has the fastest turn around on e-mails I've ever seen, Sandy Lowe. Thank you.

Lastly, of course, I want to thank you, the reader, for completing the circle. Enjoy!

Dedication

For my dad whose mind, blessedly, is still as sharp
as a much-loved wood chisel.

CHAPTER ONE

Mac scowled at the scatter of puzzle pieces on the round wooden table. It was ridiculous to even try. The damned macular degeneration robbed him of any clarity, except out of the corners of his eyes. Morgan had given him the puzzle, hoping it would bring purpose to his life. He couldn't blame her. She was trying to make the best of a bad situation. No one wanted useless elderly parents moving in.

He cocked his head to the side, giving his left eye a shot at the confetti of interlocking pieces. It wasn't one of the thousand-piece puzzles they did together when she was a girl. Same kind of picture though: windmill, bunches of tulips. Morgan always liked the ones of faraway places.

"Try that one," Effie said, pointing to a blue edge piece.

He picked up the piece and locked it into place. "Bingo." At least he and Effie were in this together. He couldn't imagine going through this humiliating stage of his life alone—even if she did make him fit the pieces together, as if *she* weren't actually doing the puzzle. But they were coping as best they could, yes siree Bob. "I'm going to put some water on for tea. You want some?"

"I'm good," she said without looking up.

"Well, don't do anything crazy while I'm gone."

She wrenched her attention away from the puzzle long enough to stick her tongue out at him then went back to scanning the pieces.

Since the remodel, Morgan and Treat's house was all angles, etched glass, and fancy blond wood furniture. Mac supposed all the houses in the trendy Tower District of Fresno had been similarly done up. The artsy section of town made a point of disassociating itself from the rest of the city's conservative style. He supposed that's what had attracted his daughter and her...wife. Boy, that was hard to get used to. Not that he didn't like Treat, but two women getting married? Of course, things hadn't been going too well between the two of them. He'd heard the whispered arguments, seen the sad looks. But it was none of his business. Morgan had made that clear on more than one occasion.

He walked past Morgan's god-awful collection of Mexican folk art—all skeletons and gaudy colors—into the kitchen with its high-maintenance granite countertops and impractical open shelving. Bright canisters marked *Flour, Sugar, Cornmeal* sat by the stove, all of them empty, save for the coffee one, which was always full of some special organic blend or other. The coffee maker itself looked like something made for outer space. Above the stove, Rosie the Riveter held her fist in the air: *We can do it!* She made Mac feel tired.

He filled the stainless steel kettle, flipped the front burner to high, and searched through a drawer of assorted teas for the one he'd finally figured out was actually tea. It was some gourmet brand they liked. Not all that different from good old Lipton's in his opinion.

"You building a boat in there?" Effie yelled.

Ignoring her, he plucked out a tea bag, dropped it into a mug, then returned to the living room. "God knows what all those other teas are," he said, joining Effie at the puzzle. "Saw one called *Women's Liberty.* It's supposed to *promote healthy hormone balance.*"

"If it helps with night sweats, I say more power to her. Remember how I used to wake up drenched in the middle of the night?"

Mac dimly recalled Effie flinging the sheets back and charging out of bed to stand under the ceiling fan. "I guess."

They stared at the puzzle for some time, neither of them finding a match. Effie pointed out a couple, but they weren't fits. Mac drifted off into his thoughts. Was that a new liver spot on his hand? A bruise? He barely recognized his hands anymore. His knuckles had gotten huge.

He pushed his chair back. "Water should be boiled by now."

"I'll get it. I've got to go to the bathroom anyway."

He watched her get up from the table and shuffle her way past the windowsill of wilting African violets to the kitchen. She was still an attractive woman, had kept her figure more or less, except for that soft little belly and her hair turning into a dandelion puff. Of course, he'd never say that to her.

"You old coot!" she called from the kitchen. "The kettle's barely even warm!"

"Is the whistle top on it?"

"Wasn't, but is now."

Mac massaged his forehead. Time had gotten so wobbly. A minute could last an hour. A whole day could slip by in a second. It was because there was nothing to do here. Sure, there were things that needed fixing, the spring on the door of the outside shed had a hinge that could use some adjusting, the downstairs bathroom sink had a drip, but he didn't have any tools here, not even a hammer or a screwdriver. And he couldn't drive to pick any up; they'd taken his license over a year ago. The bitter irony of it. He'd owned and run Ronzio's Hardware for over forty-five years and now didn't have a tool to his name! Of course, Treat had a motley collection out in the garage, but it was against Mac's principles to go rooting around in someone else's toolbox, a woman's no less. Resigned, he picked up the puzzle box top. There was a small bridge in the upper right-hand corner he hadn't noticed earlier. He searched for pieces of gray stone. That couldn't be so hard. He spotted one and locked it into place. "Got one!"

Effie returned to the table. "Well, bully for you."

Mac scanned for more gray stone. He was hot on the trail. He began sorting all the possible bridge pieces into a pile. They looked a lot like the slats on the windmill. Or were they wall pieces? His eyes began to sting. He rubbed them. He coughed a couple of times.

An intermittent shrilling blasted from the kitchen. He was momentarily confused. Teakettle? Hearing aid? No! Smoke alarm! He bolted up from the chair, his thighs banging painfully into the table, had to slow down around the carpet's edge—if you weren't careful you could catch your shoe—then tore into the kitchen.

It was filled with smoke! More coughing. More stinging eyes. He grabbed a dishtowel and reached over to turn off the burner. Success! Except the room was billowing black clouds. Morgan would kill him.

"You said you put the whistle top on the kettle!" he yelled to Effie.

Then he remembered. Effie was dead.

CHAPTER TWO

Morgan stood in her gutted kitchen and sniffed. It still stunk of smoke. They'd pulled the sheetrock, cabinets, and Pergo, and still that damn stench. Her recent cataract surgery made the exposed beams with their vein-like wiring and the splintery subfloor look all the more jarring. Like standing inside a corpse, she thought. She flipped on the big square floor fan and cranked open a window.

The idea of standing inside death fit her mood. It had been a hellish two weeks. Coming home to a house billowing black smoke; rushing her coughing, wheezing, disoriented father to the doctor who was more concerned about her dad being left unsupervised than he was about his symptoms. "He needs twenty-four hour care," the white-coated thirty-something said, steepling those ten arrogant fingers whose sole purpose seemed to be to accuse her of elder negligence. Then there'd been all the calls to the home insurance agency who suggested "a little TSP and good ol' elbow grease" would do the trick, as if just a potholder had caught fire. Add to this the zillion calls to adult live-in facilities with their mile-long wait lists, while her dad's house, still on the market after two long years, was as unsold now as the day they'd put it up for sale. They were going to need that money to pay the astronomical fees for eldercare. Then, miracle of miracles, there was a spate of deaths at Sunset Villa—not her first choice for an adult live-in facility, but doable, at least until something better showed up. Of course, the officious director who'd contacted her hadn't called it a "spate of deaths," she'd phrased it, "beds opening up," but anybody could tell what that meant.

And now he was there.

And she was here.

And she'd become the kind of person who put an elderly parent in a home.

The way he'd looked at her as she was leaving him there—not desperate, not begging her to stay, but resigned. Her hero-of-a-dad, the man to whom all of Fresno had once come to get things fixed, Mac Ronzio of Ronzio's Hardware, family-owned since 1949, stuck in an unfixable situation.

It wasn't as though she'd moved him in against his will. The teakettle incident had scared him too. Still, watching him meticulously arrange his few belongings on the dresser top had just about ripped out her innards: comb, photo of him and his beloved Effie, the little blue ceramic bowl for his change, the one Morgan herself made for him in third grade. The items looked so lonely in that foreign landscape.

Morgan returned her attention to what was left of her kitchen. Was it too wasteful to turn up the air conditioning with the window open? She decided not and cranked it open, wiping leftover greasy fingerprints of soot onto her jeans. Then she dropped what felt like her ten-ton purse onto a stack of clean sheetrock in what used to be her beautiful, sunlit breakfast nook, and stared at the mess that was her life. Apparently it wasn't bad enough that every other aspect of her life was floundering; now her kitchen—the hearth of the home she loved so much—was also a wreck.

She stepped cautiously over the snaky orange extension cord into the small laundry room, weaved her way through stacks of crammed boxes filled with flatware, pots and pans, dishes, and the rest of her kitchen junk, and opened the fridge. She hadn't eaten since, well, lunch when she'd ordered a side of fries instead of coleslaw with her BLT. But one couldn't worry about calories at a time like this. She pawed through the meat and cheese drawer of the fridge and found half of a block of smoked mozzarella under a baggie of suspect sliced ham. She ignored the sliced ham and broke off a chunk of cheese. She was a terrible daughter, a terrible person. She placed the chunk in her mouth and began chewing without tasting. Putting her father in an old folks farm. How could she?

She broke off another chunk, even though she was still chewing the first, her face wet with tears. Staring at this new chunk and hating herself for wanting it, she reminded herself of one of the positives of this terrible move: she and Treat were getting their house back, or what was left of it. Her dad living with them had put a terrible strain on their relationship. The two of them had had virtually no alone time. It didn't help that the only available room to put him in was directly across the hall from theirs, which had pretty much put a stop to making love. Morgan would freeze up at the slightest sound from him. So they were doing it less and less, choosing instead to watch TV. It was just...hard.

She plopped down next to her purse on the pile of crisp new sheetrock. Even before the kitchen incident, she'd known something had to change—and not just because her relationship was suffering. Her dad was becoming disoriented. She'd come home from work and hear him talking to himself, or worse, to her dead mom. It was heartbreaking.

And Sunset Villa wasn't *that* bad. They had a nice staff, experienced. One might even call it classy with its landscaped courtyard and Victorian décor. And she'd visit. A lot. The one bright spot of being furloughed was that she'd have plenty of time.

She looked at her watch. Fernando would be back from lunch any minute. But where was Treat? They were going to discuss cabinets. Morgan wiped the tears from her face and heaved herself off the sheetrock. Treat had promised to get off early so she could be in on the discussion.

Morgan stuck the last bit of cheese back in the fridge. Something must have come up. No doubt, something to do with Marky Gottlieb, Wonder Woman of Harmony Systems who, if their literature was to be believed, was "Unifying America's Workplace One Success at a Time." The two seemed to be in constant meetings these days, "brainstorming sessions" Treat called them. But how much brainstorming could it take to put together a sensitivity training for Treat's crew? Yes, Morgan understood that Treat was under a lot of pressure from corporate since having lost not one, but *two,* large, woman-owned accounts, and yes, she understood that Martha's Organics would be moving their merchandise in next month and corporate was breathing down Treat's neck to civilize her overly-testosteroned staff, but honestly, in weaker moments, Morgan was beginning to wonder if Marky was the reason Treat had started going to the gym and carrying around baggies of cut-up carrots and celery instead of her usual fried pork skins.

Morgan took the teakettle's rooster-shaped whistle top from the windowsill and stuck it in the shoebox with the serving spoons and spatulas. She was just being paranoid. If there was one thing Treat was, it was loyal.

She wandered into the living room where her dad's puzzle lay scattered on the table and began sweeping the pieces into the box, accidentally sweeping up a fortune-cookie fortune she'd gotten earlier in the week from yet another dinner of Chinese takeout: *Happy thoughts makes a happy life.*

The front door jangled open.

"Hey, hon," she said. "I was just about to give up on you."

"That's okay, *hon*," Fernando replied.

She looked up. Treat's contractor nephew was standing in the open doorway. He looked exhausted. "Hey, Fernando," she said. "Treat's not here yet."

He glanced up from his Android, his eyes ringed with dark circles. "I just got her text. She's running late."

Morgan made herself smile. There was probably a text waiting on her phone too. "Still no sleep? Is little Gustavo still colicky?"

"It's Alma who's getting no sleep. But my mom's coming over today to give her a break."

"You want something to drink?"

"I'm good. Had a big soda with lunch." He pocketed his phone and rubbed his bloodshot eyes. "Treat said we should go ahead and start. She'll catch up later."

"All righty then. Let's get to it."

They discussed cabinet styles and features, replacing the old hot water heater with a tankless and whether or not they wanted a lazy Susan by the stove. Still, no Treat. Morgan tried not to be annoyed, but life was hard for her too.

She tugged at the collar of her T-shirt. A hot flash was blooming in her chest and would soon been crawling up her neck and sprouting a mustache of perspiration. "So, you have what you need to give us a couple of estimates? One with the tankless, one without. And maybe, for the hell of it, let us know what a skylight would cost. I'm sure we can't afford it, especially if we go tankless, and the insurance won't cover it..." She hated the way her face flushed during hot flashes.

"I just need to take a few measurements."

"Great. I'll be upstairs if you need me."

He looked up from his clipboard. "I just realized, no Mac. Today was the day, huh? You took him to that place."

That place. It was all she could do to keep from bursting into tears again. Damn her hormones! "Yup." She could feel beads of sweat popping out on her lip.

Fernando cocked his head, his Mayan features a portrait of kindness. "Alma and I will take Gustavo by for a visit later in the week. That'll perk the old guy up."

Morgan managed to get out, "Dad would love that," before snatching up her purse and all but charging up the stairs, stopping only to grab her laptop from the living room couch.

Once in the bedroom, she tossed her purse and laptop onto the end of the bed and belly-flopped down next to them. *If only I could stay here a whole week,* she thought, her weary muscles sinking into the luscious memory foam topper Treat had bought them for Christmas. Her lower lip began to tingle. No! She hauled herself up, swung her legs off the bed, and dragged her feet into the bathroom. Sure enough, little blisters were beginning to gather on the edge of her lip. Tomorrow there would be an oozing canker sore in the shape of South America. It never failed.

She popped a couple of lysine capsules, peed, and popped a couple more for good measure, then returned to the bed, plumped the pillows up against the headboard, and powered up her laptop. *Happy thoughts!* She was not a bad person for putting her father away. Tons of people did. The adult care facilities were full of people's parents. Which, speaking of...

She reached for her purse, pulled out her iPhone, and auto-dialed her brother. He picked up on the second ring.

"Hey, Morgan. What's up?"

"I just wanted you to know we got Dad all squared away," she said in her chirpiest voice.

"Sorry. What was that?"

"I was just calling to say I got Dad all squared away."

"Oh, good. Good. Thanks for taking care of that."

Did he even know what she was referring to? "In the retirement home," she added.

"Right," he said. "That was today."

"Are you in the middle of something? Would there be a better time to talk?"

"No. This is good. I'm just on my way to a show a house—Stay in your own lane, asshole!"

Morgan pictured him, Bluetooth stuck in his ear, zigzagging through traffic. "I'll e-mail you his address and phone number. He'd love to hear from you."

"Sure. I'll get Lanie to send flowers."

Flowers. Was he kidding? "Mike. This is Dad we're talking about."

"I know. I know. I just have a hard time being around the old guy. I never know what to say." He paused, then added: "I'm not like you, Morgan."

"Not like me in that I'm an excellent communicator, or, not like me as in I'm a spineless dishrag?"

"You know what I mean."

"Mike, I haven't been caring for Dad because I have nothing better to do with my life. I have a full-time job, a relationship..." Morgan willed her voice to sound strong. "In case you've forgotten, Dad's got macular degeneration in both eyes now. He also talks to Mom like she's still alive—and let's not forget, he set my kitchen on fire."

There was a pause on his end. Morgan hoped she was getting through.

"While we're talking all things Dad," he finally said, "would you tell the renters in his house they might want to start looking. I think I have a bite."

Finally, some good news. "That's great! We're going to need that money for Sunset Villa."

"Oh, I was meaning to talk to you about that. Nancy and I are thinking of putting in a pool."

Morgan punched the end call button and leaned back into the pillows. *Happy thoughts. Happy thoughts.* She shut her eyes.

❖

"Morgan?"

She forced her eyes open. How long had she been sleeping? Five minutes? Fifteen? She scooted up to sitting, blinked a few times. Fernando was standing in the doorway making a point not to look at her. Had she been snoring? "What can I do for you?"

"Sorry to disturb you, but I tried yelling from downstairs."

"It's fine." She cleared her throat. "What do you need?"

"We forgot to talk about the cabinets in the pantry."

"Oh, right." She covered a yawn with the back of her hand. "I'll be right down."

"Take your time."

Morgan stared briefly at a pile of clean laundry on the chair waiting to be put away, thought, *One of these days*, then headed downstairs.

Fernando and she were mid-pantry discussion when Treat walked in the door. "Fernando! How's my favorite nephew?"

"Tia," he said, chuckling. "You say that to all of us."

They hugged like they hadn't seen each other just last week, Treat, short and stocky, and the slighter but still muscular Fernando.

"Yeah, well. You really are my favorite." She tussled his curly black hair.

Morgan knew how much Treat loved him. She'd been looking out for him since he was a squirt, giving him a place to hang out when his alcoholic father, her brother, got abusive, helping him to get his contractor's license, and now she was godmother to little Gustavo.

"I think we've picked out some nice cabinets," Morgan said.

Treat slung her arm over Morgan's shoulders and kissed the top of her head. "Sorry to be late, bonita, but it's been a hella bad day."

Treat's arm around her felt so good. She rested into it.

"Those punks at the warehouse causing you grief again?" Fernando asked.

"Those cabrónes, man, treating the lady customers like they don't know shit."

"Like Poppi."

"Exactly." Treat turned to Morgan. "How'd it go with Mac?"

Morgan pinched out a smile. "Hard, but he understands. And you saw the place; it's nice." Why did she feel like she had to defend herself? Even the doctor thought an adult live-in facility was a good idea.

Treat's nod did nothing to ease Morgan's guilt. She knew Treat's opinion about putting Mac in a home. Mexicans didn't do that. They cared for their own. But surely she had to see it was the right thing to do for their relationship? *Happy thoughts. Happy thoughts...* "Shall we talk cabinets?"

Fernando pulled out his book of cabinets to bring Treat up to speed.

Treat reached for it and there was a sharp *PING!* Something hit the floor. "Shit, man. I've lost so much weight my wedding ring keeps falling off." She bent over to sweep it up. But just the sight of that smooth gold ring bolting for the door made Morgan want to puke.

CHAPTER THREE

Cora gazed at the back of Sonia's head. Her friend's bottle-red hair seemed to get redder with each salon visit. But then maybe Cora was just feeling catty because Sonia had chosen to sit next to the Villa's newest bachelor, Mac Ronzio the hardware man, on their weekly van trip to the mall. Cora, sitting directly behind Sonia, watched as Sonia put the poor man through the usual initiation. She'd been at it since he'd arrived at the Villa two weeks ago. Which was interesting. Sonia usually decided within days whether a man was worthy of her time, but here she was still evaluating this Mac, giving him yet another round of what Cora liked to think of as The Dazzle Test. There were many versions of The Dazzle Test, all of them aimed at gauging the target man's responsiveness to Sonia's overwhelming charm, myriad talents, and extraordinary life, which ran the gamut from a yearlong torrid affair in an ashram to cattle ranching in West Texas and everything in between. This particular version of *The Test* involved Sonia making him endure the story of her "actress" days, how she got her big break when the lead of *Anything Goes* twisted an ankle and was unable to go on. But was Mac sufficiently dazzled? It was difficult to tell. He was such a well-mannered fellow, probably one of those who'd stay true to his dead wife 'til the end. He certainly mentioned her enough. Undying devotion to a dead wife wasn't necessarily a deal breaker for Sonia, so long as the target man understood she was Diva of the Living.

The stoplight seemed unusually long. Cora craned her neck to see past Mac's rumpled, light blue bucket hat. A stalled car in the left turn lane. John, the latest Villa driver, a young man who seemed much more suited to herding cattle than to herding old people, was just now flicking on the blinker. He was slow on the uptake and Cora hoped he wouldn't last long. The Villa went through drivers like antacid tablets.

Sonia rested a coral-tipped finger on her cheek and said to Mac, "But here I'm talking all about me. Such a selfish girl. Are you much of a theatergoer?"

He smiled politely. "Now and then. My wife, Effie, liked to go. Bought us season tickets a couple of times."

Sonia glanced back at Cora, an appreciative eyebrow raised. "Did you hear that, Cora? Season tickets."

"Very impressive," Cora said, relieved to feel the van start moving again.

Sonia returned her attention to Mac. "You don't think this color..." She brushed her hands over her fitted, lime green blouse. "...is too much? It's so difficult to know when you have coloring like mine."

Mac cleared his throat. "I don't know that you want to take fashion tips from me, but I think you look just right."

Sonia laughed her big throaty laugh. "A man who admits to his shortcomings. I like that."

He must be experiencing culture shock, Cora thought. What with Anthony Biddle, or "the Professor," as they all liked to call him, twisting around in his seat every few minutes and shouting, "Hey, Koonzie, what do you say we step out onto the balcony for a drink!" to which Shirley Peters, sitting next to the Professor, would snap, "Turn around! You're smushing the tube on my oxygen tank!" God knows, it had taken Cora longer than two weeks to acclimate to life at the Villa: the group activities, the perky staff—and all the *old* people. She knew it was silly not to include herself in the latter group. She was eighty-one, for God's sake! But she still had two good legs, a strong heart, and a sound mind—unlike many of the residents who tottered around the halls, hair unkempt, eyes vacant as black holes. Six years it had been since she'd accepted the fact that she couldn't care for her husband, Hubert, by herself, but it seemed like an eternity.

She touched the locket he'd given her before they'd married, rubbed her thumb across its golden filigree. She'd taken to wearing it again after his death, had stuck—of all things—one of his old contact lenses in it along with a tiny photo of him taken on their honeymoon. She'd found the single lens at the bottom of one his drawers when she was cleaning them out and couldn't bring herself to throw the tiny disc away. How it even got to the Villa, she couldn't imagine. He'd stopped wearing contacts long before they'd moved there, and hadn't worn the hard type since forever. Nevertheless, it reminded her of Hubert when he was in his prime, doing his morning routine: shave, brush his teeth, slap on aftershave, and pop in those lenses. She'd watched him do it thousands of times.

A familiar knot of emotion rose in her throat. Standing by Hubert while he slowly lost his mind, one agonizing memory at a time, was the most difficult thing she'd ever endured. If it hadn't been for Sonia, she'd have gone mad.

Sonia patted her hair—as though it needed it—the quartet of gaudy wedding rings she'd taken to wearing after the death of her most recent husband glittering in a shaft of light coming through the van window. "So, Mac, what do you think of a woman who, say, likes to have the door opened for her on occasion? Do you think she's old-fashioned?"

Cora only half-listened as Mac negotiated his way around Sonia's obstacle course. She just hoped that Sonia would find him worthy of their little coterie. Otherwise, he'd be doomed to the ranks of those Sonia referred to as the "untouchables." This included anyone with the slightest trace of Alzheimer's (they'd both done their time with that), those whose conversations revolved around their ailments (bor-*ring!*), and those whose political views were shaped by their religious beliefs (could they be any more narrow-minded?). But the greatest offense, Cora knew, was not to be dazzled enough.

So far, Mac seemed to be making the cut, laughing at Sonia's jokes as he dined with them nightly. Sonia had even invited him over once or twice for their afternoon gatherings in the community room. He was more reserved than most of Sonia's men, but a good man and easy around women. More than once Cora caught herself thinking that his wife, Effie, had been a lucky woman. He also seemed to have a comfortable relationship with his daughter, who came around daily—like they all did at first. She was a nice enough sort, a little frantic, but then, she was a career woman. Who knew what she was juggling? Cora had once seen her and her "friend" kiss when they thought no one was looking, making Mac all the more interesting.

Sonia slapped Mac's arm playfully. "But would you have the guts to tell a lady if she had spinach in her teeth?"

Mac cleared his throat again, this time adding an adjustment of the bucket hat. "Depends on the lady."

Cora sighed. She'd have to pull him aside once they got to the mall. *Don't take Sonia too seriously,* she'd tell him. *Her husband Klaus died two months ago, and since then she's taken flirting to a whole new level.*

It would take a strong man to live up to Sonia's backslapping, ass-pinching, astrophysicist, Klaus. Even toward the end, when he didn't recognize Sonia at all, he'd pull her in and give her a whopping kiss on the lips. Of course, he'd try it on the nurses too. And some of the residents. Had even tried it on Cora a time or two. It had been difficult for Sonia to be lumped in with all available females. But she'd stuck by him, her fourth husband, until the end, mourned him passionately for about two weeks, then seemingly moved on to replacing him. So different from Cora's quiet mourning of her Hubert, which went on for months...was still going on. Here it was, two years after his death—six after the death of his mind—and she couldn't imagine starting up with another man. All they'd see in her was a nurse or a purse. She'd *been* the nurse and was reluctant to give up the purse, which had been out of her hands until Hubert's decline. Now it was up to her to stretch it until the end.

Cora opened her favorite white leather purse and pulled out a mint. A small pleasure. She thought about offering them around, but there weren't enough. Bug-eyed Nell, buckled into Cora's right, eyed the roll of mints hungrily. Nell was an odd one in her Coke bottle glasses, and handbag slung across her chest like a Girl Scout, but Sonia, God knew why, had taken her under her wing, offering her Emma's—God rest her soul—mah-jongg spot and inviting her to dine with them. It wasn't that Cora didn't like Nell; she just couldn't get a bead on her. Her enthusiasm, about *everything*, was unsettling. She was sharp as a tack though, Cora gave her that, a real plus at the Villa.

"Would you like one, Nell?"

"Would I? I've had a sweet tooth since last night! That cottage-cheesy peach dessert in no way cut the mustard."

Cora noticed that Nell was wearing an electronic wristband again, resulting, she assumed, from the butterfly incident. It had to be. Word had it, Nell saw a butterfly through the long window by the front door and stepped out for a closer look then wandered down the block after it, a definite no-no at the Villa. One had to go through the proper procedures if one wanted to leave the premises. If you failed to do so, you got *the band*, which would set off an alarm if you walked through any of the exit doors, a policy implemented some years back when one of the Alzheimer's residents wound up dehydrated in a ditch off the highway.

Hubert had hated that band. He'd had no idea where he was, if he'd just taken a bite of Salisbury steak or tied his shoes, but he'd scratch his wrist raw trying to tear off that band.

"I hope the candy shop has finished its remodel," Nell said.

She really did look like a housefly in those thick glasses. "You and your caramels!"

"Well, I miss them."

Sonia twisted around in her seat. "One more day of listening to you whine about caramels and we'll be driven to the nut house." She put her finger to her temple. "Oh wait, we already live there."

Those in the van lucid enough to understand her laughed, including cantankerous old Irv Perloff, who never laughed at anything.

John made the turn into the mall parking lot. "Ready for shopping?" He always asked this in a talk show host voice, which Cora found annoying. But it was just another of the many little irritations of living at the Villa.

She'd considered moving after Hubert's death, but couldn't imagine where she'd go. Her friends were all here now. And she wouldn't dream of moving in with either of her boys. Their lives were full enough without taking her in. That, and they'd never offered.

John pulled up to the loading zone, shut off the engine, and cranked on the emergency brake. "All ashore who are going ashore!"

Cora braced herself for the unloading. It was going to be difficult getting out of the van. The larger bus, in for repairs, was so much roomier. At least they wouldn't have to stand around while

John helped out the wheelchair-bound. Unfortunate that they'd been deprived of the weekly outing due to lack of space in the van, but there was nothing to be done about it. As it was, the residents were required to wait outside the doors of the mall until everyone was unloaded and the van parked. Honestly, it was like being in grade school.

Mac followed Sonia off the van. Cora could see why Sonia was so taken with him. He was tall for one thing, a lovely feature in a man, and he moved with unpretentious elegance; and he was good with tools, improvising them out of the most unusual objects: a dime for a screwdriver, nail clippers for a staple remover. She wondered if he'd ever smoked. Hubert had smoked a pipe. It was one of the things she missed most after his death, the smell of that pipe.

"Our turn," Nell said.

Cora waited for Nell to scoot around the end of the seat then followed. John took her hand to steady her as she stepped down into the ghastly Fresno heat.

"Thank you, John."

"You bet, Mrs. Whittaker."

Sonia and Mac were already standing to the left of the mall door with a few others.

Cora and Nell strolled across the sidewalk to them. "So, Mac, what do you think of our mall?" Cora asked.

"I used to come here with Effie. She liked the bath shop."

He had the most beautiful blue eyes, sad though, as if something in him weren't quite resolved. Not unusual at the Villa. He'd come here to die, after all. And how many of us, she thought to herself, have done everything we've wanted to do with our lives?

She turned her attention to the unloading, shading her eyes from the blazing afternoon sun. John was helping Shirley Peters and her backpack of oxygen off the van. Two more to go. It could be a while.

"This is ridiculous," Sonia said. "We should go inside before we all melt."

Cora sighed. Once a single member of the group broke ranks, everything fell apart. Sonia knew it, too. They'd both been there for the Geraldine Thomas fiasco. It took hours to find her sleeping on one of the display couches at Macy's. "Be patient, Sonia. It'll just be a few more minutes." But Sonia would have none of it. She pushed through the door into the mall. Several others followed.

Cora was just about to join them—it *was* awfully hot—when she spotted the Professor striding across the parking lot toward a classic car parked next to the road. Normally a real lamb, he couldn't be trusted around classic cars. He'd spent his post-retirement, pre-Alzheimer's years restoring old cars and was now zeroing in on the old Pontiac like it was an empty podium waiting for his oration. Cora shot a look at the van. John was still inside. He couldn't possibly get to the Professor quickly enough. She'd have to round him up herself. She grabbed Nell. "Gather everyone inside the doors. I'm going after the Professor."

Nell scanned the parking lot until she spotted him. "Oh, dear."

The Professor was making good time, weaving through the parked cars. Cora trotted around the front of the van into the lot then heard a loud cracking thud followed by Shirley Peter's "Holy Crap!" Cora spun around. An SUV sporting a teenage driver, who was just now looking up from his texting, had plowed into the back of the van. But there was no time to deal with that, the Professor was picking up speed. She took a second to wave at John, to indicate that she was going after the Professor, then dashed off in hot pursuit. Poor John looked totally distraught.

It took her a good ten minutes to return the Professor to the fold. There was no forcing him. She had to make up a story about his being needed for an important meeting with a university president. John, now across the parking lot, appeared to be knee-deep in a heated argument with the kid from the SUV. He'd had to chase the hooligan down. The Villa residents, all back on the sidewalk, stood gaping at the action. Cora did a quick count: six on the sidewalk, two still in the van, she and the Professor, Sonia standing with Nell...But wait. Someone was missing. Mac!

CHAPTER FOUR

Mac sat on a toilet seat in the roomy handicapped stall of the men's restroom, pants still up. He needed space. Privacy. On the ride over, he'd been struck with what had to be claustrophobia. He took off his hat and ran his fingers through his thick salt and pepper hair. He'd *never* had claustrophobia. But with the van walls closing in on him, the shortness of breath, what else could it be?

Someone entered the restroom. He prayed they weren't handicapped. Or coming after him. He listened, sitting straight up, stock-still, as whoever it was used the urinal and left. He collapsed forward, elbows to knees. What was becoming of him? Hiding out in a public restroom like some kind of basket case.

He took a few breaths in this fetal-like position then straightened up to stare at the mint green walls. He'd been in this restroom before when he'd come to the mall with Effie. There were several shops she liked, one for her bath salts, one for her peppermints, and one that for the life of him he couldn't remember. He'd make the trip with her about every other month. She shopped; he picked up a cup of coffee and settled into one of the comfortable overstuffed chairs to people watch. It was as entertaining as anything on TV.

He pulled a piece of toilet paper from the roll and blew his nose. Now she was gone for good, boom, just like that. The Villa had scared her off. All the ridiculous activities—game night, crafts day, exercise class. But she could have snuck in at night. He stayed awake waiting.

Signing up for the mall trip had been a stupid idea. Squeezed in the van with all those women. And the Professor, boy, was that guy a piece of work. He kept calling Mac "Koonzie." Who the hell was Koonzie?

Mac twisted his wedding ring round and round on his finger. He was an outdated product, like that last box of Sen-Sen breath mints. How long had it sat in the display at Ronzio's before he'd finally tossed it? A year? Two? He kept it there out of sheer stubbornness, sure that one day—

"I hate to bust in on your little pity party, but you are one sorry sight sitting there on the toilet comparing yourself to a box of outdated candy."

"Effie…"

She was standing in the corner of the stall, looking as soft and comfy as ever in her green cardigan, pumpkin-colored turtleneck, and tan corduroy slacks. Thank goodness she hadn't appeared to him as her young self, as she sometimes did. He'd hate for young Effie to see him like this, hiding out in a mall restroom sniveling into a piece of toilet paper.

"I thought you'd left me for good."

"For heaven's sake, Mac. I was just giving you time to adjust to your new life."

"New life? Is that what you call it? Socked away in the Old Folks Farm?"

"I'm not here to talk about that. I'm here to remind you that you still owe me."

"Owe you?"

She leveled him with a steely look. "Why do you think you're stuck in the Villa?"

"A misunderstanding. I thought you said you'd put the whistle top on the kettle."

"My point, exactly."

"Effie—"

"I'm dead, Mac. D. E. A. D. Dead."

He knew what she said was true. Of course he did. But he knew it in the way that he knew the Earth was flying around the sun at a gazillion miles per hour. It wasn't something to focus on.

"You've got to stop acting like I'm not."

Mac chuckled. Dead or not, Effie was by far the most dominant presence in his life. They'd been together for sixty-two years—*sixty-two*. He wasn't even sure if this Effie, the one who'd started showing up after her death two years ago, was a ghost or something he'd cobbled together from memories and expectations. He'd tried to figure it out in those first few months, attempting to control her actions and words with his mind. But there was no controlling Effie, there never was. Over time, he quit worrying about the distinction; ghost or memory, he was glad to have her around.

"So, what's this that I owe you?"

"Later. First we've got to spring you from the Villa."

"Spring me from—Are you nuts? Where would I go? Besides…" He held up his wristband. "I can't get away."

"That's why we have to make our move now. When you're already out."

Was she kidding?

She huddled up next to him, close enough that they were almost touching—almost—and spoke through the side of her mouth, secret agent like. "When we drove in we passed that golf-carty thing."

He looked at her, incredulous. "The utility cart?"

"Exactly. That cute little four-wheeler the janitor drives around in. It was parked out by the loading dock—unattended." Effie wiggled her eyebrows.

"Effie. You need *keys*. And they only go about fifteen miles per hour."

Effie let out an exasperated sigh. "So you're not even going to try? You're just going to let your kids turn *you* into the problem—"

"I nearly burned Morgan's house down!"

She rolled her eyes. "Anybody could have done that."

"But anybody didn't. I did. I can't be trusted anymore."

She scowled at him over the rims of her tiger print dime-store glasses. "Do you really believe that? That you've gotten so old that all there is left to do is roll over and die?"

Mac scowled at the multiplying liver spots on his hands. Did he? Was there really nothing left for him? He'd been doing *fine* before the fire. Sure, he'd left the sprinkler on that time and nearly flooded out the basement, and he was forever forgetting to turn out lights, but he'd done those kinds of things when he was young too. No crime there. Maybe Effie was right. He was just a casualty of Morgan and Treat's struggles. They were having such a rough time. As for his son,

Mike, he hadn't even seen the Villa yet. Said he wouldn't be able to make it out until September.

"You in there, old man?" Effie said.

"Just thinking."

"Well, you better think quick. Our window of opportunity won't last forever."

The thought of the van ride home was enough to give him hives, the trio of women who'd more or less kidnapped him into their little cadre, the Professor calling him Koonzie—and the Villa itself with its dark wood paneling, fake plants, and attendants in noiseless white shoes. Claustrophobia began creeping its way back into his chest. "So what's this plan you have cooked up?"

Effie started toward the stall door. "Follow me." She turned to look at him. "Oh, come on, Mac. What have you got to lose?"

What indeed? He'd already lost everything he cared about. Except his kids. Truth be told, he was worried about Morgan. She'd been carrying the world on her shoulders as of late. What with her hours being cut back, and now with whatever was going on between her and Treat, she'd be devastated if something happened to him. She'd blame herself.

Effie folded her arms across her chest. "And don't tell me you're not going to do it because of that daughter of ours. That's just an excuse and you know it."

Was it? Mac wasn't so sure. But what was he really risking? Chances were the utility cart wouldn't even be there by now.

He tested one knee, then the other. Stiff, for sure. But workable. As were his feet, his hips. He stood, unlatched the lock on the stall, and followed Effie into the suffocating tunnel-like hallway. The walls were stark white and dotted with delivery entrances. Effie stood at the end with a glowing red "exit" sign above her. "I figure we can get to the loading dock this way," she said.

He crept down the hall and gently pushed the metal bar on the door. It clicked open onto a flood of heat and light—and fresh air. And there, parked in the loading dock, waiting dutifully like a chariot, was the utility cart, its keys dangling from the ignition. He glanced around, the sense of claustrophobia lifting. A young man snoozed on a plastic chair, his feet propped on a bucket.

Effie slid into the shotgun seat. "Cowabunga!"

CHAPTER FIVE

Morgan willed the chatting busboy to snap to and come clear her plate. There were two bites left of her Heartland Chicken Pot Pie. One bite really, at least for Morgan who had a tendency to gobble, but two bites for anyone else so it still counted. A health rag she'd read promised that a person could lose weight simply by adhering to this two-bite regime.

The bit of flaky crust and chunk of tender chicken looked so harmless just sitting there, the fluting of the pastry, the slight sheen on the milky sauce...Damn her cataract surgery! Her new eyes made everything look so delicious. She took a sip of water. Then another.

Marie Callender's was far enough off-campus that hopefully nobody from work would spot her. She was in no mood. Her office in Human Resources was revamping the *Campus Policies, Procedures, and Programs*, a bear of a job. On top of which, they were dealing with a particularly sticky whistle-blowing case. Everyone in the office was cranky. Especially since they were squeezing all this work around the staff's various furlough schedules.

She signaled the waiter. "I'm finished with this," she said sealing the deal by tossing her crumpled napkin on the plate.

He shot an annoyed look at the oblivious busboy then swept up the plate himself. "Dessert?"

"No. Thank you. But I will have a cup of coffee. Three creams, please."

"Will do." He glided off in his beautifully athletic body.

Youth. They had no idea what they had.

She eyed her cell phone on the table, its list of current voice mails, all of them listened to but for one: Treat's. There was the text from her too: LISTEN TO MY VOICE MAIL. PLEASE. Treat was a proud woman. This was as close to begging as she got.

Treat had crossed the line with Marky Gottlieb. She must have. Coming home so late the night before. Then feeding Morgan all that hogwash about "Marky's sudden brainstorm" and the two of them "loosing track of time" as she waded through her ocean of guilt to the bathroom then shut herself in there for close to a half hour before slinking into the bedroom. Morgan pretended to be asleep when she finally slipped into bed, and Treat went along with it—the coward. Then the two of them just lay for who knew how long—Treat steeping in her puddle guilt; Morgan a tight ball of self-righteous anger and hurt—until finally Morgan couldn't stand it anymore and grabbed her pillow and moved to the guest room. Treat had called out "Honey?" but hadn't had the guts to brave the slammed door.

It wasn't supposed to go like this. Once they'd gotten her dad moved out, everything was supposed to get better.

She should have seen it coming. Treat coming home from her sessions with Marky all pumped up about the corporate trainer's "amazing ideas" and "disciplined business protocol," her "cool iPad apps." It didn't hurt that Marky was gorgeous—if you liked that muscled femme look—and probably fifteen years younger.

Morgan checked the time. 2:05.

Treat and Marky would be smack in the middle of the sensitivity training for Treat's bunch of roughneck warehouse workers. Morgan pinched the bridge of her nose, wishing she could take back the day she handed that stupid Harmony Systems brochure to her. Hundreds of glossy tri-folds passed through Morgan's office, all of them promising miraculous results in teambuilding, brainstorming, ice breaking, leadership skills. Ninety percent of them wound up in the trash. Why, *why,* then when Treat moaned about needing to put together a sensitivity training workshop for her warehouse staff, had Morgan given her *that* one?

She tossed the phone into her purse. She needed to leave if she was going to get in that visit to her dad. It was his two-week anniversary at the Villa, and she'd promised to bring him cupcakes from his favorite bakery.

The waiter delivered her coffee. She noticed she didn't ask for a to-go cup. She'd swing by her dad's after work. Take him a cupcake then.

She ripped open the plastic cream buckets, one, two, three, and swirled their contents into the oily brew. Outside the window, a couple of kids in the parking lot were making out, the girl pressed up against the chassis of a pickup, the boy pressed into her.

She and Treat had been like that once, unable to keep their hands off each other. Not as openly, of course. Not in Fresno, land of homophobes, right-to-lifers, and meth labs. But in the early months of their courtship, Morgan was so sleep-deprived she could barely keep her eyes open at work. It was irresponsible. And yet somehow the world still managed to turn.

She took a swig of the bitter coffee then pulled her phone back out. She'd intentionally left the house before Treat had a chance to say anything about the night before, slinking down the stairs to wash up in the powder room off the living room, rubbing some baking soda on her teeth, and grabbing something to wear out of the laundry. It was a lame response but the best she could come up with on next to no sleep. And now there was this damn voice mail. Visions of Treat and Marky Gottlieb playing tonsil hockey in the back of Treat's hybrid 4Runner chased around her brain. Or had there been more to it than that? Listening to the voice mail would probably shed light on the gravity of the alert. Code red? Orange? But did it matter? Really? Their relationship was in trouble. No voice mail could change that.

She plucked the promotional dessert card from its perky chrome stand and glared at the Kahlúa Cream Cheese Pie with its towers of creamy chocolate. She signaled the waiter. "Is it possible to order just half a slice?"

He graced her with a tip-procuring smile. "I'm afraid not. But I could give you a take home box. You could eat what you want then—"

"What the hell. Bring it on."

He swooshed off, leaving her to hate herself in private.

She scrolled through her e-mails. Maybe the whistle-blowing case would take her mind off her pathetically keening heart. But her brain would not behave. Who cared about the woman's petty issues? Morgan's apocalypse was here. Now.

She stared at the photo on her screen saver: Treat and her on their wedding day.

Six years ago, they'd been married during those crazy two weeks when the mayor of San Francisco offered marriage licenses regardless of gender. On impulse, Treat rented a tux and Morgan bought a wedding gown at Goodwill for thirty-five dollars. They booked a hotel room on Nob Hill and after a wonderfully romantic night—the champagne they drank!—woke at five o'clock in the morning to join hundreds of gay couples at city hall. Neither of them cared about the legal and religious implications. The legal had been taken care of years earlier when they'd had a lawyer draw up the paperwork ensuring them most of the same rights as heterosexual couples. And the religious? Who could believe in a God that would care one way or the other about a silly ceremony? For them, getting married was political. They wanted to add to the numbers, to step up and say, *We're here!* But it had been hard not to get caught up in the emotion of the day. Behind them stood two charming gentlemen, easily in their eighties, each wearing a tux with a red rose tucked in the lapel. Getting married meant the world to them. And the flowers! Some group had arranged for each couple to be given a bouquet with a card—sent from all over the country. Morgan and Treat got one from Georgia. It read: *Blessings to you on your wedding day. My daughter is gay, and I hope some day that she will be able to marry her loved one.* By the time Morgan and Treat reached the exhausted clerk, the sanctity of what they were doing had wheedled its way in. As they left the courthouse, arm in arm, Treat said, "You know this means forever."

And a teary-eyed Morgan replied, "'til death do us part."

Morgan picked up her napkin and blew her nose. Where was that damn piece of pie? She craned her head around looking for the waiter. He spotted her and held up a finger.

She returned to her coffee. How could she not trust Treat? Treat, the woman who'd taught her to love, who'd seen past the cautious, stingy, white-girl love she'd offered up, countering it with full-bodied, wholehearted Mexican pasión. She flashed on Treat's father, a proud Mexican in his fancy cowboy duds, publicly proclaiming love for his wife while everyone knew he was servicing several mistresses on the side. Treat hated that about her father. Still.

Morgan took another sip of coffee. The kids in the parking lot were now so curled into one another Morgan couldn't tell whose limbs were whose. She checked her watch. To hell with the pie. It was time to fight for her relationship. She'd call the office and tell them she was running late then swing by that new store in the mall whose ad she'd seen in the circulars, All About Romance. It boasted "everything you need for your boudoir and more." Surely she could find something—

The waiter sailed up to the table with her pie. "Sorry about the wait. I had to—"

"I need my bill," she said, sliding the pie into the to-go box. It was time to be proactive. Time to get her girl back.

CHAPTER SIX

"What was I supposed to do, tell the man he wasn't allowed to go to the bathroom?" Sonia's arched eyebrow made it clear that Cora's attempt to chastise her was beyond ridiculous.

She was right, of course. Prohibiting Mac from going to the restroom would have been unreasonable. And possibly messy. The Professor's attempted escape, the SUV plowing into the van, and Cora's realization that if she'd rounded the van two seconds later, she would have been hit had her wound tighter than an eight-day clock. She rested a hand on her fluttering heart and, for the sole purpose of calming herself, counted the residents gathered around the mall entrance again. All still there. Except Mac. Everything was in order—if the Professor standing behind a trashcan shouting "Class! Class!" could be considered order.

She took a deep breath, recalling the millions of times her mother had counseled her to "roll with the punches." This was usually followed by her singsonging, "or you'll be a Cautious Cora." How Cora hated that nickname! Hated her mother for coining it, hated her even more for passing it on to Hubert who pulled it out from time to time, sometimes to tease, other times to make a point, both of which Cora found irksome. He was equally, if not more, cautious than she was.

Shielding her eyes from the afternoon sun, she squinted across the crowded parking lot to where John and the SUV driver were arguing. Could the teenager really think John was to blame? Much as she didn't care for John's driving, this was clearly not his fault. She considered walking over to see if she could be of help. She checked her watch. "Mac's been in there an awfully long time."

"Prostate," Sonia said.

"Or constipation," Nell added. "That cheesecake last night was awfully rich."

Cora glanced around for a little shade. There was none. It wasn't good for the residents to be out in the sun like this. She couldn't imagine any of them had thought to apply sun block.

"I knew we were in for some excitement today," Nell said. "Felt it in my bones. But a van wreck! Do you suppose it'll make the news? I mean, we might get stranded here."

Sonia plucked a small mirror from her purse. "Hardly a wreck, Nell." She checked her lipstick. "Fender bender is more like it. And being stranded here sounds perfectly awful." She shot a look at Shirley Peters fretting over her oxygen tank. "But if it comes to that, I say we eat Shirley first."

Cora slapped her friend's arm. "Sonia!"

"What? The woman is a waste of a good oxygen tank."

Cora shook her head, chuckling. This little incident was going to spread quite the buzz through the Villa. The evening's dining room conversation filled with: *You should have been there! Such a close call! I saw my life pass before my eyes!* "I feel like I'm back in my schoolteacher days," she said. "Lord, I hated field trips. I'd spend the whole day counting heads." She noticed something sharp digging into her foot and rested against the planter to root it out.

"Well, everything is right as rain," Sonia said. "John is taking care of the wreck, everyone from the Villa is out of the van and safe, Mac will be back shortly—"

"I wouldn't count on that," Nell said.

"Nell," Sonia said. "You seem determined to give our Cora an ulcer."

Cora found the bit of grit stuck to the sole of her Clarks sandal and tossed it into a planter of heat-stricken petunias.

Nell pointed to the side alley where a utility cart was coming up on the turn. "What do you call that?"

Cora squinted into the sun. The driver was wearing a light blue bucket hat. "Oh my God!"

"What the hell!" Sonia said.

Cora took a step forward as if she might be able to catch up with Mac, which was silly; he was much too far away. "We have to get John."

"On it." Sonia strode toward the parking lot only to stop just shy of the van. Cora assumed she was watching for oncoming traffic, but Sonia beckoned to her urgently. Cora hustled over, Nell, annoyingly, at her heels.

Sonia pointed through the open door of the van. "The keys!"

"So?"

"You used to drive a school bus."

Cora tried to make sense of what she was saying. Then did. "I couldn't."

"Why not? John's got his hands full."

"But—"

"Cora, in the time it takes us to rush across the parking lot to tell John, we could snatch the van and catch up with Mac."

"Brilliant!" Nell said.

Cora shot a look a John. He was well out of shouting distance and clearly clueless about Mac's escape. And she'd driven buses bigger than this—a *long* time ago. Still. Something had to be done. Fast. What if Mac took to the highway? Visions of him getting T-boned at an intersection blasted through her brain. It was no time to be a stick in the mud. No time to be Cautious Cora. She charged around the front of the van and hoisted herself in. "Well? Are you coming?" she shouted to Sonia through the open passenger door.

Sonia grabbed the door rail and hoisted herself into the front passenger seat. Nell, uninvited, clambered into the back.

One door slam, two, then three, and they were ready to go.

Cora made a quick study of the console. An automatic. Piece of cake. She turned the key and pressed the accelerator. She could do this. "Hang on, ladies. We're going to nab ourselves a runner." She could.

CHAPTER SEVEN

The breeze on Mac's face was exhilarating as he navigated down the wide avenue in the utility cart. If he turned his head to the side and used the corner of his eye, he could see the road and other cars pretty damn well. The power of an engine—albeit a dinky one—was intoxicating.

But he worried.

"Why are you turning?" Effie asked accusingly.

"It can't be legal to drive this thing on the main roads. It may not be legal to drive it on a city street at all." It sure as hell wasn't legal to drive a stolen vehicle. It'd been over a year since he'd sideswiped that parked car and lost his license. The accident hadn't even been his fault. A cardboard box was in the middle of the road.

He reduced his speed to read the sign: Not a Through Street. Of course! He drove to the end of the residential cul-de-sac and turned around. Maybe escaping wasn't such a good idea. Did he really want another run-in with the police?

The neighborhood was clearly affluent. Even with his feeble eyesight, he could make out the blue and white First Alarm signs neatly plunked in each landscaped yard as if stating: *We have items worth stealing!* The only person outside was a Mexican gardener pruning a tree.

They'd raised Morgan in a neighborhood much like this, their house the only one on the block without the sculpted hedges and perfect money-green lawn. Effie wouldn't have it. Nor would she let him hire a gardener. She liked her garden unruly, the leggy blossom-heavy limbs of the Cecile Brunner arching over the front window, the Mexican sage shooting up purple spikes, the lawn turning California-tan in the summer. It was her silent rebellion at having to live in Fresno.

"Oh, for heaven's sake, Mac. Why are we stopping?"

He turned off the motor. "Because I have no idea where we're going."

"To Santa Cruz. It's time to make good on that promise, old man."

It was the last thing he expected her to say. And the only thing.

He turned to look at her, knowing what he would see: Effie, eighteen and cute as a button in her white wide-legged slacks and pale blue sleeveless blouse, her curly hair clipped back on the side with a sparkly barrette, the outfit she was wearing the night they met.

What a night that had been! He and his sunburned pals snapping with possibilities, their weekend at the beach turning out so much better than their hayseed imaginations ever dreamed: meeting up with a posse of local girls, going to a jazz club on the Santa Cruz Wharf—and the dancing. Not that he was much of a dancer, but he kept up okay, and when he didn't, Effie just laughed, took hold of his hands, and the two of them spun around like lunatics. When they stepped outside into the cool night to catch their breath, the sea lions were barking up a storm. They leaned on the wharf's railing, she inside his arms, and looked across the undulating water to the Santa Cruz Beach Boardwalk with its brightly lit roller coaster and colorful merry-go-round. The muffled screams from the amusement park floated across the water. It was there that she told him she'd never leave her ocean. Never.

She told him again six months later when he proposed.

And again a month later when he proposed for a second time. This time, though, he was set on convincing her to give Fresno a try. He was next in line to take over the family business, he told her. And Fresno would be a great place to make a family. She squinted at him, doubtful. "Promise we'll move to Santa Cruz if I hate Fresno?" Of course he'd promised. He would have said anything to win her. And so she accepted his hand, and Fresno, and they were married that year.

It wasn't long before Effie was pregnant. They delivered the happy news at his parents' annual Fourth of July backyard barbeque. Within seconds, Effie was kidnapped by his domineering mother and overbearing aunts and subjected to endless advice about child birthing and rearing while he, oblivious, drank and played Ping-Pong with the men. On the walk home, Effie begged him to move back to Santa Cruz. "They've got all these family names they say I have to use!" she'd said. "And schools all picked out." He reasoned with her. His dad was close to retirement; Ronzio's Hardware would soon be theirs. His parents would have no say over them then. Besides, he said, Fresno wasn't forever; they could retire in Santa Cruz.

She made him cross his heart.

In the meantime, he tried to placate her by taking weekend trips to the seaside town. They'd take Morgan to the beach, the redwoods, the amusement park. But always, when it came time to leave, Effie looked at him with those disarming eyes of hers, why couldn't they move back? Pretty soon he just stopped going, told her to take a friend, which she did many times throughout their marriage. She'd come home with stories of dolphins swimming close to shore, a bobcat at the park, a new outdoor restaurant on the garden mall, always trying to persuade him to pack up shop. Once both of their kids moved out, the financial alibi he'd been leaning on crumbled. They had plenty to retire. Still he couldn't leave. He'd been weighing out sacks of nails since he was nine, cutting chain since he was thirteen. All his friends were in Fresno, friends he'd had since childhood. They'd become Effie's friends too, but that wasn't the same, as she was so fond of reminding him. Then she had her stroke and his chance to make good on the promise was gone forever. Three weeks later, a Home Depot moved in down the block. Ronzio's Hardware closed within the year...

"You in there, old man?"

Mac startled. How long had he been sitting here? He glanced around. The Mexican gardener was still at work on the tree. He wiped perspiration from the back of his neck. It was hot. "Good question."

"What's that supposed to mean?"

She was back to being his soft white-haired Effie with the thick waist and freckled hands. This always shook him up. The way she changed. And him, slipping off into the past. It was getting harder and harder to get back.

"Well?" she said, impatience perched between her eyebrows.

He was afraid she was just something his jumbled brain was making up. Should he tell her? No. It would hurt her feelings. Besides, he owed her an apology. She'd given him so much and was so patient, and he'd been nothing but selfish and weak. What a stupid man he was!

"Effie, I—"

"You're changing the subject."

"What subject?"

"Santa Cruz!"

Oh. Right. "Effie, Santa Cruz is a hundred and fifty miles away. There's no way this cart could take us that far."

She patted her thinning hair. "Always excuses."

"Think of our kids. It would worry them no end."

"Maybe Morgan. Lately, she's been a ball of worry. I don't see that this one little thing will change that. As for Mike, the only things he seems to worry about are his real estate deals."

"She's got a lot on her plate. And taking me in didn't help matters."

"She didn't have to take you in. Nor did she have to stick you in that…home."

"It wasn't just her. Mike was in on it too."

A suited man came out of one of the houses, glanced at him briefly, then got into his car and drove off.

"You don't know what it's like," he said in a hushed voice. "You just fell asleep and just…died. Didn't have this slow march to death."

"Hey. I had some very scary minutes there when my body started shutting down. It was like a switchboard. Click. Off goes the liver. Click. The spleen—"

"Would you stop?"

"Click. There go the kidneys. Click. And I tried to wake you, but you just lay there snoring. Click. Click. Click—"

"Stop! Stop!"

Mac hated to think about that night. He woke up with her still-warm hand clenched around his wrist.

"I'm sorry," he said.

"Thanks for keeping them from trying to revive me."

"It wasn't easy."

"I know."

They sat quietly for a few minutes, Mac thinking about that night, Effie thinking about who knew what?

"If you hadn't died, we might still have moved to Santa Cruz."

"Oh, please."

He pulled a hanky from his pants pocket, blew his nose, then glanced around to make sure the Mexican gardener was minding his business. "So what happens when I get pulled over for driving a golf cart on the freeway? Me, a fugitive with no license."

"We take that hurdle when we get there."

He whapped the wheel with his thumbs, pictured the drive. A hundred and fifty miles at least, including the narrow sunbaked Pacheco Pass and dark, twisty Hecker Pass. But what really worried him was his mind. How could it not? He'd been stuck at the same dining table as the Professor that one time. The guy had spent the whole lunch talking to Mac as if he were some unruly student, corralling him to attention. "Sit down! Listen! Take out your notes!"

What if he turned into that? Slipping into the past and not being able to get back? He reckoned the drive would be okay. He'd done it enough times, especially when he was courting Effie. He'd flick on the radio, roll down all the windows…He stopped himself. Stay focused. Santa Cruz. Utility cart. But really, besides being an impossible endeavor, what did he have to lose? His life? Being tossed out of the Villa? Who cared? He reached down to turn the key in the ignition then saw something his muddled brain must have been making up: on the cross street, up ahead, Sunset Villa's van whizzing by with his new friend Cora at the wheel.

CHAPTER EIGHT

A ll About Romance turned out to be a Bed, Bath, and Beyond of courtship, but with tasteful lighting. Morgan stood just inside the door acclimating to the pulsating colors, textures, and aromas beckoning her into its depths. A tall salesgirl with heaps of curly blond hair and wearing a flattering low-cut tux-like uniform greeted her. "Welcome to All About Romance. Can I help you find anything?" Her voice was breathy, seductive, and bored.

Morgan stammered, "I'm fine. I just need to…well…which way is the alcohol?"

Rapunzel pointed with a sharp red fingernail. "Just follow the little cupids to your right."

Morgan looked up. Sure enough, little cherubs hung from the ceiling, each one holding a frilly heart that said things like, *This way to the libations!* or *Follow me for that special toy!*

Unable to muster the courage to ask this young thing where the lingerie was, she set out on her mission. Turned out all cherubs led to *The Lingerie Lounge* situated at the center of the store where acres of lingerie were grouped by titillation preferences. Naughty pink and white lace nighties were set apart from garish black and red lace-up corsets as if they might contaminate one another. Leather had a section all to itself.

It had been eons since Morgan purchased lingerie, but this was war. Giving the Miss Muffet and Dana Dominatrix ensembles a wide berth, she beelined for a rack of tasteful satin and lace separates. But did they carry plus sizes? She flipped through the rack and found not only 1X but 2X and 3. Which made sense. Youngsters couldn't afford prices like these. Nor did they need the wares. This place preyed on middle-aged women trying to revive the passion in their relationships.

No matter. She picked out a pair of sexy silk pajamas and a bustier and panties set and strode over to the dressing room. The girl working there didn't look old enough to drive. "Just the two things?" she asked, her slut-red lips curving into a condescending little pout.

Morgan was determined not to take the girl's obvious middle-age phobia personally. "Yes."

The dressing cubicle was painted a rich pink and had mirrors on all sides causing lines of mini-Morgans to shoot off into infinity. Doing her best to ignore them, Morgan slipped off her linen slacks and cream-colored cotton blouse and struggled into the first of her choices, a little hook-and-eye ivory-colored lace bustier with matching panties. Negotiating the tiny hooks into the tiny eyes was nearly impossible. Her fingers felt like bananas. Yanking up the panties was even worse. The "whisper-light" fabric rolled into a rope as she pulled the panties up her thighs then had to be unrolled and smoothed over her own panties—kept on for sanitary reasons.

She took a deep breath then braved a look into the carnival mirror. It was jarring. The lines of mini-Morgans reflected every unflattering angle: a pale belt of naked fat hovered around her middle like one of Saturn's rings, her thighs looked like they'd been left out in hail storm, doughy flesh bulged from the armpits of the push-up bra feature of the bustier like some forest fungus, and her butt sagged like a bag of wet groceries.

Just move on, she told herself as she began negotiating the tiny hooks.

Her phone rang. Treat? Unable to stop herself, she bent to retrieve it from her purse. She could at least look. One of her breasts spilled out of the bustier. She checked the number while simultaneously trying to shove the breast into the molded cup then thought: Why bother, I'm just going to take the thing off. The call was from work. She tossed the phone back in her purse and returned to the miniscule hooks. Threads from the lacy fabric had somehow wound themselves around several of the dainty enclosures and were now holding her hostage. Her phone rang again. Again, it was work. Connie, her assistant, wouldn't call twice unless it was damn important. Morgan picked up. "What's up?"

"I'm so sorry to bother you, but our whistle-blower case just escalated."

Morgan stared at herself in the mirror: one boob out, one in; lacy bikini underwear cutting into her cotton hipsters. "What's going on?"

"She's hired a lawyer. I've got him on the phone now. I think you should talk to him. He's threatening all kinds of evil stuff."

Morgan sat on the heart-shaped stool. Her belly looked enormous. She returned to standing. "Put him on."

The click of the transfer.

"This is Morgan Ronzio. I've been handling Alice Pyle's case. How can I help you?"

"Dick Deetz. I'll be conducting Ms. Pyle's complaint from now on."

Morgan inwardly groaned. She'd dealt with Dick Deetz on several occasions, and each time, he acted like it was their first interaction. She wasn't sure if this was a strategic move on his part or if he was socially inept. Either way, he was a pain in the ass. And probably the only lawyer sleazy enough to agree to represent the infamous Alice Pyle. "And how can I help you, Mr. Deetz?" She sucked in her stomach and checked out her profile.

"Ms. Pyle filed a report with you months ago, and still the harassment continues. If the university is not prepared to take action on its own, we're ready to litigate."

Good luck with that, Morgan thought. Alice Pyle was a serial whistle-blower whose work resume read more like a grievance chronicle. Every job she took ended in a disability, sexual harassment, or whistle-blowing claim, but God forbid Morgan should mention this. Dick Deetz would jump all over it. "Dick, I can assure you that we take Ms. Pyle's report very seriously…" With her free hand, she went back to trying to extricate herself from the evil bustier. "…but I'm sure you can respect that there are proper channels for dealing with the type of accusations made by your client." The damn thing was knotted together. "We have a duty to make sure that all allegations of misconduct are thoroughly investigated to protect all parties involved."

"Only one person needs protecting," Dick shot back in his nasal voice, "and if the university doesn't provide a remedy, the courts will. We're not talking about a simple hostile work place claim. I have documented incidents of overt harassment."

Morgan gave up on unhooking the camisole and moved on to removing the bikini underwear. "I'm sure you know that if you file a lawsuit, this whole matter will become public?" The panties were taking her underwear with it. "Why not give us time to fully investigate and take appropriate action." She tried using her elbow to hold her underwear in place while peeling off the bikinis. "Is it really in your client's best interest to have her personal life splashed all over public pleadings?" The panties were so tangled she had to take them both off. The scar from her fibroid surgery looked like it was smiling.

"Of course, it's in the university's best interest to sweep this whole matter under the rug," Dick Deetz said. "While you drag your feet, my client suffers continued harassment from her boss."

Morgan stared at the million reflections of her naked butt, each one covered in identical dimples. "Dick, are you going to be at this number for the next hour? Someone's just stepped into the office."

He cleared his throat. "Are you trying to put me off? Because each day that my client has to work with—"

"I understand. And I promise I'll get back to you. I'm very concerned about the prospect of litigation."

After a bit more hemming and hawing, Dick Deetz finally agreed to resume the call later. Morgan hit end call and dropped the phone into her purse. What an idiot.

She looked at herself in the mirror. Sure, she'd let herself go a little, but she was also an intelligent, witty, and determined woman. And she had nice eyes, damn it. She ripped the bustier from her chest à la Clark Kent, patted down her hair, and reached for the next item: a black silk camisole with matching pajama pants. These slipped on easily enough, felt great, and actually fit. But were they flattering?

She raised her gaze, ready for whatever image the malevolent mirror might throw back at her. It wasn't all that bad. The pajama pants hung nicely and were devoid of the dreaded camel toe. And the camisole—well, if she ignored her woogity-woogity upper arms and too-pale skin—made the most of her cleavage. She tipped her head back, eyelids drooped, and gazed into the mirror seductively. This could work. Definitely. She was one middle-aged hottie.

But there was no time to dwell. She had to get back to work.

The pajama pants and camisole slipped off easily—a good omen—and she was back into her sensible work clothes in no time. She marched past Miss Pouty Lips armoring herself with the silent mantra: *This will be you one day, sweetie*

Alcohol was much easier to choose: Veuve Clicquot, their drink of choice since their tenth anniversary, celebrated in San Francisco. They'd drunk two whole bottles on the deck of a rented condo overlooking the Golden Gate Bridge.

On the way to the register, she picked up some scented candles— vanilla, Treat's favorite—and a bottle of sandalwood-scented bath oil. She wasn't going down without a fight.

A pretty boy wearing an assortment of leather bracelets and too much hair gel rang her up. "Looks like *you* have a fun night planned."

"Yup." She swiped her debit card and punched in her pin number. So what if she was old enough to be his grandmother? At least she didn't have to deal with homophobia on top of age-phobia. This kid was definitely queer.

Her phone rumbled in her purse. She pulled it out and glanced at the readout, expecting it to be work. Not. It was Sunset Retirement Villa. She punched *accept amount* on the card reader without even looking at the total, smiled apologetically at the cashier, then answered her phone. "Hello?"

She could hear confusion on the other end of the line, people talking, phones ringing. "Morgan Ronzio?"

She recognized the voice of the Villa's director. "Yes?"

The gay boy handed Morgan her bag of merchandise. "Have a romantic evening!"

She nodded, took the bag, and headed for the door. "Is something wrong?"

"We seem to have lost your father."

CHAPTER NINE

Sooner or later, the light was going to turn green, and Cora would have to make a decision. Right? Left? Straight? There were so many possible side streets Mac could have taken. What had she been thinking, chasing after him? And poor John. He'd be out of his gourd by now. They absconded with his van half an hour ago and were no closer to finding Mac than when they started. Enough rolling with the punches. This was going nowhere. "I say we bag it," she said.

"We've just begun!" Nell protested.

"Nell's right." Sonia was nosing through the glove box. "We can't turn back now. Mac is our friend."

Cora drummed her fingers on the wheel. Great. Two against one when it should be a standoff, but nooo, wherever Sonia went these days so went Nell. Cora noticed a bit of gradoo under one of her nails and fished it out. Sonia pretending she was in this for Mac was too much. Rescuing had been her initial impulse, or so Cora assumed, but now there was little doubt about Sonia's true motive: she wanted Constance Wright, self-righteous director of Sunset Villa—Bitch Wright, as Sonia called her—to know that she, Sonia, held the cards. She'd been trying to make the point since Candace's appointment six months ago, daring the new director to call her out, which of course she never did. She couldn't afford to. Not with the kind of money Sonia had dumped into the place and the kind of respect Sonia garnered from the rest of the staff. And it hadn't all been for naught. Thanks to Sonia's rabblerousing, they now had a dinner entrée for those who weren't allergic to every spice known to man, and who could tolerate a little salt. They also got those nice reading lights installed in the dayroom.

The stoplight turned green, but the clunker in front of them stalled. He waved his hand out the window for her to pass, but with the oncoming traffic, it wasn't safe.

Cora had to admit it felt good to be driving again. She'd never consciously stopped. By the time she'd arrived at the Villa, she was just so dog-tired, and *bitter* about neither of her sons being able to step in to help her take care of their father, that she was grateful for any assistance she could get. Being driven around and fed three times a day was a luxury. So she'd sold the Pontiac and settled into the Villa routine. She was happy to do it. Now, though, back at the wheel, she regretted selling that car.

The light turned red again. The fellow in the clunker got out, clearly resigned to push. A couple of clean-cut guys in Fresno State football jerseys jogged over to help.

"Five more minutes," she said. "If we don't find Mac in that amount of time, we turn back."

"Oooo, can we stop at Moo's Creamery?" Nell said. "It's to the right."

"This is not a lark, ladies."

"But I've never been," Nell said. "And now that the Villa's on this new non-dairy kick—"

"The Villa isn't," Sonia said dryly. "Bitch Wright is."

"I would just loooove a milkshake," Nell said.

Sonia, apparently finished snooping in the glove box—what did she think she'd find anyway?—clicked it shut. "Oh, wouldn't that be perfect, to come back with a trophy! I can just see Bitch Wright's face now as we stroll into the foyer, past her desk, slurping our lactose-filled milkshakes. It would be even better if we managed to find Mac. But either way, the milkshakes are a must."

Cora looked at her. Wasn't this taking things a little far?

Sonia pressed her palms together and pretended Cora was able say no to her. "Pleasepleaseplease?"

"Pleasepleaseplease?" Nell echoed from the backseat.

The light turned green. The young men pushed the clunker out of the road like it was nothing.

"Oh, for heaven's sake." Cora flicked on her blinker and made the turn. "We'll get milkshakes then head back."

"We're going to give up on Mac?" Nell said.

"Not give up." The giant purple cow of Moo's Creamery came up on the right.

Cora pulled into its lot and cut the engine. "Accept the fact that there are people much more qualified to find missing persons than we are."

"Cora," Sonia said with Klaus's deep German accent, "Must you alvays be so reasonable?"

Cora laughed at the private joke. Sonia was referring to the time they'd been out on the Villa's patio eating dry turkey salad sandwiches and talking about who knew what when Klaus, off in his Alzheimer's cloud, suddenly slapped his meaty hand on the table and boomed: "CORA, MUST YOU ALVAYS BE SO REASONABLE?" then went on munching his sandwich as if nothing out of the ordinary had happened. It had amused them for weeks.

Cora swung her door open. "Look. I'm driving. We grab milkshakes then head back." She gave them each a look. "Unless either of *you* want to take the wheel…"

With some effort, Nell slid open the back door. "You don't want me at the wheel. Not with these eyes."

Sonia snatched up her purse and opened the passenger side door. "Party pooper."

Strolling the blistering asphalt to the front door, Cora had to admit a milkshake sounded great. The day was heating up something awful.

Inside, they were hit with more cow paraphernalia than was tasteful, sixty-three original flavors, and a blast of glorious air-conditioning. There were no other customers.

"Exactly like I pictured it!" Nell said.

Behind the register was a boyish beauty wearing a frilly purple apron and starched purple cap. The girl's delicate features and large expressive eyes were set off by extremely short-cropped, dark brown hair, aspirin-sized holes in her earlobes and a single very large and very intricate tattoo on her forearm. She looked up guiltily from a sticker-covered laptop angled next to the register. "Don't mind me."

She folded the laptop shut. "Just doing a little homework." She flashed them a brilliant, gap-toothed smile and stashed the laptop out of sight.

Cora gestured to the tattoo of three nude goddesses wrapped around her girl's forearm. "The Three Graces," she said.

The gap-toothed girl gave Cora a second, more thorough look. "*Ve*-ry astute."

Pleased with herself, Cora glanced at Sonia hoping to gain her approval, but Sonia was too busy studying the many flavor choices posted on the wall to notice. Cora turned back to the girl. "Joy, Charm, and Beauty, right?"

"Exactly." The girl held out her arm so Cora could see the tattoo up close. It was intricately done, very colorful, and, Cora now noticed, one of the graces had an eye patch, which was certainly different.

Nell leaned in for a look. "Which one are you?"

The girl rested her chin on the back of her hands like some old timey pinup girl. "Why, beauty, of course. Can't you tell?" Then she laughed a rich, full-throated laugh. She really was charming, in an exotic kind of way, the type who seemed to glow from within. "So what can I get you ladies?"

Nell crouched so close to the glass she fogged it up. "Do we get free tastes?"

"Up to three each," the girl said.

Nell pointed to one called Bubblegum Blitz, a blue concoction with bursts of red, green, and yellow. "I'd like to try that one."

"That might not make such a good milkshake," Cora said. "You could choke on the gum."

"But good for a *taste*," Nell said.

Cora sighed. Clearly, this was going to take a while.

Sonia's phone jingled in her purse.

Cora shot her a look. The Villa? The police?

"Relax," Sonia said, but she did look concerned.

It rang again.

Sonia riffled through her carpetbag of a purse and, after another ring, found it. "Hello?" she said breathlessly.

Cora raised her eyebrows. Who?

Sonia held up a finger, plugged up her free ear, presumably to block out the creamery's peppy music, and strode over to a clutch of purple-tableclothed tables surrounding a life-size, plastic Holstein cow. Cora tried to read her body language.

"Your turn," Nell said.

"A vanilla milkshake," Cora said, barely bothering to look at the gap-toothed girl.

"That's it?" Nell said. "Sixty-three flavors to choose from and you pick vanilla?"

"It's my favorite."

"How do you know if you haven't tried the rest?"

Cora had to make an effort to keep her tone neutral. "I just know."

"If she's not going to use her three tastes," Nell said to the girl, "can I have them?"

For heaven's sake, Cora thought. Has Nell no idea what's going on here? That we could be in serious trouble for absconding with the Villa's van? Or does she simply not care?

"I don't see why not," the girl said.

Cora pulled out her wallet and shuffled through her various credit cards to make sure she had her driver's license. She had no idea where it even was and was relieved to find it tucked between her Visa and Discover card. When she looked up, Sonia was walking over to join them. "Who was it?"

"Ginny. She says the Villa is in an uproar. Miss Wright is running around telling everyone 'mum's the word'—can you imagine? But, get this, we've got quite a fan club. They had to cancel Decorating With Dried Flowers due to a group of residents who've taken over the rec room in solidarity with 'our cause.'"

"Our *cause*?" Cora said.

"Apparently, we've hit a nerve."

"But all we did was go after Mac."

"*With* the Villa's van."

Cora shook her head. "That's Sunset Villa for you. So boring something like this seems like big news."

"Holy crap!" Nell said. "We're outlaws."

Cora plucked a napkin from the dispenser and patted her damp upper lip. She felt like sticking the napkin down the front of her blouse where a crop of perspiration was drenching her new bra. "I'm surprised no one from the staff has called."

"Thelma and Louise!" Nell went on. Then, remembering there were three of them, added, "And the Sundance Kid!"

"They don't have my new number," Sonia said. "And I told Ginny under no circumstances to give it to them."

Cora watched her milkshake whirring around on the mixer. She felt all arms and legs with no center. What had she gotten them into? "Did you tell them we're on our way back?"

"And let our 'fan club' down?"

"But they think—"

"Re-*lax*. Everything's going to be fine."

The gap-toothed girl set the two milkshakes on the counter. "Are you the old ladies that ran away from Sunset Villa?"

Sonia edged in closer and spoke in a quiet voice. "You know about us?"

"I just talked to my mom on the phone. She works in the kitchen there. Says the place has gone nutso. The residents think you're some kind of heroes while the staff is all like freaking out. That is so crazy cool!"

"We should call," Cora said.

"Why?" Sonia said. "I haven't had this kind of fun since Klaus took me up in a hot air balloon."

Cora noticed the gap-toothed girl had pulled out her cell phone. "Don't you dare call the police!"

"Are you kidding? I'm posting this on Facebook."

"Not so fast," Sonia said. "Let us make some tracks first."

Nell, all but tap-dancing in her sneakers, said to Sonia, "Choose a milkshake already. And let's scram!"

Cora fumbled with the wrapping on the straw, her hands seeming to move of their own accord. "I don't know about this."

Sonia took her by the shoulders. "Cora. What have we got to lose? Being kicked out of the Villa? We've been threatening to leave for eons. Why not go out with a splash? And if we find Mac, we'll be heroes." She looked happier than she'd been in months.

Cora stared at the plastic top of her milkshake. Cautious Cora. Always dampening everybody's fun. But this was crazy, wasn't it? Then again, they were already in hot water, what would it hurt to stay out a little longer? "Well…all right. But if we don't find him soon…"

Sonia brought her hands together in a single clap. "Wouldn't it be a coup if we were the ones to rescue him? Oh, wouldn't I just love to lord that over Bitch Wright!"

"Super Woman, Bat Girl, and...and..." Nell scrunched up her face trying to think of a third.

"So what'll it be?" the gap-toothed girl to Sonia.

Nell raised a fist in the air. "Xena!"

Cora tasted creamy and cold vanilla and realized she'd brought the straw to her lips.

Sonia ordered pistachio and slapped a twenty-dollar bill on the counter. "Keep the change," she said. Which seemed prudent. The girl could so easily turn them in. But really, there was no need. As Sonia's milkshake whirred on the mixer the gap-toothed girl, clearly enamored with these three old ladies who she kept calling "freaky-wonderful," wouldn't shut up about people taking charge of their own lives and taking risks.

It seemed eons before she finally set Sonia's milkshake on the counter, saying, "Can I at least take your picture?"

Sonia shrugged. "Why not?"

"How about in front of the stolen van?" the girl said.

"Borrowed," Cora said.

"Whatever," the girl said.

Cora felt her innards lurch. "God help us."

Sonia took her hand—"Oh, come on. It'll all work out. You'll see"—and tugged her outside. Cora's legs felt like they were made of cement. Sonia nudged her toward the van. Nell took up the position on her other side.

The girl aimed her camera phone.

"Wait!" Nell said.

Panicked, Cora scanned the horizon for the police or a SWAT team, but it was just regular traffic, regular pedestrians. She turned back to Nell who was tying a large white hanky around her face like a bandito. "Must you?" Cora said.

But Sonia was getting all into it too and flipped up the collar of her blouse to obscure the lower half of her face. "How's this?"

"Perfect!" the girl said. "Especially if you tilt your head away from the camera." She turned to Cora. "Now we need something for you."

"I'm fine."

"A ski mask!" Nell said.

"Right," Sonia said. "And where are we going to find—"

"I know!" the girl said. "There's a hat in the break room. It's perfect. We'll tilt it to the side à la Al Capone." She took off into the creamery for the hat. "Wait 'til you see this hat!"

"This is ridiculous," Cora said, her mind scouring through her jumble of thoughts to find one that would put a stop to this nonsense.

"Of course," Sonia said. "At our age, what worth doing isn't?"

Nell, meanwhile, was ogling at her reflection in the creamery window, checking herself out from every angle.

The girl emerged from the creamery whapping a dusty felt fedora against her leg. "This has been in the break room forever. Some employee left it."

Sonia switched her milkshake for the hat then placed the fedora on Cora's head, tilting it so it threw a shadow across Cora's face. "Perfect!"

Cora prayed she wasn't being exposed to head lice along with everything else.

"Okay," the girl said. "Places."

Sonia took her milkshake back from the girl, pulled up her collar, and sidled next to Cora. Nell flanked her on the other side.

"To taking charge of our own destiny!" Sonia said, thrusting her milkshake out like a sword.

Nell thrust out hers. "To really living!"

And what was there left for Cora to do but thrust out hers and join them? "To extreme ridiculousness!" she said.

"Aaaaand, got it!" the girl said.

Cora stuffed the hat under her arm and attempted to undo the damage it had done to her hair—difficult given that she was holding a milkshake. "Well, this has been different," she said. "I'll give it that." She was beginning to return to her body. And while she wouldn't exactly call what they were doing fun, it certainly wasn't cautious. And that was something.

"You've got to e-mail me the photo," Sonia said to the girl.

The girl, still fiddling with the camera phone, mumbled, "Sure. I just have a few things I want to do to it first."

Cora tossed the hat onto one of the patio tables by the door and climbed into the van. "One more swoop around the neighborhood to look for Mac, then it's back to the Villa. Right, girls?" Sitting back behind the console felt good, like she still had an ounce of control.

Sonia handed the girl a slip of paper with her e-mail and followed Cora into the van, but Nell, the fool woman, was still wearing her bandana and standing in the classic pose of a fencer, milkshake held behind her, other hand clutching her straw like a rapier, and battling her reflection in the creamery window.

CHAPTER TEN

Mac held the steering wheel tight as the utility cart bounced down the rutted trashcan-lined alley. Once he'd made up his mind to humor Effie's wish for a Santa Cruz excursion, he began enjoying himself, buzzing through the old neighborhood via side streets and alleys, a meandering route, but one full of memories. "My friend Marty used to live there," he said pointing to one of the houses. He almost didn't recognize it. Back in the day, they'd stroll the alley peering over the short picket fences looking for other kids. Couldn't do that now. The yards all had tall privacy fences. "You should have seen the marble games we played back here. Yours truly was champion for a whole summer. Man, I had a stash of cat's eyes you wouldn't believe."

"This cart will never make it over Pacheco Pass."

"Hey. Not too long ago you were pretty impressed by this little unit." Mac took the corner at a quick clip and pulled into the back parking lot of a Taco Bell. Something flew off the dash and hit his foot. "Did I ever tell you about the penny candy store that used to be here?"

"We need a car. Or truck."

"Everything was one cent except for old Mrs. Walker's homemade fudge. That would set you back two whole cents. But it was worth it."

"Car or truck."

Mac pulled up next to the Dumpsters, cut the engine, and reached under his seat to see what had hit his foot. A cell phone.

"That could be useful," Effie said.

He slipped it into his jacket pocket to keep it from sliding around and got out of the cart.

"What are you doing?"

"I'm going to get me a taco."

Effie grumbled something under her breath.

"What? A guy can't feed himself if he's hungry?" He stretched his legs. His knees were a bit frozen up, but they'd do.

"Hey, old man!" a deep-pitched voice to his left said. "What do you think you're doing?"

Mac's head snapped around. A police uniform was coming at him, barrel-chested and huge.

Mac shuffled through panicky thoughts for how he could explain the stolen utility cart. Did the officer already know? Was he about to be apprehended?

The voice softened. "Hey, Mr. Ronzio, I'm just playing with you. I'm Ira Skolnick's boy, Joel."

Mac used the corner of his eye for a good look. Well, didn't that beat all? The officer was the spitting image of old Ira, only a lot more filled out. "Sure, sure, I remember you." If he recalled correctly, this was the son Ira was always worrying about. Not inclined toward college like his two older boys, Joel was kind of a lost soul. Ira was relieved when he joined the police academy. Offered him some direction.

"You were quite the little hooligan," Mac said. "Gave your dad a few sleepless nights."

Joel chortled. "Yeah. I guess I did."

"How is Ira?"

"Died a few years back." Joel smiled a painful smile. "Cancer. Mom took it pretty hard."

"Sorry to hear it." Ira, a regular at the hardware store, wasn't much of a handyman and would come in for little things, a roll of masking tape, a magnet. He was the only Jewish guy in the neighborhood. Mac always found him to be interesting, smart, and he kept up with Washington and lived by his principles—more than Mac could say for a lot of guys.

Joel pulled a hanky from his pocket and blew his nose then gestured to the utility cart. "So, you working out at the mall now?"

Mac stole a glance at the cart. Property of Fig Garden Mall was stenciled on the side. His heart started to race. "Um. Yes. Yes, I am."

Joel blew air through his lips. "Shame about Home Depot moving in," he finally said. "We were dead set against it. Dad was certain it would put you out of business."

Mac lifted his shoulders in what he hoped was a reconciled-looking shrug. "What you gonna do?"

"Yeah, well, it's not right. This whole town's been taken over by chain stores."

The two of them stood there looking at each other's shoes. Joel's were huge, size thirteen at least. After a few seconds of this joint commiserating, Joel gave his nose another honk then said, "I'm sure you know that cart isn't street legal."

Mac felt his diaphragm go taut. "Well...yes, but—"

Joel held up his hands, the hanky pinched between the index and thumb of one. "I know, I know. You're not the first from the mall to try sneaking here by the alley. Who wants to fight traffic on your lunch break? But it's against the law."

Mac glanced over to Effie. See what you got me into? But she wasn't paying him one bit of mind. She'd pulled out some knitting and was sitting there the picture of innocence, reminding him, once again, that she was dead. Alive, Effie wouldn't have been able to resist playing a part in this ridiculous charade. She'd be buttering up this Joel fellow, getting his scent off the trail. The reminder of her deadness was disorienting. Mac returned his attention to Joel but was unable to sustain eye contact. He spoke to the nameplate above Joel's left shirt pocket. "I just wanted a quick taco."

Chuckling, Joel rocked back on his heels and patted his paunch. "Boy, I can relate." Then, apparently remembering he had a job to do, snapped his fingers and pointed at Mac. "But next time *drive* a car. You hear me, Mr. Ronzio? Or I'm going to have to ticket you."

Mac nodded solemnly. "Won't happen again. Promise."

"All right then." Seemingly relieved to be past the awkward task of having to reprimand his father's friend, Joel said, "Well, I gotta get back to work," wished him well, and strode over to his patrol car.

Mac watched him drive off. That was close!

"Aren't you going to get your taco?" Effie said.

Mac glanced around to make sure no one was watching before responding. "I've lost my appetite."

A beat-up green Jetta peeled into the parking lot. Mac absent-mindedly watched a pimply teenager jump out of his car and throw on a blue Taco Bell shirt over his wrinkled T-shirt. He looked like he'd just woken up.

"You are *not* thinking about turning back," Effie said.

Surprisingly, he wasn't. In fact, he was feeling pretty good about himself. He drove his hands jauntily into his trouser pockets. "I think I handled that pretty well."

Effie rolled her eyes. "Here we go."

"No, seriously. One wrong move and I could have gone to the slammer."

"Whatever you say, dear."

Mac climbed back into the cart knowing full well it could never make it to Santa Cruz. But he had to try. The gauntlet had been thrown. He tugged his wallet from his back pocket and counted his cash. Sixty-seven bucks and a Visa card if needed. He could grab something to drink along the way. What else would he need? He rested his hands on the wheel.

"We're in too deep to go back now," Effie said.

"Just let me think."

By the drive-through, the fellow in the Jetta was peering into the side view mirror attempting, unsuccessfully, to comb his greasy hair into place with his fingers. The kid's lucky he doesn't work for his dad, Mac thought. Whenever he'd shown up late for work, his dad would give him a tongue-lashing, customers or not. And the punishment never ended there; his dad would bring it home, making him clean out soggy gutters or wriggle under the house's spidery crawlspace to insulate pipes.

"Did you see that?" Effie said.

"What?"

"That kid, before he ran into work, he tossed his keys through the window."

Mac had seen it. It just hadn't fully registered. His pulse quickened, his hands grew damp against the steering wheel. Was he supposed to steal the car? Was that it? He glanced around. No one in sight.

Effie clapped her hands together at her chest. "It's destiny."

CHAPTER ELEVEN

Breathing heavily after her dash in from the car, Morgan stared at the thin lips of the giraffe-necked Villa director. She tried to make sense of what they were saying. Mall trip? Van wreck? Stolen motorized utility cart? The director—What the hell was her name? Catherine? Clarisse?—had yet to recognize Morgan and was addressing a pudgy police officer who was scribbling notes on a dog-eared pad. The director was trying to spin the story so it absolved the Villa of any wrongdoing. An hour and fifteen minutes the woman had waited before calling her. An hour fifteen!

Morgan felt like vaulting over the reception desk and strangling her. She ground her molars while images of her dad, half-blind and zigzagging precariously down the highway in a utility cart, careened through her mind. She zeroed in on the tiny gold cross around the director's neck. She'd noticed it the day she'd moved her dad in, and it gave her pause at the time. But with everything going on, the kitchen fire, her struggling relationship, her nightmare job, she'd let it go. Now all she could think was: Why had she turned her dad over to this cross-wearing woman?

"Excuse me," Morgan said. "I'm—"

The director held up a disapproving finger indicating: Just a moment, *she* was in the middle of something *important*.

Morgan snatched a tissue from the box on the desk and blotted the sweat blooming on her upper lip. "His eyesight isn't good. He shouldn't be behind the wheel."

The director blinked a few times as if trying to get Morgan into focus. "Oh. I'm sorry. Are you—"

"Morgan Ronzio. Mac Ronzio's daughter."

The officer looked up from the note pad, his caterpillar eyebrows furrowed with concern. "Don't worry, ma'am. We'll do everything we can to find your father and bring him back safe."

Morgan hated being called ma'am, especially by a guy who was clearly her peer, but under the circumstances, chose to ignore it. "Thank you. He gets confused easily." She glared at the director. Coretta? Carla? "He shouldn't be off by himself."

The officer scrawled a note. "Do you have any guesses about where he might go?"

She plucked a brochure from the information desk to fan herself. "He's never run off before." Another glare at whatever-her-name-was. "But here are some places worth checking out." She gave him the addresses for her house, the now-defunct hardware store, and her dad and mom's old house. "I've no idea why he'd go to those last two," she added. "He's not that dim."

The police officer gave her a solicitous smile. "Any indication he was friends with the three missing women?"

"Missing women?"

"Who took after him. Who appropriated the Villa van."

A Villa employee dressed in khaki Dickies and cowboy boots stood a few feet from the director, his arms crossed so tightly around his middle it looked like he was wearing a straitjacket. He reminded her of John Boy from *The Waltons*, minus the mole. He was either somehow involved in this mess or suffering from a miserable case of indigestion.

In light of a response from Morgan—And how could she respond to this bizarre addendum? Three old ladies? Who'd stolen a van to go after her dad?—the officer continued. "Several of the..." He glanced up at the ceiling as if the word he was looking for might be hanging out there with the crown molding. "...residents reported that a Mrs...." He referred to his note pad. "Cora Whittaker, a Mrs. Sonia Faber, and a Miss Nell Carter spotted him taking off in a utility cart and, as I said, appropriated the Villa's van to go after him."

"Jesus."

"Yes. Well. Do you know if they were—"

"No idea," Morgan said. "I mean, he's made a few friends, and I believe one of them was named Cora."

"In fact," the director said. "The four of them dined together regularly."

Morgan stared at her in disbelief. "Are you suggesting they were in cahoots somehow?"

"I don't think anyone is suggesting anything," the officer said. "But we need to cover all our bases. He flipped his notebook shut. "And now, if you'll excuse me, I'm going to radio this in." He touched the brim of his hat, a la Roy Rogers, and left.

"Ms. Ronzio," the director said in a voice obviously meant to placate. "I cannot tell you how seriously we are taking this."

Morgan scanned the lobby. Old people stuck in wheelchairs, old people sitting on a bench by the door, old people huddled in the hall, all of them stirred up and confused by the police presence. The attendants looked equally useless. No wonder her dad had run away.

"Would you like a cup of tea?" the director asked like this was a reasonable question.

Morgan felt her internal thermometer rise. "No, I would not like a cup of tea." She fought to contain her anger, but it slipped out anyway, sparking her words like loose wires. "I would *like* for this to have never happened. I would *like* to find my father safe in his room so that I might surprise him with the cupcake I planned to bring this afternoon. I would *like* for him to tell me how much he's enjoying his stay here at the Villa, how it's so much better than he thought it would be."

The director looked as if she were simultaneously trying to swallow her lips and sprout new eyeballs. But Morgan didn't care. This bitch of a Christian had lost her dad.

"I-I want to assure you that in our twenty-two years of business we have never had a runaway. Never."

What was she expected to do with this bit of information? Applaud? Jump up and down? Morgan rummaged through her purse for a business card then remembered that the Villa had her phone number on file. "Call me if you find out anything."

"Where will you be?"

Not having a fucking cup of tea! Morgan felt like saying as she strode toward the door. She would have, too, if her vocal cords hadn't been strung so tight. Meanwhile, the hormone-driven arrhythmic pounding of her heart was stirring up emotions and, like screaming preschoolers wanting first crack at a piñata, each one was screaming, *Pick me! Pick me!* its fat little hand waving in the air. Resentment, despair, rage, stupefaction, vulnerability, shame, terror, helplessness, were bombarding her synapses. She weeded through looking for an appropriate one, but it was no use; she was on the verge of the mother of all hot flashes.

"Morgan?" the director called out.

"I'm going to find my dad," she managed to say, which seemed reasonable. Then, "Because *you* lost him," slipped out on its tail. She took a quick breath and yanked the door open.

"May I go with you?"

Without turning around, she knew who was asking: The John Boy fellow. *Run! Run!* her hormones screamed. But her goody-two-shoes feet betrayed her and spun her around. It was him all right, arms dangling at his sides, two sincere eyes blinking a Morse code she couldn't decipher. "Go with me?" she repeated stupidly.

With his back to the director, he mouthed the words, "please, please, please," reminding Morgan of the giant orange and white speckled fish she often watched at Wong's takeout. The poor thing was trapped in a murky aquarium not more than three times its size and would stare desperately at her while she was waiting to pick up her order.

"I was driving the van," he said, his eyes still casting an unintelligible meaning.

"And?"

"I feel responsible." His lips quivered, but still his eyes beseeched her. There was something else too. Something that wasn't ringing true.

The hot flash, now roiling in Morgan's chest, began shooting fiery tentacles up her neck. She could feel her ears burning, beads of perspiration sprouting on her lip. "He's eighty-six years old. How could you have let him out of your sight? And those poor women..." In another couple of seconds she'd be freezing.

"I know! I know. I screwed up. Big time. But I want to help. I just don't have my pick up. It's in the shop. But if you took me I could show you..."

She no longer heard his words. She was standing in front of a studio audience and Monty Hall was asking her: "Door number one or door number two?" John Boy or no John Boy? Choose the right combination of actions and win the prize. Choose wrong and you go home with the donkey.

He waited for her to say something, glancing nervously over his shoulder at the director who was now talking on the phone. The director glared at him, which, oddly, tipped the scales in his favor. Anything to piss off the self-righteous bitch. Morgan spotted the guy's nametag—John Welch—and would have laughed if her hot flash weren't threatening to suffocate her. He *was* John Boy. "Okay," she said, "but I'm leaving. Now."

He scurried after her to the Prius. "Thank you, thank you, thank you. You just kept me from getting fired."

What? That's why he wanted to come along? Why, the little—

"She was just about to give me notice when that officer arrived. And then you came..."

She flung the car door open. Why was she bringing this guy with her? It was insane.

"We should start at the mall," he said at the car. "I can show you where he took off."

She slid into the seat. The mall. Perfect. She'd dump him there. "Good idea." She fired up the engine.

On the way over, she ignored the law about pulling over to talk on your cell phone and dialed Treat. Whatever was going on between them was going to have to wait. This was an emergency.

Treat picked up on the first ring. "Bonita. Did you listen to my voice mail?"

"Not yet. Dad's fl—"

"I really wish you'd listen to it." She was speaking in a hushed tone, like she was around other people.

Morgan angled her body away from John Boy and muttered, "I really don't think an electronic version of whatever it is you have to say to me is going to help."

"I'd have said it to you in person, but you left so early, and right now we're in the middle of role-playing."

"Fine. But Dad's flown the coop."

"What?"

"They took the residents on a trip to the mall and he stole a motorized mall utility cart and split."

Treat laughed. "He what?"

"Treat. This is serious."

"Okay, okay. It's just so classic. So where is he now?"

"Nobody knows. And that's not all. Some old ladies from the Villa took off after him using the Villa's van."

"No surprise there. He is quite the chick magnet."

Morgan had to laugh at that. It was true. Her mom hadn't been dead a month when the casseroles started rolling in. Old people had to move fast, Treat had joked, because they didn't have much time.

It was a relief to be in familiar territory. Not that her dad running away was in any way familiar, but the two of them dealing with him was. They'd seen him through her mother's death, his move to their house, the selling of his belongings, the kitchen fire…

"I'm sure we'll find him," Morgan said. "I mean, how far could he get? Still…" Her voice was infuriatingly shaky. "I mean, I know this is your big day and all, but maybe you could…" Damn. She sounded like a bleating lamb.

"I'll talk to Marky. See what she thinks. It's pretty important the guys see me doing this stuff too."

Morgan flicked on her blinker. Fucking Marky. "I'm sure your employees would understand."

"Hang on, bonita—The caterers are what? Shit! Well, when did they say they could get here?—Bonita? Can I call you back? We're having a disaster here."

"Whatever."

"Not whatever. I'll call you. And hang in there. Everything's going to work out all right. And listen to my voice mail."

Morgan stuck her phone in her purse and turned up the air conditioning, hating the fact that once again her relationship had to be shoved to the back burner. She searched the road. Come on, Dad. Show yourself. She considered calling her brother, but what could he do down there in L.A.? Not that he'd do anything anyway. The guy was devoid of any sense of familial duty. Fortunately, her dad seemed to have no idea that his son was totally uninterested in his welfare. Due to innocence or denial, Morgan couldn't begin to guess, but she was determined to keep it that way.

John Boy, who'd been scanning the road like a good little cowhand, twisted around on the seat. "Wait..."

Morgan hit the brake. "Is it him?" The car behind her honked.

"False alarm."

She resumed her slow crawl forward. The car behind her whizzed past. She flicked on the radio, hoping for something calming. After flicking through all her presets, she flicked it off. The mall, a gargantuan monolith of retail, rose on their right.

"We should go to the scene of the crime," John said. "Talk to the fellow whose cart he stole."

Scene of the crime. Morgan felt like smacking him. "Lead the way."

They drove around back to the loading dock and got out of the car. A potbellied man with a thick neck was chewing out a young fellow with pocked skin and hair in a short ponytail. "Do you know how much those utility carts cost? Do you have any idea what kind of lawsuit this could bring down on us?" The young fellow gnawed on one of his fingers.

"Excuse me," Morgan said, taking the few steps up to the dock. "My elderly father was the one who took off with your cart. I'm sincerely sorry about it, but I was just wondering..." What was she wondering? If these two men knew where her father had taken off too? How could they? How could anyone?

The young fellow started stammering an apology. "I'm sorry, ma'am. I should have been paying better attention, taken the keys with me. See, the thing is, I didn't get much sleep last night on account of my ma is kinda sick. She called me up real late and asked me to come over..."

The more he rambled on, the more annoyed Morgan got. Why did everyone need her to absolve their guilt? It was *her* father who was out on the road driving around in an unfamiliar vehicle, barely able to see. Would he have gone back home? Maybe.

The fellow was still going on about how bad he felt, begging for her forgiveness. No doubt he'd want to come along too, so he could live with his pitiable self.

She was about to scream *No!* when he did. She looked at him, confused. No?

The fellow was frantically patting at his pockets. "My phone was on that cart!"

"Awesome!" John Boy said.

Morgan looked at him. Awesome?

"Don't you get it? We can call Mac!"

CHAPTER TWELVE

Milkshake between her thighs, steering wheel at her command, Cora was reminded of her school bus driving days, except then it would be a thermos of hot coffee between her thighs. She'd loved being part of the work force—waking early in the morning, Hubert heading off to do his interning at the hospital, she off to the bus yard—and hated giving it up when Hubert started his practice. But she was pregnant, and in those days a girl didn't—well, who cared what they did or didn't do? She raised two sons and that was plenty.

She turned onto Sierra Avenue, regretting slightly that she'd made such a big deal about heading straight back to the Villa. It was a beautiful day and she'd finally begun to relax, was even feeling a bit plucky. What had they done, really, except try to help? And there was still the chance they might find Mac. Wouldn't that beat all? She scanned the oncoming traffic. No sign of a golf cart. Still.

"We should stop by the cemetery," Sonia said. "We're so close."

"Oh, let's," Nell said. "Hanging out with dead people always makes me feel so alive."

Why not, Cora thought boldly, and flicked on her blinker to take the shortcut. A chat with Hubert would be great. "A quick stop."

"Goodie," Nell said. "The adventure continues!"

Sonia's Klaus and her Hubert were on opposite sides of the cemetery. She parked in the middle so each had only a brief walk. Nell said she'd be happy to just wander around. Was there anything Nell wasn't happy to do?

CLIFFORD HENDERSON

Cora strolled toward Hubert's plot feeling mildly untethered, not necessarily in a bad way, more like one of those floating seedpods she used to call "wishes," like the girl Hubert fell in love with, the one determined to prove her mother wrong, the one who used to drive to San Francisco all by herself to see a matinee.

She noticed the silk flower saddle on top of Hubert's gravestone was askew. She was tempted to leave it that way, a jaunty beret, but Hubert would hate it. He was such a stickler for symmetry. Even after losing his mind, he would stop to straighten the pictures in the Villa rec room. So like his old self.

She'd picked the plot because it was by a huge oak tree, but six months after his burial, the tree was hit with sudden oak death. Shortly after the tree's removal, the bereaved family of Robert S. Helms plopped down a life-size marble angel right where the tree used to be. Cora resented her at first—she missed her tree—but over time grew used to the angel's heavenward look of adoration.

"You keeping an eye out for Hubert?" she asked, sitting on the more modest headstone of Elma Faber. If the angel was going to stand sentry, she might as well watch over Hubert too—and someday Cora herself.

She sucked on the straw of her milkshake. Should she tell Hubert about the van? The sweet creamy vanilla seeped across her tongue. What good would telling him do? He'd just instruct her to head straight back to the Villa, because for all they'd liked to pretend that she was the cautious one, Cora always knew in her heart that for Hubert to venture out of his highly structured life, he needed a plan. To get him to travel, or take a day off, she had to prime him for months. He'd love it once they got wherever they were going, but it didn't make going any easier the next time. She often wondered if he didn't have the slightest touch of Asperger's, if that's not where her youngest boy got it. One never knew about these things. Especially back then. No one even seemed to know about Asperger's.

She cast a guilty look at the angel whose expression now seemed less adoring and more self-righteous. She and Hubert had never kept secrets. "All right, all right! I'll tell him."

Another sip of milkshake, then: "I've really done it this time, love. I took the Villa's van—without asking." She added, "And I don't regret it one bit." She could only imagine his response. Probably something along the lines of, *If you have an accident, who will pay for the damages?* Always so practical.

She missed this about him. She also missed the sound of his voice, that warm growling he was left with after his bout of esophageal cancer. The chemo and radiation made him so sick and then robbed him, permanently, of his ability to taste the foods he loved so much. But they'd survived, had ten more wonderful years before his mind started to go.

"I miss you, Hoo," she said, using the nickname she'd given him shortly after they were married, long before the harsh reality of "'til death do us part" came to roost. She dabbed her eyes with the milkshake napkin then went on to tell him how tired she was of the Villa and how she wished she hadn't sold their house. Once he'd been diagnosed with Alzheimer's, he'd gone to such measures to make the house manageable for her, color coding the circuit breakers with her nail polish, typing up instructions for changing the heater filter and rinsing the drains with his famous vinegar and baking soda mix. He'd even pruned the roses—cut them back so severely he'd almost killed them—all so that "things would be taken care of" during his decline. As if the loss of his memory would happen in a single season.

Those five years had been so desperate. Watching him go from brilliant doctor full of opinions and odd facts to a man who, at first, seemed simply old-age forgetful but then became so careless she and his associates had to convince him to retire—that had been awful! Then came the diagnosis, soon followed by those never-ending days of him losing and finding his keys, accusing her of stealing his wallet, of hiding his glasses. The paranoia was the worst. No. The worst were the lucid moments when he'd look at her with those beautiful blue eyes swimming in terror. "What's happening to me, Coe?" he'd ask. "What's going on?" The day he no longer recognized her she called a realtor, put their house up for sale, and started making arrangements for them to move into the Villa. By then she was so overwrought and exhausted she was certain that she, too, was dying.

With some effort, she heaved herself up from Elma Faber and adjusted Hubert's flower saddle. Nell was right—at least about this one thing. Standing among the dead did make a person feel alive. Shoot, she might have ten more years in her!

Or not. Phyllis Greenberg's heart attack took her out before she had a chance to say, *Pass the salt-free gravy.*

Cora's gaze drifted to the far side of the unnaturally green expanse where Sonia was sneaking one of her cigarettes, no doubt Sonia's true motive for suggesting the stop. Sonia hated how the nurses clucked at her every time she stepped out for a smoke. Not to say she didn't miss Klaus. Alzheimer's struck only eight years after they were married, and Sonia had stuck it out with him, even when the illness made him violent. That said a lot.

Nell, standing just beyond Sonia in her rumpled turquoise T-shirt over some equally rumpled light salmon-colored pajama-looking pants, was squinting up through those thick glasses at an old pepper tree as if its branches were spouting poems. Cora once heard a nurse refer to Nell as "my little Buddha." The only thing Cora knew about Buddha was from the sculptures she'd seen sitting in people's gardens. All those Buddhas ever seemed to be doing was "contemplating their navels" as Hubert would say. But Nell wasn't like that at all. Her gaze was up and out, and she gave the impression of being in a constant state of wonder, even at the smallest things. The straw in her milkshake, for instance. She was thrilled that it bended, as if that made all the difference in the world. Surely she'd seen one before. Bending straws had been around for eons!

Cora turned back to Hubert. A trail of ants was crawling across the bottom of his headstone. An involuntary shudder shot up her spine. "I miss you, Hoo, but I'm not ready to join you. Not yet. I hope you understand." She kissed her fingertips and brushed them across his name, slurped down the last of her milkshake, and began weaving through the headstones toward the living. She walked slowly, putting off the Villa as long as possible.

How strange it was to be walking across the dead. She pictured them beneath her, laid out like planks, each one loved by somebody. She made a slight detour to toss her milkshake in a trash bin, but there was no getting around that it was time to face the music. There was no reason to go on. They'd lost any scent of Mac—if they'd ever had one.

She stepped around the headstone of someone's baby. Always the saddest. Should she be worried about her sons? The Villa would certainly have contacted Donald, her eldest, by now. In a way, this gratified her. He'd been such an advocate for her staying at the Villa after Hubert's death, using the unfortunate phrase: "You'll be taken care of." Cora had tried to be patient with him. Hubert's Alzheimer's had frightened him something awful—not that he'd ever admit it, but it was obvious by the way he'd yell, "Dad, I just told you!" and "You know how to do this!" the veins in his forehead pulsing with frustration. To Cora it was always: "If you would just write it down for him!" and, "You're babying him! He needs to do things by himself!" As if Hubert could remember where to look for the notes or when to turn off a sprinkler or how to change a light bulb.

She and her eldest hadn't quite recovered from this horrific time. She couldn't shake the feeling that he somehow blamed her for Hubert's decline. She was sure her cell phone, sitting next to her bed at the Villa, was filling up with messages from him demanding she return. While her youngest, Adrian, well, the Villa had strict orders not to contact him unless she died. And Donald knew better than to call. Something like this would shoot his younger brother into one of his heartbreaking swivets. They'd just gotten him resituated tutoring at Fresno State's computer lab after his last Asperger's meltdown. No. He wouldn't hear about her little junket until his weekly visit at three o'clock sharp, and by then she'd be back and it would be just a good story.

Cora leaned over to right some toppled flowers at the headstone next to Klaus's, a Stella Pointer's. Sonia was finishing her smoke. A few headstones away, Nell was doing tai chi, learned, Cora assumed, at the Villa. Cora had tried the Tuesday afternoon class once, but couldn't get her mind to keep from making fun of its silly postures— wave hands like clouds, grasp sparrow's tail, high pat on horse—so she stuck with the Villa's Step Master.

"Well…" she said to Sonia then didn't have the heart to say what should follow.

Sonia pinched out her cigarette and slipped the butt into the plastic wrap around the pack. Her phone was in her hand. "I just called Ginny. I'm waiting for her—"

The phone rang. Sonia checked the readout and flicked it open. "So, what's the scoop?"

Cora tried to discern the information being transferred by Sonia's *Uh huh...uh huh...uh huhs* and *Reallys?* She didn't know which was more frustrating, listening to Sonia's one-sided conversation or watching Nell's achingly slow pushing and pulling. It looked as if she were wrestling with some sluggish, unseen adversary.

Sonia finally flicked the phone shut. "Get this. People at the Villa are placing bets that we'll find Mac before the police."

"You're kidding," Cora said.

"And Ginny was pretty sure the local news station was picking up the story. She overheard one of the nurses talking about it."

Nell completed a move that looked like swatting at bugs under water. "Then there's no going back."

"Now, hold on…" Cora said.

"Nell's right," Sonia said. "People are counting on us. Besides, what's the worst that could happen?"

"We could get busted for stealing the van," Nell said, her eyes glinting. "Wouldn't that be a howl! Or how about a car chase like you see in the movies."

Cora wasn't so sure. She would be the one driving; she would be the one held accountable. She stared at her Clarks sandals. They were covered in newly mowed grass. For some reason, it pleased her. It spoke of adventure, traveling uncharted waters, having the guts to drive to San Francisco to see a matinee. So what *was* stopping her? Surely, the three of them had as good a chance at finding Mac as the police. They knew him better, for one thing—and had more at stake. And she'd felt good behind the wheel, hadn't she?

She took a deep breath and thrust her shoulders back. "Okay. But if we get caught, you two have to say I kidnapped you."

Sonia placed her hands on her hips, her four diamond wedding rings sparkling in the sun. "And give you all the glory?"

"I'm serious. Blame me. That way only one of us will have to face the consequences."

"I can see it now," Sonia said, spreading her hands out like a banner, "Dotty Old Women Plead Senility in Van Stealing Caper. The jury will eat it up."

"A jury?" Nell stamped her feet excitedly. "How marvelous!"

Cora sincerely hoped it wouldn't come to that. Surely she could plea bargain or do whatever it was O.J. Simpson did. But one thing she was sure of, if she didn't step up now she'd regret it. She met Sonia's gaze. "Are you up for it?"

"Hell, yes."

"Nell?"

"Oh, yes, yes, yes!"

Cora pulled the van keys from her slacks pocket. "Ladies, let's make us some history!"

CHAPTER THIRTEEN

Outside the Taco Bell, Mac adjusted the rearview and side mirrors of the Jetta. "First stop, gas station."

Effie winced at the skull and crossbones sticker on the dashboard. "Surely we can get out of town first."

"My dear, much as you like to believe that cars run on faith and good intentions…"

"But we're making a getaway."

"There is no way I'm taking this car on the road without checking the oil and tires. I'm traveling with special cargo, you know."

"Thanks for the thought, dear, but I'm already dead."

He'd forgotten…again. "Either way." He fired up the Jetta.

"Oh, look, a sunroof!"

Mac was just about to push the button for her when a burst of god-awful music blared from his waist.

"What on earth?" Effie said.

Mac remembered the cell phone and reached into his pocket.

"Don't answer it," Effie said.

"It could be important."

"Not for you."

It rang four times then stopped. He went back to the sunroof, feeling mildly unsettled. Why? It wasn't his phone to answer.

The window slid back—a miracle considering the condition of the car. The dashboard was faded and cracked from the sun, the seats stained from who knew what, and trash was strewn everywhere, including a couple of empty beer bottles. Those would have to go.

The phone started up again.

"Just ignore it," Effie said.

Mac tried, but its volume worried him. A group of Taco-Bell-bag-toting teenagers was walking toward them. He didn't want to draw any attention—an old man sitting in a beat-up car, rock and roll booming from his phone. He considered tossing the phone out the window, but that would look really strange. He hit the green answer button just to shut the damn thing up then held it to his ear trying to look natural as the teenagers passed.

"Hello? Hello?" a familiar voice said.

Mac felt his stomach tighten. "It's Morgan," he whispered to Effie.

"Hang up," Effie said.

"Dad? Is that you?"

He cleared his throat. She sounded worried. He hated that.

"Is there someone there with you? Are you being taken somewhere against your will?"

Mac considered telling her the truth, but Morgan wouldn't understand. Hell, he barely did himself. "Just me."

Effie let out a disgusted, "Huh!"

Morgan's sigh was brimming with anxiety. "Dad. Thank God."

He scowled at Effie then said to Morgan. "I'm just fine, honey, just fine."

"Fine? You ran away."

He pictured her on the other end of the line, his sweet daughter, always so responsible, blaming herself for his escape, his crime. It was wrong to put her through this. "It's your mother. She has this idea we should go to Santa Cruz." The second he said it he knew he shouldn't have, especially the part about Effie.

"What?" she said. She wasn't worried now, she was mad.

"I understand that this might be difficult..." He paused, trying to figure out in which direction to backpedal.

"Difficult? My dad breaks out of a retirement home, steals... what is it, a golf cart? And now he's telling me that my dead mom wants him to drive to Santa Cruz? Difficult? Nooo. This is easy peasy. Just another boring day in the life of Morgan Louise Ronzio."

Mac whispered to Effie, "She's pretty upset."

"Tell me you're not talking to my dead mother," Morgan said.

"I was just explaining—"

"Where are you, Dad? I'm coming to get you."

"Don't tell her," Effie said.

"I can't tell you."

"Mom's idea or yours?"

"Well—"

"Dad, this is crazy. Dangerous. Santa Cruz is…well…a long way away. If something should happen to you…"

"Honey, whatever happens to me is not your fault."

"Oh, *that* makes me feel better."

"I just meant—"

"Dad. You're—"

"I know. And my eyes aren't good. But that's why—"

"She's making you, isn't she?"

Mac had to think about this. "Yes…and no."

Morgan moaned. "Why didn't you tell me you wanted out of the Villa?"

Mac stuck the phone under his armpit. "Maybe Santa Cruz isn't such a good idea."

"The hell it isn't," Effie said.

"I think she's crying."

"Oh, for heaven's sake. Tell her it's just a little day trip."

"She's very worked up."

"Of course she is. She's convinced herself you've lost all your mental faculties."

Mac returned the phone to his ear. Morgan was trying to reason with him. "Are you even listening to me?" she said.

"If we leave now," Effie said, "We can catch the sunset."

"Dad. Mom is dead. Do you hear me? Dead."

Mac tipped his head back and stared at what looked like cigarette burns on the interior roof fabric. What ever made him believe that his wife and daughter's passionate tug of war—using him as the rope— would stop when Effie died? It always ended the same way, with him hurting one of them. He brought his attention back to the view outside his windshield. A Honda sedan was pulling up to the drive-through window.

"Morgan?"

"Yes, Dad?"

"I love you. I hope you know that."

"Don't you dare hang up on me."

"I'm sorry, Pumpkin." He punched the red button and slipped the phone into his pocket.

"Atta boy," Effie said. "Now let's make tracks. Ira's boy could come back any minute. Someone's bound to call in the stolen utility cart sooner or later—if they haven't already."

He pushed in the clutch and took the Jetta through all the gears. It had been a while since he'd driven a manual.

"You can do this, Macky," Effie said gently.

He practiced shifting one more time then added gas and backed out.

Driving on the road took some getting used to. He couldn't shake the feeling that the Jetta was blinking: *Stolen! Stolen! Stolen!* He anticipated red lights, slowing to a near crawl before intersections then, deciding his lack of speed was drawing attention, sped up at the last minute. Effie continued to encourage him, but he could tell he was making her nervous.

A Rotten Robbie appeared on his side of the street. He pulled up to a pump and cut the engine. What a relief. With trembling fingers he dug his credit card from his wallet then got out of the car and proceeded to fill the tank. He felt like he was in a dream, his hands and feet moving through water. Was anyone watching? He glanced around. Didn't seem to be. He had to search around for the hood latch, but once he found it he raised the hood and checked the dipstick. The oil was low. He wiggled the sparkplugs, tightened a couple of loose wires. The routine started to calm his nerves. He shut the hood and pulled over to the air pump.

"Not the tires," Effie whined.

"Number one reason for accidents is that people don't maintain their tires."

"Remind me, next time I'm looking for someone to drive a getaway car, not to ask you."

"Fine by me."

The air hose was unwieldy; he had to flick it like a whip to get to the back tires, which were both low. He missed tinkering with cars.

On several occasions he'd offered to work on Morgan's, but each time wound up in the tangle of her and Treat's relationship. It was Treat's job to take care of the cars, she'd said. Which meant Treat took them to the dealer. Not that it mattered. Cars these days were all computerized. A shame, really. But like everything else, they'd gotten too darn complicated.

Once the tires were filled, he headed inside to buy a quart of oil. A piece of plywood covered the bottom half of the door where the glass had been knocked out. A kid about the age of the Jetta's owner was sitting behind the counter fiddling with a smart phone. Mac worried that the Jetta kid and this kid might be friends, and that this kid might recognize the car. "Someone kick in your door?" he asked, trying to sound nonchalant.

The kid shrugged without looking up. "Don't know. It was like that when I got here this morning."

And he didn't wonder? What a punk. "Where's your oil?"

"Cooking? Tanning?"

"*Motor* oil."

"Over by the freezer case."

Mac made his way through the cookies and snacks remembering when gas stations used to be just a place to get gas. He picked up a quart of ten-forty and returned to the cashier.

"That all?" the kid said.

A tray of blinking bracelets sat on the counter next to an assortment of lighters, some that doubled as bottle openers. Mac plucked a pack of gum from the rack beneath the counter. "This too."

The kid rang him up.

Mac pulled a ten from his wallet. Damn, he missed the days when gas station attendants had grease under their fingernails. "Don't want to drive around with my oil low. Could throw a rod."

"Tell me!" the kid said. "Me and my friend were driving to Santa Cruz to get out of the heat. Had to spend the whole weekend in Los Banos. Man, talk about hot!"

Mac couldn't help feeling smug. "I'll have to tell the wife. We're driving to Santa Cruz ourselves and she didn't want me to stop to check the oil."

"You done the right thing, mister. For sure you don't want to get stuck in Los Banos. That place sucks."

Mac stuffed the change into his wallet. "Don't I get a paper funnel?"

The kid looked at him like he was a dinosaur. "Nobody uses those any more. Not since the bottles."

Mac tried to cover his embarrassment by chucking. "Well, thank you, anyway." He pushed back through the broken door and walked around the building to the Jetta. The funnel thing was just a little slip. No biggy. He popped the hood. It's not like he didn't know his way around cars. The more he thought about it, the more he realized he was doing the Jetta owner a favor. The kid wasn't going to need the car for a few hours anyway; most shifts were at least six. Hell, he probably didn't even know his car was gone yet. And when Mac got it back, it was going to be in much better shape. Maybe he'd give the kid a few pointers about keeping the car up. It was a good one, and could last for many more years—with proper maintenance.

Oil topped off, he checked the spark plugs and hoses again—one could never be too careful—then dropped the hood. Slam! If he'd had more time he would have picked up a can of Coke and poured it on the battery clamps. There were bunions of corrosion. Maybe once he got to Santa Cruz.

He opened the back door.

"Now what?" Effie said.

"I'm just going to get rid of some of this trash."

"Oh, for heaven's sake."

"Effie, it's against the law to drive with open alcohol containers in the car."

"I'm not even going to state the obvious."

He stuffed the bottles and other trash into a crumpled Taco Bell bag and tossed it into a nearby trashcan. He considered running the car through the adjacent carwash, but knew Effie would make his life miserable. He slipped behind the wheel. "Ready?"

"I was fifteen minutes ago."

Ignoring her, he pulled out onto the street.

By the time they'd reached the outskirts of town, he was starting to get excited about the trip. They were out by Treat's warehouse, an ugly section of city, industrial, but today it was adventure's gateway. He pulled onto the on-ramp. The pack was moving fast. Best to stay in the slow lane.

"Do you suppose the radio works?" Effie asked.

He pressed the ON button. A rapper guy shouted something about pussy poppin'. He pressed another button. The bass pounded louder. Another button and the music stopped altogether and the readout flashed AUX. What did that mean? He flipped the radio off. "The kid's tricked the car out with some new radio."

"Just as well. You don't need the distraction."

"What's that supposed to mean?"

"You haven't driven in a while. It's only natural you should be nervous."

"I'm not nervous. I'm cautious."

Morgan would have called Treat the second she'd heard. She called her about every little thing. It was amazing Treat put up with it.

They came up on a white panel van traveling at a moderate speed. The back of the van was decorated in sprigs of wheat and loaves of bread. He'd tail him as long as he could.

"Remember how angry you were when Morgan first brought Treat home?" Effie asked.

"Why are you bringing that up?"

"Just something to think about."

It wasn't like Effie not to have an agenda. "Right."

But it was true. He'd been such an ass when Morgan first brought her home. It wasn't the fact that Treat was a woman. He'd gotten used to that. Morgan had gone through several girlfriends before Treat: the one who died her hair black and was always reciting depressing poetry, the one who wore a suit and tie and combed her hair back like a man, the one who managed to bring politics into every conversation, the one who was just plain dull. But Treat was going to be different, or so Effie'd promised him. She'd met her a week earlier and thought she was delightful. Never said a word about her being Mexican. That was the shocker. But he behaved himself, at least that night— made sure everybody's beer was fresh, asked lots of questions about her work—but boy did he complain to Effie the next morning over Sunday breakfast. "A Mexican? You've got to be kidding me."

"Just listen to yourself," Effie said. "You're sounding very closed-minded."

"Close-minded! Because I have the guts to say our girl and a Mexican girl have nothing in common?"

"Because all you're seeing is skin color." He remembered how she cracked an egg on the edge of the pan. She might as well have been cracking it over his head. "Really, Mac. You can be so inflexible." How she dropped it into sizzling oil. "Change, that's what life is about. A series of adjustments, one after the next after the next—and the sooner you get that the happier you'll be." He'd watched that egg popping in the hot oil and thought to himself, I bet that little fella could tell you a thing or two about adjustments. He was expecting to be a rooster! But as usual, she'd turned out to be right. Treat was good for Morgan, and, more importantly, good for his and Effie's relationship with Morgan. She was so family oriented. And generous. And she knew everyone. Best of all, she was a Niners fan.

The panel van took an exit. But that was okay. Mac was back into the swing of driving. He'd always been a good driver, could drive anything, Effie used to brag. And if he kept his head angled just right, he could see no problem. Just stay in the slow lane and cruise to the coast, he told himself.

Effie pointed ahead. "Look! Chickens!"

Up ahead there was a flatbed stacked high with crates of red chickens. Each crate looked to have twelve or so chickens crammed into it. One chicken, stuffed into a crate and on its side, had squeezed its sorry little head through the slats and had a wild, desperate look in its eye.

"Those poor things," Effie said.

They drove in the truck's wake until Mac couldn't stand it anymore. He glanced once, twice, three times in his rearview and side mirrors to gain the courage to pass.

"You can do it," Effie said softly.

He took a deep breath, flicked on his blinker, and drifted into the fast lane, keeping his foot pressed down on the accelerator until the flatbed of chickens was just a dot in his rearview mirror.

CHAPTER FOURTEEN

Morgan stood on the loading dock staring at her phone in disbelief. Her mild-mannered father had hung up on her. She punched redial. The phone rang four times then: *Dude. This is Dirk's phone. But not Dirk. Leave a message and the real Dirk—*

She punched it off. Then just stood there some more, unable to come up with any logical course of action. She sensed John Boy and the two mall employees, behind her, waiting for her to say something. A button on the filthy wall in front of her had a small sign underneath: Ring For Service. She felt like ringing and ringing and ringing.

"So do you think I'll get my phone back?" the Real Dirk finally asked.

That's what he was worried about? Fury shot through her veins like thousands of tiny scud missiles, each one raring to blow something to smithereens. She was Medusa with writhing snake hair and eyes that could turn people to stone, the three-headed hag Hecate with a whistling purple cloak and death-eating heart, the multi-armed Kali with an insatiable lust for blood. She aimed her eye upon he who mocked her with mundane cell phone concerns, and spoke in a quiet, seething voice. "I have no idea if you'll get your phone back, Dirk, and frankly, I don't care. If you'd kept a better watch on your little carty thingy, my half-blind, delusional, eighty-six-year-old dad would not be out there in the world somewhere, lost, confused, and vulnerable to who knows what."

She targeted her gaze on the smug potbellied man, lest he feel vindicated by her not including him in her tirade. "I'm also of the opinion that someone was remiss in his managerial duties, letting his employees sleep on the job. I can't imagine your employer is going to be too happy about the publicity this oversight will elicit—"

She felt a warm hand on her arm and spun around, ready to lay into—

John Boy, looking genuinely concerned, damn him. Her diaphragm began to quiver, her eyes to sting. Tears blurring everything, she turned her back on the three of them and dug through her purse for a tissue, an old receipt, anything on which to blow her dribbling nose. She was vaguely aware of John Boy speaking to the other two, but she paid him no mind; she needed a tissue! Her nose was draining like a busted pipe. She felt him take her arm, lead her to the car in those damn cowboy boots of his. She didn't protest, just followed along like somebody's dotty old grandmother, wiping at her nose with the back of her hand.

"Your anger is totally understandable," he said.

An embarrassing laugh-sob erupted from her lips. What in God's name was understandable about any of this? Hands quivering and covered in snot, she opened the car door and, kneeling on the seat, reached across to the passenger side to pop open the glove box for something to blow her nose on. She came up with a crumpled Subway Sandwich napkin.

"Did you notice any unusual sounds when you spoke to your dad?" he asked her derriere.

What was he talking about? Morgan blew her nose and backed out of the car, shoving the snotty napkin in the ashtray along the way.

"I saw a TV show about woman who was locked in the trunk of a car," he said, "but she was able to identify her location by the sounds she heard outside and called it in to the police. So I was thinking—"

Mercifully, her phone rang. She couldn't stand one more second of his nonsense.

His eyes grew wide. "Maybe it's him."

She allowed herself a second of hope. Maybe it *was* him! She plopped sideways onto the driver's seat and snatched the phone from her purse. The readout said Treat. She shook her head and picked up. "Hey there."

"Any news?"

Morgan leaned over hoping to find another napkin in the glove box. Her nose was still going gangbusters. "I just talked to him." Unable to find one, she resorted to the used one in the ashtray. A piece of gum was now stuck to it. She used it anyway. "He's got a cell phone with him." She gave John, apparently planning to just stand there and listen to her conversation, a blunt look. *Space, please!* The look he returned was either abashed or insulted, she didn't care, just so long as he got the message, which he did, dragging his boots over to a nearby lamppost. She gave her nose one more blow then filled Treat in.

"He might return of his own free will," Treat said, "come, say, dinner time. It's not like he doesn't know his way around Fresno. Shit. The guy has a built-in compass. And you know how he hates to miss a meal."

"Did you even hear what I said? He's headed to Santa Cruz."

"Come on, in a golf cart? He's just trying to make a point. It's not easy for a guy who's been independent his whole life to be put away. He's a proud guy."

There it was again, the unspoken accusation that Morgan was wrong to move her dad into the Villa. She glared at the console. "I take it you can't get away," Morgan said coolly.

"I'll skip out as soon as we're done with the role-playing. Marky feels it's important for me to explain why I'm missing the ropes course—it's pretty weird for me to have set this whole thing up and then bail halfway through—but between sessions, I'll tell them what's going on. Oh, and I think I've averted most of *my* disaster—thanks for asking—our caterer got us mixed up with a gig at some country club and was all set up over there. Jesus."

Morgan's head throbbed. "Sorry…"

"There's nothing to be sorry for. Just acknowledge that I have a life too."

"I do, it's just—"

"Can we talk about this later? They're finishing up in the auditorium. I'll call you, okay?"

"Maybe we'll get lucky and you won't have to leave."

Silence on the other end of the line. Was Treat multitasking her? "Well, call me ASAP if that's the case," Treat said at last. "Otherwise, I'll call you as soon as I can get out of here."

"Okay."

Morgan punched end call, stared at her phone for a few seconds fighting the urge to call back and tell Treat that she loved her, and was sorry, then tossed the phone back in her purse. After a couple of gravelly-sounding neck rolls, a quick massage to the jaw, she was ready to go. She had to be.

John Boy, sitting on the base of the lamppost, was futzing with his phone.

"Coast is clear!" she called over.

Either he didn't hear or pretended not to.

"John!"

He looked up.

"Shall we?" she said.

He shrugged and trotted to her side of the car. She willed back her impatience. "I say we circle the area a few times then, if we don't find him, I'll take you back."

"Whatever." He rounded the car and dropped his lanky body into the passenger seat. "You could at least *try* to remember if you heard anything."

So it was back to that again: John Boy, Private Investigator. "Okay. I'll *try*." She was sure she hadn't heard a thing, but shut her eyes anyway, if only to get him off her back. "Motors running," she said, dully, "like cars at a stoplight or something..." And then damn if she didn't remember hearing something else too. Her breath quickened. "And there was a kind of robotic sounding...I don't know...voice? Like maybe a loudspeaker? But that's not right. More like an intercom..."

"A drive-through!" John said.

He was right. "Oh my God, that makes total sense. Dad loves fast food."

He pulled out a smart phone and searched for one in the area. It turned out there were quite a few.

"Let's start with the ones closest to the mall," she said feeling a surge of confidence. Maybe her Let's-Make-A-Deal-door-number-John-Boy wasn't such a bad choice after all. "Any Dairy Queens? Those are his fave." She started the car then had a thought. "I should call the police. Let them know what we've learned."

"Let's just hope we find all of them."

The dispatcher took the information about fast food restaurants and Santa Cruz. "I'll pass on your information," the detached voice said. The jerk might as well have been yawning. Morgan dialed the Villa next.

"What's your boss's name?" she asked John Boy.

He looked desperate. "You're calling the Villa?"

"The more everybody knows, the better chance we have to find him. Now, what's her name?"

"Constance Wright. But don't tell her I'm with you, okay? And ask if the ladies are back yet."

The receptionist picked up, robbing Morgan the chance of asking why. She stated who she was and whom she wanted to speak with. Constance Wright was on the line in seconds, and before Morgan could get out why she'd called, Constance resumed her efforts to barricade the Villa from a lawsuit, reminding Morgan of the teenage SUV driver plowing into the van—surely no one could blame them for that—and assuring Morgan that, regardless, John would be fired. Morgan refrained from mentioning that there should have been another attendant in the van, not just a driver. She wasn't about to quibble now, not with her dad on the loose. Instead, she calmly gave the witch what information she had then put an end to the backlash of empty assurances by hanging up.

"What did she say?" John Boy said.

"She's going to fire you." She shifted the car into reverse and checked her mirrors. "Now, where are we going?"

"What about the ladies?"

"I didn't ask. But I'm sure she would have mentioned if they'd returned."

John Boy groaned.

"We've got no time for this. What does your phone say?"

He checked the readout. "Jack in the Box point five miles away."

She pulled out of the parking lot and onto the street. "Keep your eyes peeled."

"Go left at the light."

Morgan cruised into the turn lane. "You don't seem surprised. About her firing you."

"She's already left me two messages saying the same thing. I'm going to pretend I didn't get them."

"Why?"

"Because we're going to find your dad and the ladies and then she won't fire me."

His optimism touched her. "You really like this job."

"I'm good at it."

She couldn't help but lift an eyebrow.

"Hey. The accident wasn't my fault. My van was parked."

She had a momentary flash of compassion. He was going to go down for this, even if it wasn't his doing. "I just don't see how you could have lost track of him. And the van."

"You should have been there. It was crazy. The dude who hit us was like jacked up on something."

The light changed and she made the turn, wishing it led to somewhere besides blaming herself.

CHAPTER FIFTEEN

Cora gauged the passing cars to be traveling close to seventy mph, but she stayed at a comfortable fifty-five. Life was moving fast enough without her speeding too. They hadn't been gone from the cemetery fifteen minutes when Ginny called back with the news that she'd eavesdropped on a phone call between Constance Wright and Mac's daughter, and that Mac was believed to be heading toward the seaside town of Santa Cruz. And now here the three of them were, cruising down CA-99 and headed for westbound 152.

If only it were just she and Sonia. Sonia she understood. Sonia was predictable—although she'd hate to be thought so. The way she masked her insecurities with that brassy bravado, always needing to establish that she was the queen bee, especially around men. But these were things Cora could count on. Certainly it got a bit tiresome at times, but what she got back in return was Sonia's splendid wit and steadfast friendship. That Sonia was diehard loyal in her friendships always seemed to Cora a marvelous inconsistency. But Nell! She was like a butterfly changing flight pattern with each new pretty flower. How quickly at the cemetery she'd jumped onto the idea of going after Mac then just as quickly onto the idea of heading west to Santa Cruz, never once considering the consequences. Cora was beginning to wonder if their whole excursion wasn't riding on Nell's rudderless flying carpet of enthusiasm.

She came up on an ancient, sputtering Eldorado, its back fender wired in place. She flicked on her blinker to pass. Stop kidding yourself, she silently scolded herself while changing lanes, the only reason for your pettiness is not having Sonia to yourself. She accelerated past the Eldorado then back into the slow lane, glancing briefly at Nell in the rearview mirror. She was gazing dreamily out the window.

"You keeping your eyes open for Mac?" Cora asked.

"Wide open," Nell said. "Isn't it all so wonderful?"

So much for the mission end of things.

Sonia took a small pocket mirror from her purse to check her makeup and hair. "I could use a restroom."

"And you didn't mention this when we were in Madera because...?"

"I hate giving in to this damn bladder. It's so fucking needy."

Cora chuckled. Just the mention of bladders set hers off. "Next station," she promised.

"I've always wanted to go to Santa Cruz," Nell said. "I've heard they have musicians that play on the street, just like in Europe. And a boardwalk on the ocean."

"That they do," Cora said. "And a lovely little garden mall full of quaint shops."

An exit came up on the right, but the only thing she could see was a giant grain silo. She pressed on. "I suppose Mac could have hitchhiked," she said.

"Or taken a bus," Sonia said. "There's no way that utility cart could do this highway."

"Maybe he's walking," Nell said.

Cora maneuvered around a squished cardboard box in the road. Mac wasn't that delusional, was he? She tried to recall if she'd ever heard him talk about Santa Cruz, but another thought niggled its way forward: the trip wasn't about Mac, not anymore. Her palms began to perspire, her heart quickened. She needed to think of something else, on the double, fill her mind with some kind of bubblegum that would keep her from pursuing this mutinous line of thought. A road trip game! The kind she used to play with the kids on the school bus. That should do the trick.

"Nell," she said, in her brightest voice. "What kind of food best describes you?"

"What is this?" Sonia said. "Some kind of culinary Rorschach?"

"A game," Nell said. "What fun!"

"Can we use drinks?" Sonia asked.

Cora shook her head. She should have seen this coming. "Sure."

"Then I can tell you what *I* am: Two fingers of Jack Daniel's. Neat. I may initially burn the back of your throat, but after that, I go down smoooooth."

Cora laughed. "You did take a bit of getting used to."

"And now…" Sonia reached over and gave Cora's thigh a pat. "You love me."

"You still burn from time to time."

"Well…yes. But that's what makes me so scrump-dilly-icious."

Cora signaled to pass a slow-moving pickup with a *Blessed are the Peacemakers* bumper sticker. The contradiction of the graphic, a gun and a dove, rankled.

"Fish food!" Nell chirped from the backseat. "That's me. Or will be."

Cora glanced at Sonia. Wasn't that a tad morbid? Sonia just laughed and said, "Perfect!" Then asked, "And you, Cora?"

Cora hadn't expected her turn to come up so quickly and couldn't think of a thing. The usual suspects, the one she used to tell the kids—apple pie, chicken soup, toast and butter—all comfort foods, didn't seem right anymore.

"I know what you are," Nell said. "A treasure cake! Like my mother used to make. She'd fill a yellow cake with little charms so that every piece had something wonderful tucked into it. They were so much fun. So magical."

Cora flushed. Here she'd been so critical of Nell. "Why, thank you."

Sonia slapped the dashboard. "Hallelujah! A Pilot Travel Center. Restrooms, here we come!"

❖

It took a moment for Cora to adjust to the pulsing music, pungent aromas, and aisles crammed with garish merchandise that greeted them inside the gigantic travel center. Hubert had been a sucker for roadside depots. A self-proclaimed non-shopper, he'd roam the aisles marveling at the travel paraphernalia: cups with snap-on lids, mini first aid kits, Swiss army knives, but depots like this one always made Cora feel like she was in retail purgatory.

Nell picked up a pair of glasses featuring an attached reading light. "Aren't these clever."

Sonia didn't stop to look. "Just get me to a damn bathroom before I wee my pants."

Cora followed and was heartened to find that the restroom had six remarkably clean and empty stalls. She chose one on the far end directly across from Sonia's. Nell pushed through the door and beelined for the stall next to Cora's.

The wobbly lock on Cora's stall door took a little doing, but once she had it secured, she tugged a seat cover from an overstocked dispenser, laid it on the seat, and thankful for the elastic waist of her L.L. Bean slacks, slipped them off and sat. And sat. And sat. Her pee simply would not come. No big surprise there. She was keyed up. It was still annoying. She noticed a bit of graffiti etched into the metal wall above the toilet paper holder: *Wherever you go, there you are.* She'd heard the saying before, of course, but under the circumstances, it was highly apropos. With this thought, her urine released. It wasn't the only thing that released. Next door, Nell let out a stunning fart.

"What the hell was that?" Sonia asked from her stall.

"Sorry," Nell said. "It was the milkshake."

Cora giggled. Nell joined in, snorting and gulping, then Sonia in that husky chortle of hers. Their giggles swelled into laughter like Cora hadn't experienced in years. Cora had to brace herself against the metal door to catch her breath before exiting her stall.

A teenage blonde, parading her bare midriff, gaped and backed away as if their hysterics might be contagious. Cora couldn't be bothered and strode past her to the sink to wash her hands.

As they made their way back through the aisles of merchandise, stopping to remark at this and that, Cora couldn't believe how light she felt. And not just because she'd relieved her bladder. The world was opening its doors to her.

They approached the food court.

"What do you say to a cup of coffee, ladies?" Cora said.

"Or a milkshake," Nell said, setting them off again.

An attractive, middle-aged woman waited patiently behind the counter at Dairy Queen, poised to take their order.

"Sorry," Cora gasped. "We're just a little punchy."

"Take your time," she said, smiling. "There's no one else in line."

Cora always hated seeing mature women saddled with jobs that seemed beneath them—definitely the case with this willowy cashier— but the woman seemed contented enough watching the three of them acting like lunatics.

Sonia wiped the tears from her eyes with a napkin, trying desperately to regain composure. "Don't mind us. Today's been a trip."

"Not just a trip," Nell said. "A whole vacation!"

The woman pushed back her Dairy Queen visor and gave them a closer look, her lovely brow furrowing. "Wait. I know you."

Cora searched her school bus driving days for a student who might have grown into this lovely woman.

"I just saw your video on Facebook."

Cora felt her innards shrivel. "You must be mistaken."

"Nope. Definitely you." The cashier leaned in conspiratorially. "On Isis LaFlair's Vlog." She glanced over her shoulder to make sure her fellow employees were otherwise occupied then briefly scanned the dining area before she honed back in on the three of them. Her eyes flicked from one to the next. "You haven't seen it yet," she surmised.

Cora stole a look at Sonia and Nell who both shrugged. "What are you talking about?"

Nell rubbed her gnarled hands together. "It sounds exciting!"

The cashier pulled a smartphone from her apron pocket. "Just tell me if any customers are coming."

"You got it, doll," Nell said, and spun around to plant herself facing the restaurant, her stance wide, her arms crossed over her chest, like some burly thug.

"The point, Nell, is *not* to draw attention," Sonia said.

"My daughter is a big fan of this site and sent me the link," the cashier said, scrolling through her phone. "I was just on break and I was—oh, here it is." She thrust out the phone.

Cora had to put on her glasses to see the tiny screen.

It was the gap-toothed girl from Moo's Creamery! Only she was wearing a pirate's hat and eye patch.

"Welcome," the girl said, seeming every bit as charismatic as she'd been at the creamery. "I'm Captain Isis LaFlair—aka Beeee-auty, and this is Three Graces"—she held up her tattoo—"my online video log broadcasting from the bowels of conservative Fresno, Ca-li-for-ni-a, where 'normal' rules and the rest of us play the fools. If this is your first time joining me…" She held up a plastic hook hand. "Arg! And greetings! It's time to let me entertain you with *real* people leading *real* lives." She leaned in close to the camera and spoke in a hushed tone. "My latest undercover gig is scooping ice cream at a mom-and-pop creamery; my mission: to secretly film the vile and the wonderful, the angels and the demons—all of them off guard, all of them true to themselves."

She looked from side to side as if checking to see if the coast was clear. "Your little pirate has lucked her way into a killer story this time, mateys. These ladies are the real thing. They've escaped from one of America's saddest institutions—the oooold foooolks hooome." This last bit she said while patting her hand over her mouth. Next the small screen revealed the three of them in front of the van—Cora in that silly fedora, Sonia with her collar pulled up, and Nell with the bandana tied over her nose and mouth—thrusting out their milkshakes like swords.

"To taking charge of our own destiny!" the miniature Sonia said.

"To really living!" the miniature Nell said.

"To extreme ridiculousness!" her own miniature self said.

But that wasn't the end of it. The girl left the camera on, sound turned off, while tiny Cora and Sonia removed their disguises and Nell mock fenced with her reflection. Only the girl had somehow added little comic eye patches, whose intention, it was clear, was to obscure their identities, but instead the patches floated disconcertingly around their faces, as if the girl didn't quite have the skill to pull it off.

"These runaway grannies," the girl said over the muted video footage, "are taking life by the huevos and living it on their own terms. And just in case this video reaches out beyond this pit of a town and you see these grannies on the road, don't turn them in! Harbor them in your homes; give them money. Support the dream that a person can grow old without shriveling into a useless burden on society! Remember: This could be you someday."

The image of the girl returned. "And that's it for this week's episode of Three Graces Video Log. I'm Isis LaFlair—aka Beeee-auty—vlogging my way to other kindred spirits in a world full of dull.

You can find me on Facebook, Twitter, and in the world at large. Vive the Runaway Grannies!" The video froze mid saucy wink.

"That little rat!" Sonia said. "She didn't just take our picture; she videoed us. That's why she was making such a big deal about balancing the camera on the windowsill."

Cora was too bowled over to speak. Not just at the audacity of the gap-toothed girl, but also because the video made it look like Cora was the ringleader, charging back to the van, barking at Nell to quit fooling around with her reflection. "This is a nightmare," she said.

"I think it's inspiring," the cashier said, "But you do need to be careful. You've got a ton of hits on the video. And tons of shares. People are posting it on Facebook and Twitter."

"How could this happen?" Cora said. "We haven't been gone that long." She glanced at her watch. "Not even two hours."

"And tons of comments," the cashier went on. She started scrolling. "'I want to be like this when I grow up.' 'These guys are cool.' 'I wish this were my grandmother.' You have tons of fans."

"What a world," Nell said, her voice filled with awe.

Sonia slapped a ten on the counter. "This is to keep your mouth shut."

The cashier looked hurt. "I would never—"

"Make sure you don't," Sonia said. "Now, how about three coffees?"

Cora, uncomfortable with Sonia's brusqueness—the woman had helped them after all—smiled. "Thank you..." She glanced at the cashier's nametag. "Joy." An odd coincidence, she thought, that the woman should bear the name of one of the three graces. Usually, she was a sucker for this kind of synchronicity, it made her feel as if she were where she was supposed to be, but now she could barely hold on to the thought of it. Her whole body was tingling with a kind of terrified excitement. It had been so long since she'd felt...what... noticed? Seen? Now she was a person of interest! She took her coffee from the counter and headed stupidly toward the door.

"Isn't it something?" Nell said, padding after her to the exit. "What a single day can bring?"

Sonia lingered at the counter fixing her coffee. She looked classy in her tailored cream-colored slacks and lime green blouse. Cora had always thought her hair a bit too red, but today it looked chic. For that matter, Nell was quite an interesting-looking woman too. Even with the thick glasses. Her short, white, unkempt hair and mismatched clothing, complete with grass stained knees, gave her an eccentric style, artistic, as if she had much more important things on her mind than fashion.

Cora brought the cup of coffee to her lips. It tasted luscious.

Back on the road and buzzing on caffeine, Cora sped past a beat-up camper van pulling a tarped trailer. They were coming up to the San Luis Reservoir.

"I'm going to call Ginny," Sonia said. "Ask her to start a rumor that we're headed to Mexico."

"Maybe she can get someone to post it on that video thingy. Do a hit or whatever," Nell said, "the way those other people did."

"Good idea," Sonia said. "We can get them to say they saw us."

"Look!" Nell pointed out the window to a bunch of windsurfers. "Water skeeters!"

Cora eased into a pullout. It was a fantastic sight, the surfboards with their brightly colored sails cutting tracks through the sparkling water, frothy whitecaps roiling, endless sky stretching out to forever.

"I'm getting out," Sonia said, flinging her door open. "I want to feel that air."

Cora turned off the van and followed suit, as did Nell. They followed Sonia down to a little promontory to watch. The gray-blue water surrounded by tanned, live-oak-dotted hills was gusting a strong, hot wind—wonderfully refreshing. Cora felt years of dusty thoughts being blown from her head.

What a dazzling world it was! People whizzing across the water while others whizzed around the Internet. Cora had never really spent much time with social networking. A friend had helped her set up a Facebook page on one of the community computers at the Villa, but she never had anything to say, and found the things her "friends" said trite or self-aggrandizing. Now, gazing out at the wind surfers making patterns across the water's surface, she reflected on the notion of a World Wide Web, but the Web she envisioned was much bigger than the one on the computer. It connected her to every being on the planet, and was so subtle, so responsive, she felt that the simple act of placing her warm hand on her cheek could change the future of everything.

Chapter Sixteen

C ruising down the main drag, Mac barely recognized Los Banos. The quaint agricultural town of his youth was now all built up with chain restaurants and flashy stores.

"A shame, isn't it?" Effie said. She'd been in her mid-thirties for the last half hour, the age when she'd first started going to her groups, wearing dangly jewelry, a hideous paisley pantsuit, and her hair long—her folksinger phase. It had been a difficult time in their marriage. She'd come home from this political group, that self-expression or environmental group, all fired up and expect him to get fired up too.

"Progress," he said. "It happens."

"Just happens? Is that what you think, Mac?"

His throat was parched. He scanned the passing stores for a place to pick up something to drink.

"I'm *talking* to you," she said.

"And I'm *ignoring* you," he shot back.

"I'm serious, Mac. Progress doesn't just happen. People make it happen."

He wanted one of those bottled iced teas. A Walmart was up ahead, but he wasn't about to wait in some long line of women with their carts full of groceries, or deal with the confusing self checkout where things never swiped properly. That is if you could even find what you were looking for. The employees were never any help. They all hated their jobs and acted put out if you actually needed something from them. At Ronzio's Hardware, people came in with all kinds of questions: how to repair the plug on a lamp, what gauge of chain would be best to hold a potted fern, what size nail was needed to build a birdhouse. He always took the time—

"There's a place," Effie said.

A bright yellow storefront with an ornate mural was up ahead. The mural was of the brown-skinned virgin, her feet surrounded in red roses. Lupita, that's what Treat called her. Not that Treat was in the least bit religious. Nor was she very Mexican. Or so he gathered from her family's nickname for her: Pinto Bean, they called her, brown on the outside, white on the inside. But she was a good woman. And good for Morgan.

He pulled up to Lupita's feet. The sweet rice drink that Treat occasionally brought home would be the perfect thing. "You want anything?" he asked Effie.

She scowled and pulled out her knitting as if to say, *Go ahead. Leave me here in the car.*

He left the window open for her.

Walking toward the store's entrance, he glanced around to see if anyone recognized the stolen car. But why would they? He was seventy miles away. The kid probably hadn't even noticed the car was gone yet.

Then again...

He pushed open the glass door, which was covered in beer ads and community flyers, and was hit with the smell of something delicious. Grilled beef? Pork? Above him, colorful piñatas swayed slightly from the draft of the swinging door. A small group of Mexican men, their work boots covered in mud, stood by a taco bar speaking in Spanish and laughing.

Mac strolled past a shelf filled with an odd assortment of canned goods, colorful blankets, and thirty-two-ounce bottles of orange Fanta, trying to shake the feeling that he didn't belong. What was the name of that rice drink? He searched the refrigerator cases crammed with dairy products, eggs, sandwich meats, bottled sodas and water, but couldn't find anything that even looked close. Then he remembered that Treat always brought it home in large soda cups. He spotted the soda fountain. Of course! But when he walked over to it, he found just the usual: Coke, Mr. Pibb, Barq's Root Beer, 7UP, Mountain Dew...

He did a sidelong glance at the men by the taco bar. If only he spoke Spanish! He'd saunter over and work his way into their conversation, gripe about the weather a little, the price of gas, then casually work the drink into the conversation. It's how it was done. Or at least how it was done at Ronzio's. He used to love watching Fresno newcomers edge their way into the conversation by the coffee machine. They'd hang around the knobs and handles eavesdropping on the huddle of men circling the complimentary coffee talking remodels or local politics. It never took long. The guys were happy to welcome in a stray.

He took another futile look through the refrigerator case. I should just ask, he thought. I'm a paying customer. He studied the scene. No one was manning the taco bar's counter, but someone was whistling in the tiny offset kitchen. At the front of the store, a gaggle of brown-skinned children were trying to get a young cashier to figure out how much candy their loose change would buy. No one was paying any attention to the old white man. He noticed an umbrella stand of hand-carved canes tucked in next to a shelf of sugary pink pastries. He picked one up, tried it out. The curve of the turtle's back fit nicely in his palm. He checked the price. Twelve dollars, what a steal! He moseyed it down the aisle and back. He liked its feel, how it detected a bit of loose linoleum before his eyes or feet did. This could come in handy, he thought. He stabbed the air with it. Very handy. He allowed the cane to walk him over to the men at the taco bar. "Excuse me, gentlemen, I was wondering if you know of a Mexican rice drink. Sweet."

The men looked at him blankly. He mimed taking a drink.

"Ah," a short fat fellow said then pointed toward the beer case. "Cerveza!"

Mac shook his head, and, tucking the cane under his arm—a nice fit—grabbed a bag of rice from a nearby shelf and mimed pressing it into liquid.

Clearly amused and definitely puzzled, the short fat guy looked to his friends to see if they had any idea what Mac was talking about. They shrugged, shook their heads, and talked among themselves in Spanish, but none of them seemed to have the slightest idea. Mac tried again only this time after miming the rice bit he included sipping it from a straw causing the guys to laugh outright, but they were good-natured about it; they clearly wanted to understand. "José!" the short fat one yelled past the counter. "Vienen aquí!"

The whistler came out from the kitchen wiping his hands on his apron. He was a pleasant-looking fellow with several gold teeth. "Sí?"

The short fat guy said something to him and motioned toward Mac.

"You looking for something?" the cook asked Mac.

"Yes. A drink made of rice. Sweet."

"Horchata. Sure." He pointed to a drink dispenser on the counter. "Here."

If it had been a dog it would have bitten him. "That's it!" Mac smiled at the guys. "I'd like one please." He'd never felt so white in his life. "My...daughter-in-law...is Mexican," he said to the group, even though they couldn't understand him. It was the first time he'd ever referred to Treat as his daughter-in-law, and it came out sounding contrived.

The cook didn't seem to notice, just translated for the men who started speaking over one another and laughing. "They say your son better watch out," the cook said. "Mexican women can be ve-ry tricky."

Mac felt ridiculously happy to be included in their banter. "I'll be sure to tell...him," he said, a disloyalty to Morgan and Treat, but two women being married was difficult to explain in any language.

After getting his drink and settling up for his purchases, he bade the men farewell, a little waggle of the cane and a wave, "Adiós!" then pushed back outside into the bright day. The temperature was skyrocketing, but he was so pleased with himself he barely felt the heat. He took a sip of his horchata. Light and sweet, thoroughly refreshing. He pulled the cell phone from his pocket and negotiated the tiny buttons to dial Treat's number, impressing himself that he remembered it. She picked up on the first ring. "Theresa Mendoza."

"Hey, Treat, guess what I'm doing?"

"Mac! Where are you?"

Oh. Right. He'd forgotten he was a fugitive. "I'm drinking a horchata outside of a place called..." He glanced over his shoulder. "El Toro Mercado."

"Mac. Do you know how crazy you're making Morgan? She's worried sick about you."

He pictured Treat, phone pressed to her ear, wearing her work khakis and short-sleeved polo. She was only about five-four, but made up for it in strength. The girl could lift a fifty-pound sack of cement like it was nothing.

"I'm fine. I just…" He had no idea how to finish this sentence, so he took another sip of horchata.

"Where's this mercado? I'll come get you."

"Don't you dare tell her." Effie, suddenly standing next to him, was back to her old-aged self, and looking none too pleased.

He turned away from her. What had he been thinking, calling Treat? "I'm sorry about your kitchen."

"Is that what this is about?" Treat said. "You're feeling guilty?"

Mac stared at a couple of crows fighting over a shiny wrapper, snatching it back and forth.

"Mac. Where's this mercado?"

"I have to go."

"Mac!"

He didn't respond, but he couldn't hang up either.

"Mac, you still there?"

One of the crows swiped the wrapper and took it to the top of the building, the other close on its tail.

"Listen, Mac, if you're still there, I don't know what it is you're doing, but if anything should happen to you, your daughter will be destroyed." There was a pause on her end of the line. He could hear her breathing. "Do you hear me?"

"I'm *fine*," he said finally.

"Well, make sure you stay that way. Now tell me where—"

Mac folded the phone shut.

"Atta boy," Effie said.

He took another sip of horchata then braced himself with his cane to sit down on the curb. He was suddenly exhausted, and feeling very old. A couple of the guys from the taco bar came outside with greasy bags of food and spoke to him. He didn't need to understand Spanish to know they were worried about him. Hell, he was worried about himself—he was sitting on a curb in a strange town, driving a stolen car, with no place he really wanted to go, his only companion his dead wife. He waved them off. "I'm fine. I'm fine." They gave him dubious looks but went ahead and climbed into a beat-up pickup and drove off.

I should just go back to the Villa, he said to himself, but the thought of the community room with that damn TV tuned to reality shows made the horchata start curdling in his stomach.

Effie sat next to him. "You okay?"

The crows, having given up on the bit of shiny trash, were now hopping around the parking lot squabbling.

"Just give me a minute." He felt so heavy, so tired, he thought he might sit there forever.

Chapter Seventeen

Dread settled its heavy sandbags onto Morgan's shoulders as she pulled into Taco Bell's parking lot, the last fast food restaurant listed for the area on the GPS. If they didn't find her dad here they'd hit a dead end. Even the ever-optimistic John Boy was looking glum.

It was going on three o'clock and Treat, having finally been pried from Marky Gottlieb's "amazing" program, had just called from home: no Mac there or in the neighborhood. The police had come up empty at the old house and the vacant hardware store. Morgan supposed she and John Boy could swing by and double-check them, but besides that, she couldn't think of a thing to do. Her dad had driven that little cart into thin air. Nothing left to do now but crawl into bed with a pint of Ben and Jerry's Chunky Monkey and cry her eyes out to her well-worn DVD of *Terms of Endearment*. Or go salty, surround herself with bags of Ruffles, Cheez-Its, Nacho Doritos… How well she knew herself. To make things worse, another hot flash was coming on, the perspiration sprouting from her upper lip like whiskers. That's it, she thought, I'm going to start hormone therapy— breast cancer be damned. She punched the air conditioner up a notch.

John Boy pointed toward the Dumpsters. "Look!"

A parked utility cart. But was it *the* utility cart? Morgan hadn't even cut the engine when John Boy flung open his door and bolted out. She switched off the car and followed, coaching herself not to get too excited until she knew for sure it was the one. John Boy gestured to the toolbox on the back of the cart. "Booyah! Property of Fig Garden Mall!"

Treat was right! Her dad just needed a break from the Villa's bland food. He probably had a sack of tacos in front of him right now.

He glanced around the lot. "No van though."

"Still," she said.

John Boy pumped both fists. "Yeah. Am I good or am I good?"

Laughing, she strode toward the entrance. "Well, come on, cowboy. Let's round him up." The two of them barreled through the door like a couple of gunslingers in an old Western and scanned the restaurant only to find a teenage couple whispering intimacies by the window, an obese woman sitting alone with a mound of food, and a group of young men placing an order at the counter.

Morgan's heart sank.

"I'll check the men's room," John Boy said.

Morgan got in line. Maybe the cashier, a tricked-out chola with penciled lips and thick eyeliner, would remember seeing him. She grew impatient as the girl with her heavy eyelids and slow-moving limbs took the men's orders. And then there were the super-sized drinks to be filled, ten of them at least. John Boy returned from the bathroom, shaking his head. The whole scene seemed to be happening under water while Morgan, crispy and alert, couldn't move fast enough. She took out her phone to report the found utility cart to the police. The dispatcher promised to pass on the information. She called the mall, told them she'd found the cart, gave them the location and promised to pay for any damages. She prayed they wouldn't press charges.

When the guys finally started lumbering to the condiments to wait for their order, she just about gave the last of them a flat tire stepping up to the counter. "Did an old man come in here...sometime within the last hour and a half?" she asked breathlessly. "He's not too tall...Anglo...and has big ears. Maybe a bit disoriented. "

The girl looked personally affronted to have to do something besides fill orders and drinks. "No one like that came in."

"Maybe the drive-through," John Boy said.

"Yes," Morgan said. "He would have been in a golf carty thing."

"A utility cart," John Boy said.

The girl sauntered back to another bored-looking girl and engaged her in a conversation that went well beyond asking if an old man had come through.

Morgan tipped her head back and was assaulted by an array of delectable looking meat-product tacos and lard burritos on the overhead menu.

The girl returned. "No one like that through the drive-through either."

"Are you sure?"

The girl all but rolled her eyes. "Y-*es*."

"Well, if he does come in, would you mind giving me a call?" She slid her card across the stainless steel countertop. "He's my father and his mental faculties are…well…just call me, okay?"

John Boy held the restaurant door open for Morgan. He looked miserable. "There went my job."

"We'll keep driving around. He couldn't have gotten far." She opened the car door, tossed her purse onto the backseat, and dropped heavily into her own, the adrenaline she'd felt seconds before melting into lethargy. The interior of the Prius was sweltering. She punched on the ignition and chased it with the air conditioner. It felt good to sit.

John Boy strapped his seat belt and started texting.

She didn't relish facing Treat, not after yanking her out of her big day—and Marky Gottlieb. But who was she kidding? Marky wasn't the problem. She and Treat had had so much thrown at them in the last year it was amazing they hadn't combusted before now. It wasn't just Mac moving in with them either, or Morgan's hours being cut back, or the kitchen fire. There was Treat's gang-banger nephew that kept having to be bailed out of jail, her warehouse losing those accounts. She just hoped the muscled femme wasn't taking advantage of Treat. One had to be ever vigilant not to take too much; Treat would give until it killed her.

Morgan felt herself beginning to choke up. Was this the end of their relationship? Is this how it happened? A slow crumbling into complacency? She remembered the bag of lingerie in the trunk. What a joke. Lingerie didn't stand a chance against middle age.

"What do you say I drop you back at the Villa?" she said to John Boy.

He looked up from his texting. "But you just said—"

"I know, but I might be driving around for hours. Surely you have things to do."

"Like going home and telling my parents I'm not going to be able to move out at the end of the month like I promised? That they're stuck with me until I can find another job? Can't wait to go back to *that*."

So the little cowboy had his own knotty life. She stared through the windshield at an impenetrable wall of pittosporum, her mother's favorite shrub with its tiny, scented, ivory-colored flowers, and was reminded of the hikes her mother used to trick her into as a teenager. *Just a short walk around the block, to catch up with each other.* An hour later, Morgan would come dragging after her, feet blistered, throat parched. But young Morgan never turned back, not even to pick up a pair of more appropriate shoes. It would have confirmed her deepest fear: she wasn't the woman her mother was, a belief she was never all that certain, even to this day, that Effie hadn't held herself.

"Maybe he met up with someone," John Boy said. "That would explain him leaving the cart."

But who? When her mom died, her dad might as well have too. Morgan angled out of the parking space. Had he just started walking? Decided he'd had it with life? She noticed her near-empty gas gauge. "We need gas," she said, taking a left onto the street. He'd been so bored living with her and Treat. It drove her crazy the way he'd walk up behind her while she was working at the computer then just stand there breathing down her neck.

A Rotten Robbie's was up ahead. "You want something to drink? I'm going to get myself an iced tea."

John Boy looked doubtful.

"On me," she said pulling up to the pump.

And there it was, that award-winning John Boy smile. "Hey, thanks. Want me to pump the gas?"

"That's all right. I'll meet you inside."

After getting the pump pumping, Morgan walked over to the mini mart, stepping gingerly through a mess of broken glass around a boarded-up door. A kid sat behind the counter playing games on a smartphone. John Boy was at the soda machine filling a huge cup of Coke. She joined him, choosing a medium iced tea for herself.

"I'm sorry I snapped at you back there," he said.

"When?"

"About not being able to move out. I just can't stand living there anymore."

She topped off her drink. "Understood."

"Get this. My mom had a rage attack yesterday because I called her and Dad on their way home from visiting my sister in Bakersfield to tell them to pick up some dishwashing detergent."

Morgan located the appropriate-sized lid. "Let me guess. She wanted to you to go out and get it yourself."

"Exactly. I mean, what would be the point? I'd have to make a special trip."

"And you had accumulated a pile of dishes while they were gone."

"Well, yeah. I had a few friends over."

Morgan snapped the lid into place. "You're right. You have to get out of there. You're going to be the death of your parents."

"Very funny."

The kid at the counter rang them up.

"Any chance an old man stopped in here?" John Boy asked.

Morgan paid in cash. She wanted away from the chips and M&Ms, the cookies and candy bars. She was too vulnerable.

The kid handed her the change. "What kind of old man?"

"Blue windbreaker, crisp khakis, blue bucket hat. About yea high." John Boy held his hand just below his own head.

Morgan's phone rang. She checked the readout. Treat. Was it possible her dad had showed up? She took the call outside.

"I just got a call from Mac," an excited Treat said.

Morgan's pulse quickened. "Where is he?"

"A Mexican market in Los Banos."

"What!"

"He sounded fine," Treat said.

"Back up. He's *where*?"

"Los Banos. El Toro Mercado."

"That's like, sixty, seventy miles away. How did he get there?"

"I have no idea. He hung up on—"

"You let him hang up?"

"I did not *let* him hang up."

"Sorry. I'm just—" But there was no good way to finish the sentence so she started a new one. "So, go ahead, tell me." She watched a big-bellied, ranchero pull up to a pump and wash the windows on his mud-splattered pickup as Treat brought her up to speed. The ranchero reminded her so much of Treat's playboy dad with his fancy belt buckle, boots, and hat. He was probably washing up his truck to impress some mistress. He sure wasn't doing it for his wife. Guys like him treated their wives like shit.

"And you figured this El Toro Mercado was in Los Banos how?" she asked.

"Google." Treat sounded proud of herself.

"Did you notice the number he was calling from? Or could you check?"

"A guy named Dirk Boehner."

"Good. He's still got that kid's phone. I'll try calling again."

"Oh, and I've already alerted the police."

Treat's efficiency made Morgan go mushy inside. Treat was good in a crisis. It was one of the things she loved about her. She glanced over her shoulder. Where the hell was John Boy? "Okay. I'll head that way. And it sounds like you can go back to your workshop...or whatever."

There was a silence on the other end of the line.

She shouldn't have added that whatever. Not when there wasn't the time to talk. "I mean, I really appreciate everything you've done, are doing, it's just, it doesn't sound like he's heading back home, and I thought you're probably wanting to get back to your thing with...Marky." Damn! Why couldn't she say Marky's name without sounding like a bitch?

"It's fine," Treat said flatly. "Just keep me in the loop."

Morgan pinched her lips together to keep from asking if she would indeed return to her event. She refused to sound that needy. "So I'll call you if anything changes. Okay?"

"Whatever."

Ouch. That hurt.

John Boy burst from the mini mart. "Mac stopped here! He came in to buy oil and fill up with gas. Only the guy said he was traveling with his wife."

"Hang on," she said to Treat. Then to John Boy: "Dad's traveling alone. On foot."

"He didn't actually *see* the wife," John Boy said. "Mac just talked about her."

"Did he say where he was going?"

"Santa Cruz."

"And they were *driving*?" Morgan said.

John Boy shrugged. "He bought gas and oil."

"What kind of car?"

"The guy never saw it."

Head spinning, Morgan returned to Treat. "Well, I don't know where he got it, but apparently Dad's acquired a car. And sure enough, he's heading to Santa Cruz."

"Holy crap."

"Yup. I'm going after him."

"Do you want me to come?"

She would if it was her old Treat. This new one she wasn't so sure about. "That's okay. I'm already by the freeway. And you have your thing."

She closed out the call with a clumsy good-bye. She couldn't exactly say what she really felt, not with John Boy standing there: that she appreciated all that Treat was doing, but she wasn't the kind of woman who could pull a Hillary Clinton, to smile and go on as if nothing had happened. There wasn't time for that conversation.

She turned to John Boy. "Where should I drop you?"

"No way. I just texted my mom and told her I wouldn't be home for dinner."

"John, this is ridiculous. I don't blame you for losing my dad."

He dug his hands in his pockets, his heels into the asphalt. "Sorry, but I'm in this for the long haul."

Morgan didn't have the energy to argue. "Sometimes 'long haul' is a lot longer than you expect." As she said this, she wondered if she were talking to him or Treat.

CHAPTER EIGHTEEN

"A school bus driver," Nell said. "How marvelous."

Cora chuckled. "It helped with the bills during Hubert's internship."

They were driving over Pacheco Pass. Its rolling hills, teddy bear tan, had bothered Cora no end when she first moved from the lushness of Maryland. The dryness defied her notion of summer being the verdant season, when the moist grass had to be hacked back, and frogs took up residence in every available puddle and stream. But over time, she'd come to love California's odd seasons; the hills, so dead-looking in the summer, blazed brilliant green with winter rains, and in spring—oh the spring!—the California poppies bloomed, carpeting the same hills in a fiery orange-gold. Yes, California had become her home—*was* her home.

"And when he first opened his private practice, I worked as his receptionist," she said. "I did that until I was seven months pregnant."

"Sounds simply awful," Sonia said.

"I take it you've never had to work."

Sonia squirted a pearl of moisturizer out of a tube she kept in her purse. "I always let my husbands take care of that end of things. I'd be a terrible employee anyway." She massaged the moisturizer into her hands. "I take it back. I taught dance for a while—before I was married. I was just out of college, and some girlfriends and I rented this wonderful old house in Brooklyn." She tucked the lotion back into her purse. "We all needed money so we started giving ballroom dance classes in the basement. We charged two dollars a class. Most of the classes we offered were held after school and filled with teenage girls, so they had to learn to lead *and* follow, but we also offered a couple of evening classes for adults. We got three dollars for those. That's where I met my first husband, Charles. He was already an accomplished dancer and only took the classes to court me. It was all very romantic."

"What happened to him?"

"What happens to most men, he became unbearably boring, more interested in the health of his stocks and bonds than the health of our marriage."

"So you left him."

"The tedium was killing me."

"And your second husband?"

Nell pointed out the window to the giant slash of blue water. "Can we drive to there? I want to stick my toes in."

"I don't see why not," Cora said, rolling the crick out of her neck. "I'd love to stretch my legs. Sonia?"

"Well, now that we have a reputation to uphold..."

"Ah," Cora said. "The reputation. Yes. We wouldn't want to disappoint our fans."

"We *are* the Runaway Grannies, much as I dislike being referred to as a granny."

"But aren't runaways usually running *to* somewhere? We have this vague destination centered around an impossible task—"

"Why not just see where we wind up?" Nell said impatiently.

Cora and Sonia exchanged glances. It was unlike Nell to sound vexed. Then again, she had a point. Making a plan really didn't make much sense. The whole venture had started with an impulse. Why not see where the impulse led, like the stones she and her brothers used to skip on the water, each leg of their short journeys propelling off the last.

"I say we keep going until either we can't or don't want to," Nell continued. "It could be our code."

Sonia shrugged. "Works for me."

A promising looking turnoff was up ahead. Cora flicked on her blinker and slowed down. What an idea to travel along with no plan, no goal, aiming toward an outcome that never turned out the way you expect anyway. She thought of Robert Frost's poem, "The Road Not Taken." Unlike him, she'd taken the more trodden road—getting married and having children, a doctor's wife. But nothing about it had been predictable. Still, she tended toward choices that she *thought* she could predict, fancying herself as someone who planned ahead. What would it be like not to?

She parked the bus in a dirt pullout, and the three of them hiked a short overgrown path to the water's edge where a big flat rock sat invitingly on a small sandy beach. Flanked by live oak trees and twittering with wildlife, the spot was private—a welcome oasis from the hustle-bustle of the last two and a half hours.

"This is it," Nell said. "Our very own pirate's cove."

Sonia flopped down on the rock, her prominent bosom facing skyward, and stylishly white, Capried legs crooked at the knees. "Our own little Riviera!"

Cora joined her, choosing to sit on a smooth edge of the boulder. She stretched out her legs and inhaled deeply, cherishing the sweet scent of tranquility. A warm breeze set a stand of rattlesnake grass rattling. She widened her gaze, taking in the whole of the reservoir, or what she could see from their little cove—pirate's cove as Nell called it. The teddy bear hills seemed to be hugging the water in their rolls of fur, providing a safe haven for weary travelers. A brilliant blue damselfly lighted on her knee then whirred away. She kicked off a sandal. Then the other. Perhaps wading was called for. But in a moment. For now, it felt so good to just sit.

Nell wandered along the water's edge. Sonia, it seemed, was content to nap.

Cora scanned the nearby thicket for birds. A kingfisher sat regally on a branch while something else—Rufous-sided Towhee?—was scratching around beneath. She wished briefly for her binoculars then decided it didn't matter. The moment was perfect as it was. She felt her muscles loosening, the Tin Man's rusty joints after Dorothy squirted him with oil.

Her youngest, Adrian, had played the Tin Man in a school play. She had no idea how the drama teacher talked him into it—his Asperger's made him avoid this kind of group activity—but he'd been perfect all trussed up in that refrigerator box costume, barely able to move his arms, so earnest in his interpretation of a man without a heart.

What if he'd somehow found out about what she'd done—was doing? He might nosedive back into isolation. She took a deep breath. Heart, brains, and c-c-c-courage, that's what was called for. She wouldn't be around to take care of him forever.

Sonia yawned and pulled her knees toward her chest. "There was a time I could wrap my leg around my neck."

"I'm sure all of your husbands enjoyed that little trick."

Sonia smiled devilishly. "You bet they did."

Cora refused to let Sonia's candor about sexuality make her feel like a prude, not today. She and Hubert had enjoyed a healthy enough sex life, perhaps not as adventuresome as Sonia's or the ones the women's magazines were always touting, no fancy positions or scandalous locations, or "toys" as Sonia referred to them, but they'd done all right.

Sonia propped herself on her elbows. "What's happened to Nell?"

Cora's heart skipped a beat. "I don't know." She scanned the water's edge. "She was here a minute ago."

"Shit." Sonia pushed herself up to standing.

Cora slipped on her sandals and stood as well, not sure what the worry was. Nell was a grown-up. Still, she shouted, "Nell!"

Sonia strode toward the twisty path heading into the brushy undergrowth. "Which way was she walking?"

"Thataway," Cora said, pointing to the right.

Sonia began down the path, shouting, "Nell!"

"Here!" Nell's voice came from behind a flowering shrub. "I'm fine! I'm just—" She tottered out from behind the shrub—stark naked.

Cora clapped her hand over her mouth.

But Nell was shameless, making little ouchy noises as she picked her way through the rocks and twigs. She looked so fragile, so pale and hairless, like a baby bird that had fallen prematurely from its nest. Her skin, almost translucent, made sticks of her arms and legs, while her breasts, angular and pointed, hung toward the swell of her sagging belly. "I thought I'd go for a swim," she said.

Sonia was already headed back to the rock. "For God's sake. Put your clothes back on before you scare the wildlife."

"Don't listen to her," Cora said. "You look gorgeous—like a wood nymph."

Nell laughed. "A rather ancient one."

"You're perfect."

Nell didn't seem to care one whit about what either of them thought, and continued toddling through the prickly vegetation to the water's edge where she stuck her toe in its glassy top, setting off a series of ripples in the otherwise flawless reflection of land and sky. Cora glanced at Sonia who arched an incredulous eyebrow while Nell continued on, her arms raised for balance, her toes finding their way along the reservoir's uneven bottom. Once she was up to her knees, she stood a moment, her slack butt covered in goose pimples, then she progressed quickly forward until only her head and shoulders were above the water. She turned to Cora and Sonia. "Oh, it's delicious! Once you get out a ways there's a soft bottom that squishes up between your toes."

"You do know how to swim," Cora said, only half-joking.

Nell dunked her head under and came up sparkling, her thin white hair sticking to her skull, making her look bald. "You've got to try this! It's simply too good."

Cora took a quick look around the area. No one in sight. And it was awfully hot.

"Until we can't or don't want to!" Nell said before dunking back under.

There it was again, the challenge to live.

It wasn't a question of can or can't; Cora was a capable swimmer, attending the Silver Dolphin water aerobics class twice a week. But did she *want* to? The only thing stopping her was vanity and propriety, two useless traits if ever there were any. She began shucking her clothes.

"Not you too," Sonia said.

Cora unzipped her slacks. "Until we can't or don't want to."

Sonia shook her head—priggishly, Cora thought. Which was odd. She was usually the first one to jump on this kind of thing.

"You okay?"

"Fine. Just...loving the sun."

"Well, all right, then." Cora hung her panties and new bra on a shrub. "I'm going in."

Having watched Nell's laborious and painful-looking walk to the water's edge, Cora kept her sandals on for the short trek to the shore then shucked them. The water was cold at first, but she persevered, and sure enough, when more of her was in than out, it felt wonderful, especially the parts usually covered in a bathing suit. Water caressing her breasts, her thighs, and when she scissor-kicked, entering into her, a cavern that had been dry for so long. It was all so sensuous. She floated on her back and looked up at the wispy clouds. What a small part of creation she was. Or was she creation itself? Overwhelmed by the immensity of the thought, she righted herself.

Nell was making little waterfalls with her hands, and Sonia was standing at the water's edge looking disgruntled. "Even if you can't swim," Cora said, "there's no big drop off. You can walk out as far as you want."

"I can swim," Sonia said, clearly annoyed. "It's just..." She hesitated for a moment then removed her blouse and bra. An angry scar cut across her skin where each breast should have been.

"Oh, Sonia," Cora said.

Nell just stared.

Sonia opened her arms wide, dangling her padded bra like a dead rodent, and flaunted what was gone. "I could never get myself to do the reconstructive surgery. Klaus wanted me too. Pleaded with me." She let her arms drop. "But I just couldn't do it. It seemed...I don't know...like I was doing it just for him. Or not that really...He was so kind. So understanding. I just don't *want* reconstructed breasts. I want my breasts. They take fat from your butt; did you know that? Your butt! So instead I have this." She held up the padded bra, pinching each strap like a lingerie salesperson then spoke in a sarcastically sweet tone. "The little deceiver." She flung the bra onto the sand. "My fucking body turned on me, that's what happened."

"Cancer is nothing to be ashamed of," Cora said. "In fact, just looking at you, and knowing this about you, makes me feel you're even more..." She searched for the right word.

"Kick-ass!" Nell said.

"Exactly. You are one kick-ass granny."

Sonia gave her the stink eye. "Granny?"

"As in Runaway."

"Ah." Sonia chuckled. "So you still love me?"

"Of course," Cora said.

"Even more," Nell said.

"So get your kick-ass butt in here and enjoy some of this wonderfulness."

Watching Sonia undress, Cora marveled at how it was possible to know a person so well—and not at all.

CHAPTER NINETEEN

Having finally peeled his weary, old man bones off the hot curb outside the market, and taken the reins of his burgled chariot, Mac was now cruising over Pacheco Pass, Effie riding shotgun and urging him ever forward. He was well past the lush blue water of the reservoir and wishing the next logical stop, the notorious fruit stand on steroids, Casa de Fruta, was closer. Everything along the roadside was dry dry dry, and it was naptime and he was getting sleepy. He forced his eyes open, shut, open, shut, yawned, and buzzed air through his lips making a motorboat sound to stay awake. If he could just stretch his legs, he'd be good to go. The Jetta tried to swerve into a passing eighteen-wheeler hauling cattle, but Mac held the steering wheel steady. He could do this—just keep his mind off the highway's nickname: Blood Alley. Beautiful, but deadly. She lulls you to sleep, he thought, that's what it is. He tried the radio again, randomly poking buttons on the dash. Nothing. Another yawn. His eyelids, damn it, wouldn't stay up. It was the heat. The car had no air conditioning; he was being battered with the feverish wind as it whipped past him through the open...

A deafening roar startled him awake, caused him to tap the brake. But the road ahead was clear. Shaken, he checked his rearview mirror only to see the same Mazda sedan that had been tailing him for the last fifteen minutes, looking intact, minding its own business. So what the hell *was* that? A blown a tire? Didn't feel like it; the car wasn't tugging. But what else could it be? The muffler?

"Pull over!" Effie yelled. "It's her!"

"What?"

"The ghost!"

He didn't need to look to know what age Effie was now: exactly two weeks before her stroke, the day she'd seen the Ghost of Pacheco Pass. Or thought she did.

He flicked on his blinker and reduced speed. A ranch entrance was up ahead.

"I need to ask her if she knew!" Effie yelled into the din.

He negotiated the car safely off the road and cut the motor. "Knew what?"

"If I was going to die!"

The racket continued, even after the motor was turned off, only now it sounded more like the thunderous rumble of a stagecoach— and snorting horses. Just like Effie said had happened the first time. Just like the legend of the Ghost claimed.

He turned toward Effie with the intention of getting some answers, but she was already outside the car and trotting up a short hill to...a Victorian woman? Mac squeezed his eyes shut. When he opened them again the woman was still there, wearing a long brown dress with a bustle, a hat sprouting feathers, and a valise beside each lace-up boot, exactly the way Effie described her that fall day, six years ago, when she'd returned from her spontaneous trip to Santa Cruz.

She'd woken up that morning announcing that Santa Cruz was calling her. Mac didn't think much about it. Effie could be impulsive. He just told her to drive safely and not to worry about him for dinner; he'd pick up a burger. When she returned home, after ten, she was all aflutter about some ghost she'd seen, and the pass being a portal to another world, then she'd kept him awake with her speculations about what her sighting meant: wasn't it strange how she'd had this impulse to make the trip, the ghost must be trying to tell her something. Two weeks later, she had her stroke.

Mac squinted out the car window. Effie and the Victorian lady, who looked to be about twenty, were deep in conversation. But this was crazy. *He* was crazy.

But wait. If the Victorian lady was a harbinger of death...Is that what this whole journey to Santa Cruz was about? Was he dying? Was he being warned that he only had two weeks left to live?

Traffic continued to stream by as if nothing were out of the ordinary. He stared at his frightened eyes in the sun visor mirror. Should he call Morgan? Mike?

"The poor thing." Effie was back in the front seat. "She's looking for her diamond bracelet."

Mac flipped the sun visor up. The Victorian lady was gone. "Effie—"

"You know how everyone's always going on about her looking for her child? They've got it wrong. She reached her hand out of the stagecoach and her bracelet dropped to the ground. She made the driver stop so she could look, but the other passengers didn't care about her bracelet so the brute threw her bags out of the coach and told her to catch another. The poor dear was still looking for it hours later when a second stagecoach barreled over the rise and struck her dead. Can you imagine being trampled to death by a team of horses?" Effie shuddered.

Mac pressed one hand down on the other to keep it from shaking. "What does it mean, her showing up like this?"

"I've no idea."

A train of ten or so Harley Davidsons roared down the highway. He waited for them to pass, his heart pounding alongside their earsplitting engines. "So did she know you were going to die?"

Effie leaned back against the seat and propped a foot up on the dashboard. "I told you, she's looking for her bracelet." She tightened her sneaker lace. "I think it's her greed that's trapped her on earth."

"Effie, I might be dying here! And all you can do is speculate about your little friend?"

"Oh, for heaven's sake, Mac. Are you still afraid to die?"

Mac stared at the ranch's mailbox, an elaborate brick and wrought iron thing with a wagon wheel. He needed to get to Casa de Fruta. Be around other people. Children. He started the car and looked for an opening in the traffic.

❖

Casa de Fruta was bustling with tourists wandering to and from Casa de Restaurant, Casa de Motel, Casa de Wine, Casa de Diesel,

Casa de Choo Choo, and Casa de Restrooms. Mac headed straight for the fruit stand, using his new cane to tap the road, shrubs, and sides of produce bins to test their legitimacy. He wanted to know what was of this world—and what wasn't. He passed a crate of fresh garlic and was comforted by its pungent smell.

The stand itself was just a token of the much larger indoor market where he strolled amongst bins of produce and nuts, trying to relax. He stopped at the cashews. A young family—two kids, two parents—were making a family project of filling a sack of honey-roasted peanuts next bin over.

"One more scoop," the rascally son demanded, his chubby hand tugging the hem of his mother's sundress.

"Are you going to be able to eat all this?" the father asked, tickling him.

Delighted, the boy released his mother's skirt and squirmed away. "Y-ees!"

"Okay." The mother, a model of patience, scooped more into the sack. "But that's it."

Mac felt his blood pressure ratchet down a few notches. "Cute kids," he said to the father.

"Don't let them fool you."

The mother slapped his arm playfully. "Ted!"

"Have two myself. Boy and a girl," Mac said. "'Course they're grown."

"Then you know," the father said.

"Do I," Mac said, squelching a ridiculous urge to tell them about the stolen car, the ghost, his promise to Effie, to beg them to take him wherever they were going. He pulled a paper sack from the stack and flicked it open. Who was he kidding? He should tell them to appreciate each other while they could, that life goes faster than you ever imagine. But that was just old man stuff.

"Bye bye!" the little girl said over her father's shoulder as he toted her away.

Mac filled his paper sack with cashews and picked up an apple for later. Once paid, he strolled out to the mini amusement park where a band of fat-cheeked toddlers were chasing a tired flock of puddle ducks while parents snapped photographs with tiny cameras.

He wanted to eat his nuts there, but a parked van of rowdies was blaring some god-awful music. He continued on to the outskirts of the country-fruit-stand-turned-tourist-trap, a healthy walk past several Casa-de-Something-or-Others, searching for peace and quiet, the sun-soaked asphalt sizzling up through the soles of his shoes. How quickly he'd gone from craving humanity to running from it.

He came upon an alley of retired farm equipment, rusted out tractors, grazers, backhoes, some of them a hundred years old, the people who ran them long gone. He popped a cashew in his mouth, grateful for his teeth. Several juncos were pecking around in the dust. How did one let go of this glorious earth? And what was it like in the great beyond? *Was* there a great beyond? It was the one thing Effie would never talk about. He looked around. Where was she anyway?

"Here," she said, sitting in the shade of a sprawling live oak, her legs stretched out, a satisfied smile on her face. She was back to her regular old self, dressed in her green sweater, pumpkin-colored turtleneck and tan slacks.

Using his cane, he lowered himself down next to her and leaned against the gnarled trunk of the old tree. It felt solid behind his back, real.

Perched on one of the old tractor seats, a squirrel chittered and clicked its disapproval. Mac tossed him a cashew. The squirrel would not be moved. Mac tossed another. It was obvious the squirrel wanted the nuts but was too timid to move. Mac went about munching on his own, pretending not to notice the squirrel. The nuts were delicious, coated with black pepper, and fresh. Wary, the squirrel finally found the courage to skitter off the tractor, shimmy on his belly to a nut, snatch it up, and hastily return to his post where he snacked on the tasty morsel. Then, of course, he had to have the second and made the treacherous trek over to the nut. This one he ate in place not six feet from Mac's foot. Mac tossed him another. The squirrel gamboled over and scooped up the nut as if he didn't have a care in the world. Mac's eyelids grew heavy, his grip on the bag of cashews slackening. How easily one can be baited into feeling secure, was his last conscious thought before giving in to his drooping eyelids.

CHAPTER TWENTY

"He must have a reason to want to go to Santa Cruz," John Boy said, adjusting his seat into a more reclined position. "People don't just go places for no reason. Even people with Alzheimer's have a reason. It might be a twisted reason, something from their childhood, but they have a reason." Seat to his liking, he folded his hands behind his head and spread his elbows wide, encroaching on Morgan's space. "Then again, we don't know for sure that Mac's going to Santa Cruz. Sure he *said* he was, and it sounded like that gas station dude saw him and Mac told *him* he was going to Santa Cruz, but all we really know for sure is he's in Los Banos. Did he have a connection to Los Banos?"

They were just outside of Chowchilla, and Morgan was beginning to regret caving in to the young cowboy's wish to come along. He'd been talking non-stop since leaving Fresno, a monologue that seemed to loop in on itself: why would Mac want to go to Santa Cruz, what might the reason be, people didn't just do things for no reason...

But there was a reason, and Morgan knew what it was. Her mom. Her dead mom. Morgan just couldn't make herself tell him. She wasn't in the mood to *share*. Nor did she have the energy, but the penalty for this omission was the endless drone of the cowboy's speculations.

It killed her to think of her dad doing this for her mom. Did he feel that guilty? Had the years of real estate pamphlets casually left around the house finally, belatedly, gotten to him? He'd tried so hard to make her happy: letting her rip up his neatly landscaped backyard to put in her unruly vegetable garden; sitting with her on the board of a community theater, which he hated, because they needed bodies; forgoing milk for a year because her mom read some article about it being bad for you. But this one thing, moving to Santa Cruz, he could not do. He was too much of a homeboy. Which was the problem. Her mom had been a homegirl too—only she'd given up her home for his.

They were passing the Pick-A-Part salvage yard. How old was she—eighteen? nineteen?—when her dad took her there to find a new windshield for her clunker Ford Escort. Wandering through the salvage, she had done nothing but whine about why they couldn't just buy a new one.

"I keep going over conversations I had with him," John Boy said, for the fourth or fifth time. "Maybe he let something slip."

Morgan pulled into the fast lane to pass a train of slow moving vehicles. "My mom grew up in Santa Cruz."

John Boy looked at her like she'd just spit out the winning lottery ticket. "That's it then, right? He's going back to find her." He pulled his phone from his pocket and started scrolling, a nervous tick Morgan was beginning to recognize. "If I could just get a bead on the ladies. It's like they disappeared into thin air."

"Seems unlikely they're on their way to Santa Cruz." She eased out of the passing lane.

"Everything about this whole day is unlikely. I mean for Cora to steal a van…She's like the sweetest old lady anywhere."

"Okay. Tell me about this Cora. Is she the one who looks like she came straight out of an AARP magazine?"

"What's AARP?"

She scanned the drivers and passengers in the cars they were passing. "You know, old person on the go, all happy and healthy and sporting a perfect set of teeth?"

"Short gray hair?"

"Dresses out of an L.L. Bean catalogue?"

He nodded. "That's her." He spoke while texting. "No way the kind of person to steal a van."

Morgan had to agree. The woman didn't look like she had it in her. She looked too refined. But Morgan liked her more for it. Which made no sense whatsoever. Here she was furious with her dad for running off, but found the same action in someone else's parent daring and spirited. And what of the other two women? Who were they? But her mind had no room to seriously consider any of this. "Any word from the Villa?" she asked. Not that she expected any. Not about her dad anyway. He'd call her before he called the Villa. But the police might contact them, if they found him…She fought off visions of him careening off the road into a ditch.

"Nope." He stuffed the phone back in his pocket. "Just Miss Wright wanting to make sure I know I'm fired."

"That's not very Christian of her." She was unable to keep her aversion to Bible-thumpers from coloring her tone. Why should she? It was her car, her crisis. Still, she couldn't help noticing that her comment had sucked all the air from the inside of the Prius. "You Christian?" she finally asked.

"Mormon."

Well. That made things interesting. She'd been pissed at Mormons since they'd dumped so much money into California to defeat the gay marriage bill. She'd actually been accused by Treat of making Mormon-bashing a hobby.

"Practicing?" she asked.

He crossed his arms in front of his chest and said, with an edge, "More or less."

What a crock. You either believed that you and your fellow Mormons were the only ones allowed into the highest Celestial Kingdom or you didn't.

"Why?" he asked.

This was going to feel so good. "I'm gay *and* happily married."

Then damned if she wasn't robbed the satisfaction of a good theological tussle by her ringing phone.

She checked the readout—work—and considered not picking up; not when she could grill this young upstanding Mormon about being "more or less" practicing. How wishy-washy was that? If he was going to claim Mormonism, he might have the decency to be a real posthumous-baptizing, weird-underwear-wearing Mormon. But her assistant, Connie, had been instructed not to call unless there was an emergency.

She picked up. "What's up, Connie?"

"I know you said not to bother you," Connie said, sounding frazzled, "but Dick Deetz is here—in the office."

Morgan groaned. She'd forgotten all about Dick. "Put him on," she said, belatedly realizing it meant she'd have to pull over. A phone call with Dick Deetz was sure to cause her to steer into oncoming traffic. She flicked on her blinker. She'd make it quick. Deetz knew the Pyle case was shaky or he wouldn't be using this lame intimidation tactic of showing up at the office without an appointment. She pulled onto the shoulder of the road by an assemblage of grain silos, popped on the hazard lights, and kept the engine running. Dick Deetz had fucked with the wrong woman today.

"I don't care that you're gay," John Boy said.

"Then I won't care that you're Mormon," she said before twisting away from him to take the call.

The whooshing air from passing cars rocked the Prius like a dinghy on the roiling sea.

"Ms. Ronzio? Dick Deetz here. And I have to say your follow-up on our last call does not give the impression of an HR department that is serving the needs of its constituents."

Constituents? Was he kidding? She dropped her head to her chest, counseling herself to stay professional. "Dick. I'm sorry I never called you back. I'm in the middle of a family crisis, something I'm sure you can understand."

He continued on as if she hadn't said a word. "As I mentioned to you before, Ms. Ronzio, we are ready to litigate."

It was like dealing with an automated phone service, one of those endless spirals: Press 1 for service, 2 for billing, 3 for having a meltdown because you can't talk to a real person.

"Dick. As I mentioned to you before, we are thoroughly investigating Ms. Pyle's complaints." Morgan noticed something stuck to the door handle of her car. Dried ketchup? "And until we complete this process, we can not move this case forward." She scraped the dried whatever-it-was from the door handle with her thumbnail. "And as I mentioned, just seconds ago, I am in the middle of a family crisis—"

"I don't see how this is applicable to our—"

"—and can't really give you my full attention. However, I would ask that you assure Ms. Pyle that we have her best interests in mind instead of harassing my assistant."

"Ms. Ronzio—"

"Oops. You're breaking up."

"—my client is—"

"Can't hear you."

"—suffering—"

"Are you there? Dick? Dick?" She hung up.

So much for being professional. But she didn't care. Her caring was all used up. She shifted into drive and pressed down on the accelerator. She'd lost too much time as it was. The car made a loud flap-flap-flapping sound and pulled to the right. She slammed on the brake. What the hell?

"Flat tire," John Boy said matter-of-factly. "We must have picked up a nail. Do you have a spare?"

She turned off the car, leaned her head against the steering wheel, and screamed into the horn, while John Boy, damn him, just sat there, the Good Little Mormon waiting for the Bad Lesbian to finish her unseemly display of emotion. Which made her feel like screaming louder. So she did. When he *still* didn't respond she said, "I have Triple A."

"I can change it before they get here."

Forehead pressed into the steering wheel, she studied him out of the corner of her eye. He looked awfully self-righteous, and was no doubt shocked out of his Mormon mind by her bizarre behavior. But she was tired of pretending, tired of acting the adult. "Okay, cowboy. If you think you can fix it faster than Triple A, have at it."

He flung the car door open and galloped out, no doubt relieved to have a reason to get away from the mental case old lady.

She popped the trunk and followed with the vague intention of helping, but he didn't need it, didn't want it; he was a tire-changing machine, his young muscles jacking up the Prius like it was made of cotton. She dialed her dad hoping he would pick up. He didn't. They were back in the car in less than twenty minutes.

"You're good," she conceded as they merged into the traffic.

"Yup," he said, spit-cleaning the side of his boot.

There was an awkwardness between them now, a line drawn, and not by him. He probably wasn't even old enough to have voted in the 2008 election, or if he was, he probably had no idea that it was his people who funded the hate-filled commercials that turned California to the right. "So how well do you know my dad?"

"I know him pretty good." Satisfied that his boot was as clean as he could get it, he started on the other one. "And for your information, Mormons aren't against gay people."

"Right. They just think we should stay celibate."

"Well, I don't think that."

"And you call yourself a Mormon," she said jokingly.

He glared at her briefly before reclining his seat, plugging up his ears with the headset to his phone, and shutting his eyes. The little fuck.

"Tell me truthfully," she said, speaking loud enough to be heard, "am I the first gay person you ever talked to?"

He turned up the phone's volume so she could hear the music through the headset.

"You know that can cause lasting damage to your eardrums!"

He continued to ignore her, tapping his cowboy boot to the tinny-sounding rock.

She didn't blame him really. Half an hour earlier, she'd been screaming into her steering wheel. Who was she to give him shit about anything? Her heart started in on one of its weird arrhythmic riffs. Was there no end to this menopausal hell? Her acupuncturist assured her there was, that her adrenals were just working on overdrive to help her body make the hormonal shift. Rest, she said, take time to nurture yourself.

Right.

Outside, acres of almond groves soared past, dotted with the occasional requisite bee-box outcroppings. How did those few tiny bees manage to pollinate the gazillion trees without working themselves to death?

At least John Boy had stopped with his incessant chatter. She plugged in her iPhone and selected *This American Life*, randomly choosing the podcast "What People Will Do for Love." But after a few minutes of listening to Ira Glass interviewing a young couple about their pact to sleep with as many people as possible before they got married, she felt like punching a hole in the dashboard. She put the phone to sleep and stole a peek at John Boy. His eyes were still shut, his ears still defiantly blocked up with earbuds.

Fine with her. She cherished the silence. It was beautiful outside, the sky a brilliant blue, the rows of almonds trees a never-ending musical staff. Until her mind started speculating on her dad's motives for wanting to go to Santa Cruz, a loop not all that different from John Boy's, only her loop blamed her for not being a more attentive daughter, for putting her father in that damn Villa to begin with.

She glanced at him again. She had to get him talking or she was going to drive herself mad. "Look, I'm sorry!" she yelled. "But you have to understand my position. Mormons, in general, have not been good to my people!"

He yanked an earbud from his ear. "I'm not a Mormon in general. I'm me."

"Point taken."

"So I would appreciate it if you'd stop acting like you know everything I think."

"Okay. But tell me this." She couldn't help herself. "Did you vote in the 2008 election?"

"Nope."

"Not old enough?"

"I was old enough. I just didn't, okay?"

Another of her pet peeves, but she'd leave it for now. "Well if you had voted, how would you have voted on Prop 8?"

"What was it?"

Sigh. "It amended the constitution to bar same-sex couples from marrying."

He thought for a moment. "I don't know."

Which meant he'd have voted for it at the time, but now that he'd met a real live lesbian he was having second thoughts. A good sign. He was impressionable. "I can live with that," she said. "But next time get your ass out there and vote."

For a moment, she was afraid he was going to plug himself back up again, but instead he popped out the other earbud. "You sound like my dad. Only he'd leave out the ass part."

Morgan adjusted her sun visor. Treat was going to love this: the kid likening her to a Mormon.

❖

El Toro Mercado's small parking lot was half full. Morgan angled the Prius between an old pickup with "Cheap Hawling" slopped on its side and a royal blue, low-riding Ranchero with red and yellow flames.

"Like I said, very few Mormons still practice polygamy," John Boy said.

Morgan nodded wearily. He'd been hammering her with this and other interesting characteristics of the modern Mormon for the last half hour. "Feel free to wait in the car," she said. "No use both of us going." But he was already unbuckled and out the car door. "Suit yourself."

She climbed out into the ungodly heat. Not a shade tree in sight. Just blistering cement, asphalt, and stucco. A group of teenagers was hanging out by a wonderfully gaudy mural of the Virgen de Guadalupe, the girls' short shorts, bare midriffs, and caked-on makeup in sharp contrast to the Virgen's saintliness. The lone boy, a real vato, leaned against a lowrider, cargo shorts jailin', calves and forearms covered in tattoos, bandana pulled down to his eyebrows.

Morgan discreetly plucked her panties from her butt crack.

John Boy eyed the teenagers and storefront warily. "Why would Mac come here?" he said under his breath.

Why indeed? Morgan trudged on. A molded cement planter by the door held a severely wilted petunia and a pile of cigarette butts. She pushed open the glass door plastered with beer advertisements and was rewarded by a blast of air conditioning. Had her dad totally lost it? He never shopped the Mexican groceries.

Without talking, she and John Boy wish-boned out, she taking the left, he the right. The grocery store was classic Mexican—the produce case filled with mangos, poblano and jalapeño peppers, and chayote, while colorful blankets and leather huaraches occupied the shelves next to restaurant-sized cans of hominy and lard. Under other circumstances, she would have loved it, taking her time to examine the shelf of tchotchkes, possibly even picking up a little skeleton for her collection, but today she whizzed up and down the aisles, her radar tuned to only one frequency: Dad.

She met up with John Boy by a stack of industrial-sized bags of masa.

"The guy at the taquería remembers seeing him," he said breathlessly. "Says he bought some kind of drink."

"Horchata."

"That's it."

"When?"

"About forty-five minutes ago."

The shred of hope that maybe, just maybe, her dad had ordered his horchata then hung around a spell evaporated into a cloud of desperation. Her dad could be anywhere by now.

"Oh, and no restroom," John Boy said. "I checked."

Like a boxer, bruised and bleary, and up against a monster opponent, she strode back into the hot afternoon, readying herself for the next round.

John Boy chased after her. "Now what?"

Her gut was turned inside out, devouring itself. "We head to Santa Cruz. Unless of course you want me to put you on a bus—"

"No way."

She was about to rephrase her suggestion, making it a demand, when he motioned toward the group of teenagers. "Maybe they saw his mode of transportation."

Once again, the kid was saved by a good idea. She approached the hormonal posse. A girl with way too much eyeliner was showing the other girls pictures on her phone. They giggled and pointed while Mr. Vato rested on the hood of his lowrider ogling. He was clearly too old for the girls, but they looked like the kind who could take care of themselves. How could any of them stand the heat?

"Excuse me," she said to the group. "I was wondering if you might have seen my father, an old man, in his eighties, probably drinking a horchata."

John Boy, puffed up, a tom turkey challenging another tom turkey, and added, "He'd have been wearing tan slacks, a light green short-sleeved polo, and a bucket hat."

Eyeliner Girl tossed back her thick black hair, clearly for his benefit. "Sure. He drank a horchata on the curb."

"He looked sad," another girl said.

The vato leaning on the lowrider gave John Boy a disparaging once-over. He wasn't going to let this guy move in on his territory. "I didn't see no old man."

"Before you got here," Eyeliner Girl said. "We were hanging out in Maria's car."

"Yeah," the other girl said, thrusting her hands onto her hips, and adopting a serious chola attitude. "Life doesn't start when you arrive, Car-*los*." She and Eyeliner Girl did a high five, bangles clinking.

Carlos hocked a lugey onto the hot asphalt where it sizzled into nothing.

"Did you see where he went?" Morgan asked, hoping her no-nonsense tone would cut through the mist of pheromones.

"He got into his car and drove off," Eyeliner said.

Morgan felt her pulse quickening. So he *was* driving. "What kind of car?"

Eyeliner placed a hot pink fingertip to her lip-lined lips. "I think it was green."

"Yeah," another girl said, "dark green."

Another waggled her head. "Uh-uhn. It was light. Kinda olive."

Morgan willed her irritation to heel. "Any chance you noticed the make?"

The girls looked at each other like she'd asked for the square root of pi.

"Kind of small?" Eyeliner said.

The chubbiest of the bunch shrugged. "I didn't even see it."

Carlos exhaled loudly, letting Morgan, and more importantly, John Boy, know if *he'd* been there *he* would've known what kind of car it was.

"Well, thank you," Morgan said.

John Boy flashed the girls an adorable, clearly much-practiced, lopsided smile. "Yeah. Thanks." Then tossed a cool nod to Carlos.

"No problem," Carlos said, returning the nod, man to man. Apparently, the two of them had come to some kind of manly truce, although Morgan couldn't imagine how. Nor did she spend time thinking about it. She was burning up. She needed to get some air conditioning or she was going to pass out.

She charged back to the Prius dimly aware of John Boy puppying after her. Once inside, she flicked on the motor and the air conditioning then she just sat there staring at the dashboard and soaking up the cool air. "Small…and probably green," she said to herself. Could the girls have been any more vague? Just from where she was sitting she could see two cars that fit that description.

"It's something," John Boy, said.

"I'm going to call Treat."

"Then let me drive."

Morgan hesitated.

"Come *on*. It'll eat up too much time sitting here."

Morgan's overloaded brain was slow to understand his logic. Oh. Right. No talky on cell phone while driving.

"If we hustle," he said, "we might be able to catch up with him on the pass."

She left the car running while they switched seats.

He adjusted the mirrors, the good little driver, then shifted the car into reverse. "We're going to find him."

For all his talk about hustling, he drove like a grandma, waiting until there was no car in sight before pulling out of the parking lot and stopping at a just-turned-yellow light.

She pulled out her phone and dialed Treat.

Treat picked up on the first ring. "Tell me you found him."

"I wish."

"So what's up?"

Morgan squinted at a green Lexus. "We're just leaving Los Banos." The driver was a middle-aged woman in a pink top.

"Then I'm about twenty minutes behind you. I'm hoping to meet up with you at Casa de Fruta."

"But your retreat…"

"They'll have to bond without me."

Green Toyota passing on the right. "You're not speeding, are you?" A young mother driving; baby in a car seat in back.

"Don't you worry about me, bonita. Now, what's the latest?"

Morgan filled her in on the car business.

"Where the fuck did Mac get a small, probably green car?"

Green VW Bug in the oncoming lane. "Who knows?" Middle-aged couple. "But he shouldn't be driving. Not with his eyes."

"Okay. Listen," Treat said using the competent voice she reserved for crises. "My cousin's boy is a cop in Los Banos. I'll give him a call. Ask him to keep his eyes open, in case Mac is hanging around there. Oh, and Louis, our neighbor, is keeping an eye on the house in case Mac shows up. I'll call him and tell him about the probably green car."

Morgan felt her diaphragm quiver, silly organ, but it felt so good to have Treat on board. "Thank you."

"We're going to find him, Morgan." Exactly what John Boy said a few minutes earlier, but somehow coming from Treat, the woman who made everything right, she believed it. Then Treat just had to add, "I don't suppose you've listened to my voice mail yet," ruining everything.

Morgan stared at her ankles. Were they swollen from the heat or were they always that chunky? "Not yet."

"Well, then, I'll tell you what I said."

"John's driving," she blurted, code for: I'm not alone.

"Who?"

"You know, John," she said making brief eye contact with him, "the guy from the Villa."

He wiggled his eyebrows.

"He's still with you?"

"Yup."

Morgan tried to read the silence that followed. Pissed? Disappointed?

"Okay, well, we'll talk later," Treat finally said. "After we find Mac."

"Okay." Hanging up, Morgan had the sickening feeling that she was pushing Treat into Marky Gottlieb's arms.

She focused on John Boy's driving. He was dangerously cautious. And slow slow slow. "You might try picking up the pace," she said after a few minutes of trying not to. "Dad's got a big head start on us."

"I'm going the speed limit."

"But nobody else is."

"Yeah, well, I have my job to think about. One violation and I'm toast."

"You're already toast."

"Not until Miss Wright tells me to my face."

"You don't seriously think she's going to keep you on?"

"None of this was my fault."

"It has nothing to do with that. She can't keep you on after losing a resident. It would look bad."

He hit the steering wheel with the heel of his hand. "It's not fair!"

It was tempting to come back with the jaded *life isn't,* but it made her feel too parenty.

A woman in a green Mazda roared past.

"This is insane."

They rode in gloomy silence for a few minutes. Then John Boy asked, "How did your mom die?"

Morgan kicked off her sandals and spread her toes, debating whether she wanted to dredge up that horrible night. Then decided, why not? The day couldn't get any worse.

"In her sleep, unexpectedly, the way we all hope to. But it was pretty hard on Dad, waking up next to her. Apparently, she grasped his hand as she was dying. He thinks that's what woke him up." Her mind replayed the night she got the call, her dad hysterical, yelling that the paramedics had taken Effie away, Morgan not even realizing she was dead. "I honestly don't think he saw it coming. Dad's never been one for pondering the big stuff. He kept the house painted, the car running, and the drains clear. He left lofty concerns to Mom."

Another green car whizzed by.

She'd expected to feel sad when her mom died. But she'd also expected the kind of relief she'd seen her friends experience, how they seemed to lighten, grow more confident, once that parental pressure was gone. And there were moments she was thankful her mom wasn't there to remind her of her potential and how far she was from it, or second-guess her choices. But nothing had prepared her for the blindsides of intense physical pain of missing her mother, leaving her reaching out into the void, wanting so desperately to unite, even briefly, with that essence that was her mother, and the absolute sense of loss when all she got was a busy signal.

She adjusted the vent on the dashboard to blow the tears from her eyes. Then she tried calling her dad again. One ring. Two. Please, Dad. Please. Three. Four. *Dude, this is Dirk's phone. But not Dirk. Leave a—*She punched it off. Up ahead was the python-like California Aquifer, startlingly blue thanks to her cataract-free eyes. A sign FOOD GROWS WHERE WATER FLOWS was planted into the ground.

And where the dead go, Morgan thought, nobody knows.

CHAPTER TWENTY-ONE

Cora pulled up to one of the few empty gas pumps at Casa de Diesel, relieved that the van, unlike their usual mode of transport, the Villa's bus, had only a small, almost illegible, version of the Villa's logo on the door. It was important to stay as low profile as possible.

Sonia thrust a bill forward. "Here's ten dollars."

"And ten more," Nell said, doing the same.

Cora cut the engine and took their money.

After swimming, they'd tied their bras to various shrubs—and left them there. It felt wonderfully defiant. "Be right back," she said, cranking the door open. "Don't do anything too naughty."

"No promises there," Sonia said.

"Just so long as we get to go by the fruit stand," Nell said. "I'm hankering for a nice sweet peach."

Cora chuckled. It was like driving the school bus, only the kids always whined for her to stop for the ice cream truck, which she could never do. She climbed out of the van into the blistering afternoon. What time was it anyway? Four thirty? Five? If they kept at this pace, they'd be able to do a late dinner in Santa Cruz. The wharf? She'd been once before and seen a pod of dolphins swim right past the restaurant window.

The air wafting through her linen blouse felt scrumptious. A man in overalls and a cap nodded. I'm-not-wearing-a-bra-ah, she smiled back at him.

Inside, a bored, overly made up woman in clothes much too tight for her body type worked the register. Cora got into line behind a frantic man whose credit card had been declined. Out of respect she averted her eyes while he shuffled through his wallet for another, letting them wander the racks of candy and gum, the chips and sunflower seeds, the whole time silently singing, *I'm not wearing a bra-ah; I'm not wearing a bra-ah.* To the right was a small lobby for people getting their cars serviced. Nothing but empty chairs there. A boxy TV carried on anyway. Male and female anchors, their faces chiseled and perfect, their clothing Hollywood-casual, nattered on about a cauliflower recall, joking that it wasn't going to make much of an impact. Cora tried to tune them out, focusing instead on the gloriousness of the day and her adventure. But the female anchor's next bit of news grabbed her by the throat.

"And now an unlikely story from the city of Fresno. A trio of freewheeling grannies, residents of Sunset Villa Retirement Home, have stolen the facility's van and are believed to be headed toward Mexico."

The male anchor went on. "These dames are garnering quite a bit of attention thanks to a rather colorful vlogger by the name of Isis DeFlair, who captured some video footage of them unawares and posted it on YouTube."

And there it was again, the five-second video footage of the three of them in front of the van thrusting out their milkshakes. Cora's heart began to race. She considered bolting for the door, but decided it would be too suspicious. Besides, they needed gas. She tore her gaze from the small TV to steal a peek at the cashier and the man she was helping. They were still caught up in the transaction and paying no attention to the TV. Or didn't appear to be.

"You should hear some of the comments this trio of dames is getting," the female anchor went on. "'Way to go, grannies! You're never too old to boogie,' 'I wanna be you when I grow old,' and 'Runaway Grannies for president!'"

The male chortled. "Wow, Char. They *have* hit a nerve."

"They sure have. And we're asking you, our TV audience, to log on to our website and give us your views on these lively ladies." She shuffled some papers. "I have to admit, Chuck, I admire their pluck."

The male nodded. "Let's just hope they stay safe out there."

"You bet."

"And now on to an interesting story about a girl, a shopping cart, and a car full of kittens. Just after this commercial break"

Cora stared at a woman dancing with a box of detergent.

"Ma'am?" The cashier's lavender-lidded eyes were looking at her with a mixture of annoyance and expectation.

"Oh. Yes. Um…" She glanced around. The frantic man was gone. She dug in her wallet for a ten to add to Sonia's and Nell's. "Thirty dollars on pump…" She hadn't even thought to check what number pump it was, but surely if she looked around she'd draw attention to the van—the *stolen* van.

"Which pump, ma'am?"

"The…um…one closest to the fruit stand."

"The van?"

Cora felt herself flush. "That would be the one." She forced her terrified lips into what she hoped looked like a smile, threw the cash on the counter, pivoted a hundred and eighty degrees, and beelined out the door, her Clarks sandals plodding the ground—plop plop plop—the rest of her body numb.

Sonia was sneaking one of her cigarettes by a planter and quickly crushed it out before meeting her at the van. "Something wrong? You look pale."

Cora saw her hands flip open the door to the gas tank and unscrew its top. They looked to her like someone else's hands, someone who knew what in God's name they were doing. "They were talking about us on TV."

"What? Who?"

Cora's hands picked up the pump, pushed the button for 89 octane, lifted the handle, and inserted the nozzle. "Some news show," she whispered, noticing a girl at the next pump over. "We were on it. The Runaway Grannies."

Sonia tossed her cigarette butt into the trash. She couldn't have looked more pleased. "National or local?"

"I've no idea. One of those silly talk shows." Like a desperate woman at a slot machine, Cora watched the numbers flip around on the gas pump. "They think we're headed to Mexico."

"Yes! Our plan worked."

"Shhh! We need to get out of here."

"What about Nell's peach?"

Right. Nell's Peach. Cora stared through the van window at the back of Nell's blissfully ignorant head. "Surely she can live without it."

"Who says the road will be any safer?"

"True."

Sonia scanned the area through her designer sunglasses, the tiny inset rhinestones flashing. "There must be a place where service trucks park. Then the van wouldn't be visible from the road."

"Service trucks," Cora repeated, trying to ground her scatter of worries in Sonia's logic.

"Hey," Sonia said tenderly. She rested her hands on Cora's shoulders. "We vowed to keep going until we can't or *don't want to*."

The gas clicked off.

"Cora. Look me in the eyes."

Cora twisted out of Sonia's grip to return the pump to its cradle.

"Cora."

Ashamed for being such a coward, Cora made herself turn around and look through the tinted lenses into Sonia's eyes.

"Do you want to go on with this?" Sonia asked.

"I think so."

"Think?"

What they were doing was crazy! They could all be arrested, go to jail! Yet not fifteen minutes ago, she'd sworn she was having the time of her life, and nothing had really changed, had it? Besides being poisoned by fear. And what was fear but a disbelief in herself? Cora inadvertently snorted a little air, reminding herself, ridiculously, of the poor bulls she'd seen in Spain, let loose in an arena of blood-crazed spectators only to be humiliated and ultimately killed. They never went down without a fight. Oh no, those bulls gave it their all. She thought back to the patronizing quips of the two TV anchors, their smug little chuckles, as if they couldn't imagine anyone over fifty doing something of consequence, something...gutsy. She had to prove them wrong—*would* prove them wrong if it was the last thing she did. Cora-the-bull would dance with that red cape until she dropped. She jutted her unbridled breasts forward. "I want to go on."

Sonia slapped her arm. "Atta girl."

Nell poked her head out of the van. "Everything okay?"

Cora screwed the gas cap back on. "Fine." She flipped the gas tank door shut. "In fact, it's damn wonderful."

❖

The fruit stand wasn't really a stand at all but a maze of fruit-filled bins attached to a much larger store featuring gourmet nuts and dried fruits, gift baskets, T-shirts, caps, and a wide array of tchotchkes.

Nell went straight for the peaches, bought herself the biggest, juiciest one, and headed out to a duck pond adjacent to the fruit stand while Cora and Sonia wandered around a bit. Cora was happy for a chance to stretch her legs and try out her newfound bravery. They passed a large decorated fruit and nut basket. "We should have that sent to the Villa."

Sonia snickered. "With a gift card saying, *Wish You Were Here.*"

As they zigzagged their way around the store, Cora noticed that she was actually hoping someone would recognize her. She wanted to be picked out of the crowd as someone remarkable, an event that, over the years, happened less and less. Even though, by far the most heroic thing she'd ever done was to stand by Hubert while his mind eroded. A person deserved a purple heart for that kind of devotion or to be a guest on *Oprah*, a mention in the newspaper, at least: *The Amazing Cora Whittaker Makes it Through Another Day Without Losing Her Mind or Killing Someone.* But no one in the shop gave her a second glance. She was just another harmless old lady who'd outlived her usefulness.

"I think I've had enough of overpriced fruit," she said.

Sonia popped a teriyaki almond into her mouth. "Me too. Let's blow this joint."

They found Nell out by the duck pond talking with a fellow who looked to be in his early twenties. He had a mop of curly blond hair pulled into an unruly ponytail and wore cargo shorts and a sleeveless tie-died T-shirt with *All You Need Is Om* written on the front. The white cords of some electronic device were draped around his neck.

"This is Tawn," Nell said. "I've told him we'd give him a lift to…" She turned to him.

"Mount Madonna," he said, "at the summit of Hecker Pass. It's right on your way to Santa Cruz."

She had to be kidding. A hitchhiker? Cora eyed the fellow's backpack. Maybe a transient.

"We've got plenty of seats," Nell said.

Tawn flashed a brilliant smile.

He did have good teeth. But really, their scenario was starting to sound a bit too much like Thelma and Louise. And *that* hitchhiker did something terrible to the women—robbed them or raped them, Cora couldn't remember which—and *he* had good teeth. "I'm not sure that's the way we're going," she said.

"Of course it is," Sonia said.

Cora glared at her. "We don't know for sure. Anything could happen."

"Anything could *always* happen," Sonia said.

Sonia's sudden alliance with Nell and Tawn the Transient was troublesome. Cora crossed her arms. She would not be swayed. She was brave, not stupid. "Yes, but…" Then for the life of her she couldn't think of a way to finish the sentence without revealing too much about their situation to this…this…stranger.

Nell placed her peach pit on the bench by her thigh, folded her hands on her lap, and looked up at Cora through her thick glasses. Her magnified eyes, devoid of eyelashes, were full of compassion. "Is there some reason you don't want Tawn to ride with us, Cora?"

Had they both gone mad? Allowing someone else to join them was downright reckless. Cora turned away to get her bearings and was hit full on by the white, hot summer sun. She lifted a hand to shield her eyes and spotted John from the Villa interrogating some tourists in the parking lot. The blood drained from her cheeks. She was only slightly relieved when the group shook their heads, which she assumed meant, No, we haven't seen a trio of fugitive old ladies, now would you let us get on with our summer fun? But it would only be a matter of time before John worked his way over to the duck pond and asked Tawn, the only person at Casa de Fruta she was certain would remember them. She spun around. "Fine. Let's take him."

Her sudden change in attitude clearly confused Sonia. "Cora? What's going on?"

How to tell her without blowing their cover? "I was just being silly. Now, let's go."

Tawn scratched the back of his neck. "You know, I don't want to cause any strife with you ladies."

"Nonsense. We'd love to have you." Cora pointed behind the fruit stand. "We're parked thataway. Now, go."

He flapped the back of his collar, presumably to let some cool air in. "But—"

"No buts. Let's go. Chop-chop."

Nell picked up her peach pit and tossed it in the trash. "What's the hurry?"

"The heat." She ushered Nell and Tawn in front of her, effectively herding them to the van. "It's got me feeling a little lightheaded. I'm sure I'll be fine once we make it to the van."

Sonia pinched the back of Cora's arm and whispered. "What's got into you?"

Cora let Nell and Tawn the Transient get a little ways ahead before whispering back. "John is in the parking lot."

"John?"

"Driver John? From the Villa?"

Sonia craned her head around to see.

"Don't look!" Cora hissed. "You'll draw attention to us."

"I saw him."

"Did he see you?"

"Didn't look like it. Should we tell Nell?"

"Not until we've got *Tawn* locked in the van. We can't risk him telling John he saw us." She strode forward and unlocked the van. Once everyone was in and buckled up, she revved the engine and ground the gears into first.

"Is everything all right?" Nell asked.

Cora backed out of the parking space and rounded the fruit stand where she saw John with Mac's daughter walking toward the stand— their backs, blessedly, to the van.

"We just missed John," Sonia said.

"John?"

Sonia pointed.

"Ha! That was close."

Tawn twisted around in the seat to see who Sonia was pointing at. "Who's this John?" He sounded worried.

"We're the Runaway Grannies," Nell said.

"The who?"

Cora and Sonia made eye contact. Was Nell going to tell him everything?

"If you had one of those little computers, you'd know," Nell said.

Tawn pulled a cell phone from his pocket.

"Look us up," she said. "We're famous."

Cora checked her rearview mirror one more time. John and Mac's daughter were talking to a maintenance guy. She drove beneath the underpass and merged into the westbound traffic.

"Found you," Tawn said, peering at his phone. He was silent for a few minutes, the only sound in the van coming from his phone. "Whoa...How cool. I got picked up by outlaws." He started typing something on his phone.

Sonia undid her seat belt, reached over the backseat, and snatched the phone.

"Hey!" he said.

"Hey nothing.'" Sonia pocketed the phone. "You'd lead them right to us."

"But..."

"Sorry, young man," Cora said. "But I'm afraid you're stuck with us until we feel absolutely certain you won't reveal our location."

Nell slapped his knee. "What do you think of that, dolly? You've just been kidnapped by the Runaway Grannies."

CHAPTER TWENTY-TWO

Mac was giving a tour of his childhood home to his new friend Sonia and someone else. But where were his parents? His two younger sisters? They were usually lurking around, but today the house was eerily quiet. Sonia and the other person—who the hell was it?—hung behind him oohing and aahing at the old farm table in the kitchen, the mangle in the laundry room, the pressed tin ceiling. Mac felt vaguely guilty about having Sonia there. What would his mother think?

He led them up the secret twisty staircase to his secret tower room. It wasn't always there, but this time it was. The room was cramped and stuffy with its angled ceiling, creaky floors, and dusty curtains, but it was filled with the most wonderful things: a radio flyer, a fleet of model airplanes, a brightly colored Chinese kite, and a robin's nest with two perfect blue eggs. And then, smack in the middle of the room, was the dreaded freestanding oval mirror with its spidery crack down the middle. His father's gray felt fedora sat by the mirror's wooden claw feet, begging to be tried on. Warily, he picked up the hat, set it on his head, and adopted what felt like a fearless stance for the mirror. He wasn't there! The mirror held only a cracked reflection of the room.

Something touched his hand.

He startled awake. The squirrel was tugging at the sack of nuts. Mac shooed him away, his head thick with...What had he been dreaming? He closed his eyes to remember. The room. He'd been back in the secret room...A blue jay squawked in a nearby tree. An insect buzzed past. Mac was traveling at top speed down a busy thoroughfare, supine, as if he were in a luge, only there was no luge, no track—and he was going *backwards*, careening around cars, pedestrians, cyclists. He craned his head around to make sure he wasn't going to smash into anything or anyone, but each obstacle was miraculously avoided. Trust, he told himself. Trust. But how disconcerting to be facing the past while zooming into the future.

Something brushed by his hand.

The squirrel! Only this time the little bugger had stolen the sack of nuts and was dragging it over to an old combine. Mac stretched his hands over his head. The tree trunk was digging into his spine. His left leg was asleep. He rolled his ankles and wrists a couple of times then pushed himself up into a more comfortable position. How long had he been sleeping? He checked his watch. Five fifteen.

"About time you woke up," Effie said. She was standing by the road with her hands on her hips. "We should get moving if we want to get to Santa Cruz while there's still some light."

Mac rolled onto his hands and knees and fought his way to standing. His hips felt cranky and tight; his lower back ached. "And what, may I ask, are we going to do when we get there?"

"Come *on*. We're burning daylight."

Mac lumbered behind the combine and unzipped his pants. No one was around, so why the hell not?

Effie turned her back. "Oh please!"

"Hey," he said. "I've got needs too."

Once he'd relieved himself—it took a little doing; he hadn't peed outside in years and his pecker froze up—he walked over to the empty sack and, careful not to strain his back, bent down to pick it up. Nuts were scattered everywhere. The squirrel chattered at him from a scrawny oak. "Don't worry," Mac said. "I'm leaving the good stuff for you." He crumpled the bag into a fist-sized ball and shoved it in his trouser pocket.

On the walk back to the car he passed a cherry 1954 four-door Buick Riviera, just like the family car they'd had when he was a teenager, the one he'd backed into a post while ogling his high school crush, Ava Hansen. Every day, he'd wait for his dad to confront him about the dent, and every day, his dad didn't. It was hell. Finally, he figured out his dad was waiting for him to fess up. Once he did, all his dad said was, "Took you long enough." But it had been plenty. Hell yeah, it had.

Mac noticed a smashed pigeon seconds before stepping on it. He stopped to give it a good look; its wings were spread out like an angel's, its decimated head covered in ants. The poor thing probably never saw it coming, he thought, was just pecking at a tossed hamburger bun, or potato chip, when, whoop, out of nowhere a car flattened it. Using his cane, he pried the carcass from the asphalt and pushed it to the curb. It was the least he could do. But wait. Was that Cora and Sonia walking to the fruit stand? It couldn't be. Could it? No way. What would they be doing here? He watched the two women until they disappeared inside the store then shook his head. There was no trusting his eyes.

"Go ahead," Effie said. "Say it."

"What?"

"That all us old ladies look alike."

Mac chuckled. "You said it, I didn't." But it was odd. He'd thought he spotted Cora earlier too. He needed a friend to talk to, that's what it was. Someone sensible, like Cora, who would tell him that what he was doing was stupid, dangerous, and that he should stop.

When he got back to where he'd parked the Jetta, he half expected it'd be gone. Or he hoped it would be. Better yet, he thought, it'd be surrounded by cops. They'd lock him in the back of a patrol car and take him to the station. Morgan would have to post his bail.

But the Jetta was just sitting there as he'd left it, tucked between two SUVs. Sighing, he pulled the keys from his pocket and let himself in.

"You all buckled up?" he asked Effie.

"Very funny."

He hadn't meant it to be funny. He didn't tell her that though. Just started up the car and shifted into reverse.

Chapter Twenty-three

M organ sat in the cramped restroom stall at Casa de Fruta trying to prolong the inevitable: her dad would not be found here, or anywhere, and she would be burdened with the everlasting guilt of knowing her selfishness led to his disappearance. Or worse, they *would* find him, bloodied and broken and wrapped around a tree or signpost in that damn green car. He'd reach for her through the shattered car window, his liver-spotted hand limp and streaked with blood. Through a crushed windpipe, he'd utter, "Better this than the Villa."

There was a loud rapping on the stall door. "You having a baby in there or what?"

Mortified, Morgan hiked up her slacks, grateful for the slight elasticity woven into the fabric—so civilized—and twisted around to flush the toilet, clearly an activity the designer of the pint-sized stall hadn't given much thought to. Once twisted around, it was too arduous to untwist so she unlocked the door from behind and backed out of the stall avoiding eye contact with the line of impatient women. She washed up and left.

Outside, she stretched her arms up over her head to work out a kink from her restroom contortions. Flashing her bare muffin top at a vanload of tourists was the least of her worries. She spotted John Boy talking on his cell phone by the car. He looked stressed.

I should call Treat, she thought, tell her we're at Casa de Fruta, see how close she is to catching up.

Morgan wasn't about to wait. She'd used up her waiting the night before, lying there pretending to read, watching the hours click by.

She decided to hold off calling until she and John Boy had searched the place and were ready to leave. *Well, sorry, babe, but you didn't get here in time.* That was the message she wanted to send. Nothing desperate. Just: *Don't think you're indispensible.* It was a stupid game and Morgan hated herself for playing it.

She walked past the duck pond where children were romping around and chasing ducks, an ancient white-haired woman was sharing a peach with a young traveler, and a group of teenage boys were drinking sodas and smoking, their carefreeness in stark contrast to her own stressed out state. She reached John Boy as he was shoving his phone into his pocket.

"My coworker says there's still no news about the van," he said. "The ladies are MIA." He massaged his skull. "I am so fucked."

"I didn't think Mormons used those kinds of words."

"Would you lay off with the Mormon cracks?" Butt on the car hood, he slumped over and dropped his head into his hands.

Crying? Morgan wasn't sure. But the display of naked emotion made her feel way too squirmy. "Look, I'm sure the ladies will turn up." In truth, she'd forgotten all about them. And the stolen van. He had good reason to be freaking out. He hadn't lost one elderly person, but four.

He lifted his head. No tears, thank God. But he did look utterly bereft. "Well, I'm glad *you're* sure."

Sarcasm. Good. She could deal with that. "Why worry about the future? There's nothing we can do about it anyway."

He scowled at her.

"You're right," she said holding up her palms. "I've been reading too much Eckhart Tolle."

"And he is…"

"Just some enlightened guy—who hasn't lost a vanload of old women."

John Boy snickered. "Or an aging father."

"Yeah." She slapped the roof of the Prius. "So fuck him. Let's go search this place. See if we can't find us one crazy old man."

"Right."

They combed every Casa, stopping to ask people if they'd seen Mac. Morgan was boiling hot, and miserable in her work clothes.

She could only imagine how hot John Boy felt in his boots and jeans. But he didn't complain, just walked into each Casa and started all over again with the "Excuse me. Have you seen..." Morgan let him do most of the talking while she scanned the different areas for her dad. She bought a bottle of chilled, overpriced Chardonnay at Casa de Wine, wishing she could guzzle it on the spot.

They were on their way back to the Prius, Morgan pulling out her phone, John Boy texting someone, when Treat came careening into the parking lot in her hybrid 4Runner. Superdyke to save the day! She lowered her window. "Hey, kids."

"Jesus," Morgan said. "How fast were you driving?"

"Pedal to the metal, bebé."

"I *guess*."

Treat ignored the bitterness in Morgan's voice. "So what's the scoop?"

Morgan studied her wife. So handsome with her short ponytail of black curls, her beautiful chocolate eyes. No wonder women were always throwing themselves at her, especially straight ones, who wanted to "test out" their feelings. She made a woman feel like she was in good hands. No doubt it was those very hands that Marky Gottlieb found so—Morgan cut that train of thought off at the pass. "Still no sign. We were just about to head to Santa Cruz."

"Well, hop in."

"And we're going to do what with my car?"

"Pick it up after we find him."

Morgan had to admit she was *somewhat* relieved to have her uber-capable wife join them, but her sudden appearance was also disorienting. Morgan wanted to be able to find her dad without Treat. Whether to hurt her, or prove to herself she could live without her, she wasn't sure. But something was changing in their relationship, and Morgan refused to be the helpless, weepy spouse who "never saw it coming." She saw it, felt it, and even though she didn't understand it—not yet, not fully, not until she and Treat had a chance to talk—she was prepared to deal with it, even if it meant...divorce.

The thought of divorce made her stomach cramp.

If only John Boy weren't standing there. No doubt he was waiting to be introduced. God forbid, his first experience with a lesbian relationship should be one with a troubled couple. She put on a happy face and turned toward him. "Treat, this is—"

"Hey, John," Treat said. "Thanks for helping out my girl."

John Boy shook his head. "I'm in this for myself. My job's on the line."

"You know each other?" Morgan said.

"Sure. John's the one I get to slip Mac extra pudding cups."

"Yeah," he said. "And I need to talk to you about that. He nearly got me busted by telling one of the orderlies." He looked down at his boots, noticed a little dust, and rubbed it off on his jeans leg. "Not that it matters now."

"Shouldn't we go?" Morgan said.

Treat didn't budge. "Did you listen to my voice mail?"

Morgan looked her straight in the eyes. "Nope."

Treat cocked her head and said "Chica..." so tenderly Morgan had to fight from mushing out. But she would not give in. Not when fidelity was at stake. So she just kept staring into Treat's eyes, and Treat into hers, the two of them deadlocked, each born Year of the Dog, Morgan, the pit bull, or that's what Treat always said, claiming that once she bit into something, she wouldn't let up, and Treat a goddamn Latin Lassie—only with that luscious streak of bad that made her so damn interesting. The stare was intense. Steaming.

It took John Boy clearing his throat and saying, "So...what do you say we do this thing," to break the spell.

Treat cracked a smile.

Blushing, Morgan turned toward him. "Last chance to get put on a bus and returned to Fresno."

"I'll pass."

"Then jump in," Treat said. "We're burning daylight."

Morgan strode around the front of the 4Runner to the passenger side while John Boy slid into the backseat. Treat rested her hand on Morgan's seat to look over her shoulder as she backed the 4Runner out of the parking space. "Come on, Mac old boy," she said, "work with us."

Morgan turned the air conditioning up a notch. "You getting enough air back there?"

John clicked his seat belt. "All good."

Treat wove them through a group of Japanese tourists. "Here's something you may or may not know. The old ladies that stole the Villa bus? The press has turned them into heroes. The Rockin' Runaway Grannies they're calling them. Of course, the Villa is going crazy. Such bad publicity."

John Boy groaned. "This just gets worse and worse."

"Did the news mention Dad?" Morgan asked.

"Not that I know of. Maybe you should try calling again."

"He won't pick up."

Treat didn't say anything, just pulled out of the parking lot and onto the highway.

Morgan dug out her phone and dialed. One ring. Two. Three.

"Hello?"

Morgan glanced at Treat. It's him! "Dad?"

"Morgan?"

"Where are you?"

"Heading to Santa Cruz, like I told you."

"But you're driving?"

"Actually, I'm pulling over so we can talk. It's illegal to talk while driving."

"Where did you get the car?"

It was quiet on his end.

"Dad!"

"I'm going to give it back."

"What do you mean 'give it back'?"

Treat momentarily took her eyes off the road. "He stole it?"

Morgan shrugged. Her dad would never...would he?

"Ask him."

"Did you...steal the car?"

Again, silence.

"You need to tell me where you are.... Dad...*Dad*..." Morgan tossed the phone onto the seat. "He hung up."

"Did he steal the car?" Treat asked again.

Morgan rubbed her temples. "I have no idea."

"Holy crap," John Boy said.

"Mac, Mac, Mac," Treat chuckled. "What have you got yourself into?"

Morgan blew down the front of her blouse to discourage an incoming hot flash. "It's not funny."

"Come on. We'd expect it from someone in my family. But Mac? Mr. Rotary-Club-Chamber-of-Commerce Mac?"

"At least we know he's okay," John Boy said, the implication being that they didn't even know that much about his old ladies.

"Well, I for one," Treat said, "am glad he decided to head to Santa Cruz instead of inland. I wouldn't mind having me one of those sourdough bread bowls of chowder on the wharf once we get there."

"If he gets there," Morgan said. "He's half blind."

"He sees more than he lets on. He does that side-eye thing."

John Boy laughed. "So true. Makes him look all demony."

Morgan slumped down in her seat, eyeing the beads of perspiration on the side of Treat's soda cup. "Can I have an ice cube from your drink?"

Treat nodded.

Morgan popped the top off the drink and plucked out a cube.

"Tell me you're not a little glad to be heading into some cooler weather," Treat said.

She stuck the cube in her mouth and spoke around it. "I'll never forgive myself if something happens to him." She wiped a bit of deliciously cold ice-drool from her chin.

Treat rested her hand on Morgan's thigh. "His mind is spry, chica. He knows what he's doing. Think about it. It's not easy to steal a utility cart. And now a car—"

"We don't know that for sure."

"True. But he's figured out a way to get to Santa Cruz. That takes cojones."

"I'm with her," John Boy said. "You're underestimating your dad. He's a cool dude."

Morgan thought about the lingerie sitting in the trunk of her car. How proactive she'd been feeling earlier, upbeat even. Keep your mind on the lingerie, she told herself, mind on the lingerie. She leaned back and closed her eyes then slipped the ice cube from her lips, ran it slowly down her chin and throat, and dropped it down her cleavage. She opened a single eye to see if Treat had noticed. Yup. She was just returning her focus to the road, grinning and shaking her head. Good.

Chapter Twenty-four

"Can I have my phone back?" Tawn reached through the space between the driver's seat and the passenger's one.

Sonia zipped it up her purse. "Sorry. You're a security risk."

"Can't have you squealing," Nell said.

"But I wouldn't—"

Cora swerved to avoid a tire strip on the road. "Sit down and fasten your seat belt." This was no time to get careless.

"What was John doing there?" Nell asked.

"Looking for us, obviously. I hope our little caper hasn't jeopardized his job." Cora glanced in the rearview. "Does it look like we're being followed?"

Sonia swiveled around in her seat. "I don't see his pickup. And let's not forget, Mac was the one who started this whole thing. We were just trying to help. If anyone's to blame for John losing his job—"

"Mac's daughter might be driving. Do we know what kind of car she drives?"

"Whatever happened to them believing we were going to Mexico?" Sonia asked.

"Obviously, *someone* believed it. Otherwise the TV—"

"Wait," Tawn said. "You guys were on TV?"

Cora felt like screaming. Why did Nell get them mixed up with this guy? He made things so much more complicated. She peered at him in the mirror. He was sitting next to Nell—still no seat belt—worrying his knuckles off and eyeballing the interior of the van as if looking for an escape hatch. Ironic, considering not ten minutes ago she was afraid of the harm *he* might do to *them*. "So what's your business at this place you're headed?"

"Mount Madonna?"

"Oh. I like the sound of that," Nell said. "Makes me think of a mountainous woman with pendulous breasts and huge birthing hips."

"Makes me think of one of the nuns at my elementary school," Sonia said. "We were all convinced she was the Virgin Mary. She was so good it gave me a damn tummy ache." She chuckled. "I used to leave tacks on her chair."

"Mount Madonna is a retreat center for the healing arts," Tawn said in an annoyingly self-righteous tone. "Very sacred, and the home of an amazing teacher, Baba Hari Dass. I'm doing a month-long teacher training in Ashtanga Yoga."

"Very…enlightening," Cora said. "We'll see if we can get you there."

"'See?'"

Cora flicked on her blinker to pass a slow-moving truck. "As you may or may not have noticed, we're fugitives."

"Running from the law," Nell said.

"I know, but—"

"What she's trying to say, *Tawn*…" Sonia drew out his name like a schoolyard bully. "…is that our top priority is to cover our own asses."

"Our own asses!" Nell laughed.

"But I've been saving up forever," Tawn said.

Honestly, it was like talking to a three-year-old. Cora put on her most sensitive voice. "As I said, we'll do the best we can."

"Maybe we should off him and dump the body by the side of the road," Sonia said.

Cora flashed her a look. "Behave."

"Why? It's never gotten me anywhere before."

Cora glanced in her rearview mirror. "Are you sure we're not being followed?"

Sonia twisted around again. "No, I'm not sure. For all I know they've got the FBI tailing us."

"Or the CIA!" Nell said.

"*Please,* can I have my phone back?" Tawn whined.

No one bothered to answer.

Outside, the late-day wind was picking up. Cora held the van steady. So much had happened since heading out for the mall, and all because of that single impulse to rescue Mac. Mac. She'd barely given him a thought in the last hour. Was he all right? Was he still headed to Santa Cruz? Why? What was he thinking nabbing that utility cart? That the rinky-dink thing would take him to the coast?

Then again, he'd been miserable at the Villa, prone to wandering around the community garden talking to himself. Lonely and displaced, but sharp as a tack at dinner. And a marvelous bridge player. He caught on so quickly. And been so helpful with the sticky drawer in her room, rubbing the track with soap.

The strum of a stringed instrument startled her out of her brooding. She stole a peek in the rearview. Tawn had a ukulele on his lap.

"A concert," Nell said. "How absolutely perfect."

"I'm not that good," he said. "Join in if you want."

Singing? Cora almost laughed. She didn't suppose Bonnie and Clyde ever sang when they were on the run, or Pretty Boy Floyd, or Jesse James. But the kid was obviously nervous—totally understandable. He'd gotten himself mixed up with the wrong people. "I can't imagine we know any of the same songs."

"'This Land is Your Land'?"

Sonia slapped her knee. "My Russian father would be thrilled. When that song came out, he said it should be our national anthem."

Tawn began strumming.

Nell joined in right away, her airy trill floating over Tawn's melodious tenor. Sonia, after a bit of eye rolling and one "Oh for God's sake," took up the tune on the third chorus. She was horribly tone deaf, but either didn't know or didn't care. Cora worried about how all this singing would appear to passing drivers so didn't join in. Not until they started in on "Yellow Bird," then she couldn't help herself. Hubert loved that song. "Michael Row Your Boat Ashore" came next and she sang along with that too. Then "Puff the Magic Dragon."

Tawn was a better musician than he'd let on, strumming along on songs he claimed not to know: "I'm Forever Blowing Bubbles," "Mairzy Dotes and Dozy Dotes." They'd just started "Bali Hai" when she saw a highway patrol car zooming up behind them, lights flashing.

"Police," she said. "Behind us. Flashing their lights."

Sonia twisted around in her seat. "Crap!"

Nell twisted around too. "A chase scene!"

"Nell." Pulse racing, Cora gripped the steering wheel. "I am not going to try to outrun the police."

Tawn crawled into the wayback for a better look. "He's coming up fast."

"Don't they usually use a siren?" Nell asked.

Cora tried to steady her breathing while slowing the van, her mind a jumble of possible consequences: getting fingerprinted, having a mug shot taken, calling Donald to make her bail, hiring a lawyer... Was there such a thing as the dementia defense?

The police car got closer and closer...

Then, mercifully, sped past.

Tawn pumped his fist. "Yes!"

"Thank God," Sonia said.

Cora let out a long exhale. "That was close." She swiped her forehead with the back of her hand. "Somebody hand me a Kleenex. I'm soaked."

Sonia dug one out for her. "I thought we were cooked."

"Me too," Nell said. "I was picturing myself being slapped around in some dusky interrogation room, a coupla dicks watching through a one-way mirror, one with a cup of stale coffee, the other with a cigarette dangling from his lips."

"Any cops think they're gonna take you ladies down without a fight ain't met you yet," Tawn said.

Sonia slapped the roof of the van. "Booyah!"

There was a road sign up ahead: Gilroy 15 miles. But Cora needed a stop before that. She was a nervous wreck. A ranch entrance was just past the sign. "I'm going to pull over," she said. "Stretch my legs."

"We could all use a breather," Sonia said.

The gate was flanked by two huge live oak trees, for which Cora was grateful. After bumping over the cattle guard, she angled the van in so it was somewhat hidden from the road then cut the engine and propped the door open. Despite its stifling heat, the fresh air was a relief, as was the solid earth beneath her feet. She held up her hand to shade her eyes and noticed it was trembling.

"You okay?" Sonia asked.

"I just need a moment." A spiraling black cloud of blackbirds swirled around in the sky.

Nell, standing by one of the live oaks, stretched her arms up over her head and let out a loud, happy groan ending it with: "That was thrilling!"

Tawn flipped himself up into a handstand by the front of the van. His shirt fell around his armpits. Cora sighed. He had the six-pack Hubert had always wanted.

"That's some trick, Dolly," Nell said.

"Gives me energy," he said, his giant Teva-clad feet swaying in the air. He came down abruptly, his face a knot of concern. "Ladies, I don't mean to alarm you. But there's a security camera up in the tree."

Cora turned to look.

"*Don't* all look at once," he said.

Cora froze, mid head lift.

"Choose one person to look," he said. "So it doesn't look suspicious. It rotates so it may not have caught us getting out of the van. Meaning, I could conceivably be your driver."

"I'll look," Sonia said. She faked a yawn, masking her peek. "Damn. He's right."

"I suggest you ladies start acting feeble and treating me like I'm in charge."

"Excuse me?" Cora said.

"Act old," he said.

"We are old," Cora said

"Well, act older."

She knew what he meant, saw the logic, but it grated in so many ways. First, to be taking orders from this youngster. And second to think that it would be more conceivable that Tawn, with his mop of curly hair, tie-dyed sleeveless T-shirt, and cargo shorts would make a more believable driver than one of them. But he was right; three old ladies being driven around by a young man would make more sense to people, and be a great cover, so she joined Sonia and Nell in trying to appear dithering.

"Now, Cora," he said, "I'm going to help you into the back of the van. Slip me the keys once you're inside."

Was he suggesting *he* take over the wheel?

"Devious," Nell said. "I like it."

Sonia, thank God, wasn't as easily swept up. "Have you ever even driven a van?" she asked.

"Hell, yes. Drove one across the country last summer. It was a stick shift too."

Sonia turned to Cora. "He barely looks old enough."

Cora couldn't agree more. Besides, she'd heard that splinter of condescension in his voice when he'd said, *Now, Cora.* There was no telling what he'd do if she relinquished the wheel to him. While his intentions seemed earnest, the young were quick to treat their elders like they couldn't think for themselves, railroading them to suit their own needs. Could they trust him? If he were forced to choose between his agenda and theirs, would he turn them over to the authorities?

Nell placed a hand on Cora's arm. "No fear."

Cora shook it off. She wasn't afraid; she was savvy. Still, a part of her envied Nell; she was so trusting, so able to change course in an instant, like one of the blackbirds in the spiraling flock—so unlike herself who survived on lists and plans. "Mom the control freak" Donald had once called her.

Sonia was staring at Tawn like she wished she could read his mind. She obviously had reservations too, which eased Cora a bit. "What do you think?" Cora asked her.

"I don't see we have much of a choice. The camera's catching you getting into the driver's seat would look suspicious."

"It's the perfect cover," Nell said. "The reason Tawn is here."

No, Cora thought, the reason Tawn is here is because you invited him along. But there was no denying the circumstances. "Okay, kiddo," she said, doing her best to look ancient and disoriented. "We'll give you a chance." She walked over to the van. "One."

"But if you screw with us in any way," Sonia added. "I'm going to call every contact on your phone and tell them you're a disgusting perv who molested three helpless old ladies. Got that?"

Tawn laughed. "You ladies are calling the shots." Then he gave Cora a hand into the passenger's seat. "I'm just the lowly getaway driver."

"You got that right," Cora said.

Chapter Twenty-five

Mac had forgotten how 152 zigzagged through Garlic Capital of the World Gilroy. He kept on the lookout for signs—difficult with his rotten vision. Effie wasn't much help. White-haired and mature, she was trying to direct him, but her memory was coming up short. "The turn's right up here," she said, pointing. "Oh wait. No. Maybe the next one. Yes. This is it. I'm sure. Oh, wait…"

The car's lack of air conditioning hadn't bothered him on the open road; the two windows did the trick, the hot air blowing past him exhilarating. But crawling through Gilroy's outlet centers and fast food restaurants, he was broiling in the stink of garlic.

So much for the days when Gilroy was all fields and farm workers, when you were happy just to find a gas station with a soda machine. Now you were lucky if you could snake through the traffic without being channeled into some shopping center parking lot.

"I think it's at this next intersection," Effie said.

Mac flicked on his left blinker. He couldn't stop thinking about the phone call with Morgan. He'd picked up with the intention of telling her not to worry then gotten all mealymouthed when she asked if he'd stolen the car. Had the theft been reported yet? He glanced around for cops. Or was she guessing? For all he knew she'd been calling from the police station and there were officers listening in. Either way about it, his little girl was upset and he was the cause.

"This is it," Effie said, wagging her finger. "Turn!"

He cranked the wheel left.

A car's brakes screeched. There was honking. A young man yelled, "Jesus Christ, Grandpa! Watch where the fuck you're going!"

Mac waved an apology, his heart slamming in his chest.

"Don't blame me," Effie said, "I'm just the navigator."

Mac searched for a spot to pull over. He was too shaken up to keep driving. He swung into a garlic outlet's parking lot and cut the engine. Took a few shuddering breaths. Then a couple more. Could have been worse, he told himself, much worse. Outside, a large welcome sign advertised weekend garlic tastings.

"I love this place," Effie said. "Dad used to take us here as kids. 'Course it was much smaller then, a mom-and-pop stand. We'd get strands of braided garlic, pickled garlic, and our favorite, garlic ice cream—sounds icky, but it's wonderful."

"I nearly had an accident and you're talking ice cream?"

"Oh, poof. The guy was driving too fast."

"I cut into his lane."

She was quiet a few seconds. "So what are you saying?"

Mac unlatched his seat belt and let his head drop back. He breathed in more sweltering inland air, giving his heart time to resume its steady tha-thump, tha-thump. He was too old to be taking this kind of trip, too old to be driving at all. "I could have gotten us both killed."

She smoothed her corduroy slacks. "We'd be together."

It was his turn to be silent. What *was* he sticking around for, anyway? Since moving into the Villa—hell, in with his daughter—his life had become sorrier than a bent nail. He didn't have the strength or acuity to do the things he loved, the woodworking, the tinkering with cars, golf. And his social life, what a joke! That came to a screeching halt the day he lost his driver's license.

"This isn't about us," he said finally.

"Then who?"

"Our kids."

Effie glared out the window. "You're an excellent driver, Mac."

He followed her gaze to a picture of a Mr. and Mrs. Garlic holding hands and looking as if the world held nothing but promise. So simple when there's just two to think about, but when children are added...

"And you've gotten us this far."

The woman would not let up. "Our kids would be devastated to lose me in a car wreck. Especially Morgan. She'd never stop blaming herself." He turned to his wife, hoping for once she'd see things his way. No such luck. She was now young and pregnant and looking about as interested in his problems as a butterfly.

"Garlic ice cream would be perfect right now," she said—so cute in her seersucker pedal pushers and loose sleeveless blouse.

A lot of guys he knew didn't like how their wives looked pregnant, but he loved her swollen belly, the filling out of her hips and breasts. She looked succulent, ripe.

She wrapped a chestnut-colored curl around her finger. "You've never even tried it."

She was right about that. He hadn't done a *lot* of things. Hadn't followed through with the clarinet because of his obligation to the family business, hadn't bought that motorcycle because it made her nervous, hadn't invested in that car parts shop next to Ronzio's because his dad didn't think it was prudent, never even made the Glider Festival in Lost Hills because it was held on the weekends when the store was busiest. Wasn't it time he did something unpredictable? Irresponsible? Go out in a blaze of glory instead of slowly rusting away like an old junkyard car.

"We're almost there," she pleaded, her sneakered feet stretched out and wagging in front of her. "There's just Hecker Pass, Watsonville, and then—voila!—the cool, cool air of Santa Cruz."

Mac tapped the steering wheel a few times with his callused thumbs. He could do without the ice cream, but brisk ocean air was exactly what he needed to get out of this funk.

"And I'm telling you," she said in a singsong voice, "that garlic ice cream is goo-ood."

"What about my eyes?"

"Oh, phooey. I'll be your eyes."

How could he say no to her? This girl who'd left her friends and family and moved from her beloved hometown of Santa Cruz to be with him; this girl who'd braved three terrible months of morning sickness then six more of backbreaking pregnancy and a grueling twenty-four hour labor to give him a son, then went through the whole thing again to give him a beautiful daughter; this girl who'd patiently listened to his mother and aunts advise her on raising their kids only to disregard them and do it her own way; this girl who was now asking for the simplest thing, that he take her on one last trip to the ocean that she so loved. "You promise to keep your eyes on the road? Keep me from any more potential accidents?"

She held up her two fingers, Girl Scout style. "Promise."

CHAPTER TWENTY-SIX

Morgan watched gloomily as a convoy of flatbeds hauling giant crates of tomatoes rumbled past. She pictured the tasteless, genetically modified orbs traveling to factories where they'd be dumped onto conveyor belts, dropped into vats, and pulverized into sauce, ketchup, and tomato paste. The lucky among them would appear atop withered iceberg lettuce salads where they'd be dressed with gloppy mixtures seasoned with heaps of salt and MSG. The rest pulverized into sauce.

There hadn't been a green car in over fifteen minutes.

Treat and John Boy were speculating on whether the Giants had a chance at making it to the playoffs, Treat acting as if everything between her and Morgan was hunky-dory. Which Morgan appreciated. Mostly. Morgan had dated spewers in the past, and she had friends that were like that—Alice from work was a spewer of epic proportion, dragging Morgan into her extramarital dramas, trying to get Morgan to take sides. It was exhausting, and Morgan was grateful that Treat wasn't like that. Still, the pretense that everything was all sparkly-good between them was unsettling.

"Ever been to a game?" Treat asked John Boy.

"Once. Tickets are so expensive. But it was boss."

"I'll see if I can get you into one."

"No way."

"Yeah. I have a cousin who works at the stadium. He's gotten us in a coupla times. Right, sweetie?"

Morgan nodded.

Part of the problem was they hadn't made love in forever. Well…a few months, anyway. Not that they made love all that often to begin with. Two or three times a month. Work and life's other demands left them exhausted and happy to just cuddle up with a movie and ice cream. But it wasn't just a question of convenience. Making love meant a descent into the carnal: a dangerous place—vulnerable and wild. It was so much easier not to go there, to simply ignore the part of their relationship that craved naked flesh. But once they had everything just right—a bottle of wine, soft music, low lighting—their love was howlingly passionate, each of them climaxing multiple times; and every time they promised, eyes dewy with devotion, to do it more often. Then two more weeks would pass.

This time felt different. It had been rocky since her dad moved into the guest room across the hall from theirs—the thought of him hearing her gasp, *OhGodOhGodYes!Yes!Yes!* was enough to shoot her clitoris into a permanent coma—but it continued even after they'd moved him into the Villa. They'd fought a lot during the transition. Treat was opposed to moving him out, even though it cut into their intimacy and he'd nearly burned down their kitchen, it offended her Mexican Code of Honor, while Morgan felt she had no choice. She was drowning. And then there was the strain Treat was under from work and her drama-spewing family, the latest crisis being her married-with-three-children younger brother knocking up a prostitute. So like the head of the Hernandez family, Treat's dad, who'd torn up the family with his mistresses.

Morgan noted the car had gone quiet. "You okay back there?" she asked John Boy.

"Yeah. Just checking my e-mail."

She glanced at her partner of twenty years, wife of six—twelve years younger and fertile as a teenager. She looked cute as ever in her pressed shorts and brand new yellow tee, her outfit for the big in-service, the one that was going to make everything right with corporate.

"You haven't said much about the retreat."

Treat stiffened. She thought Morgan was asking about Marky. A reasonable assumption, but wrong. Morgan had moved on from Marky with her zero percent body fat. Whatever came down the night before had clearly been difficult for Treat. You could see it in the tautness of her mouth, the way she gripped the steering wheel; she was suffering, and that made Morgan sad, and mad, and some other emotion that felt like staring down a hurricane.

"Were the guys responsive?" she asked, making a point to clear her voice of any accusatory undercurrents.

Treat gripped the steering wheel even tighter. "Relatively."

Morgan watched the needle on the speedometer tick to the right. Treat always drove fast when she was stressed. How could Morgan let her know she wasn't asking about The Big Whatever that had happened the night before? She twisted around in her seat to John Boy who was hunched over his smartphone, his long legs splayed like a grasshopper, oblivious to the emotional shift that had taken place. Sorry, fella, she thought, but I'm yanking you into this. We need an impartial buffer or we're going to start head tripping each other. "Treat manages a warehouse and put together this retreat for her guys—"

"Not for them," Treat interjected. "For corporate. The guys are happy to go on the way they are."

"For corporate then," Morgan said, relieved to have rerouted the conversation onto dry land. She went on to explain the months of planning Treat put in for her knuckle-dragging staff.

"They're just guys," Treat said.

"Who think women should stay barefoot and pregnant."

"But they're okay with you as their boss?" John Boy asked.

"It took a while," Treat said.

"Years," Morgan said.

"But they tolerate me now."

"More than tolerate. They love her."

"Yeah, well, what do they know?" Treat said. "Anyway, Stu Williams—"

"A real cabrón," Morgan said.

"Cabrón?" John Boy said.

"Asshole."

"Deals with our female clients like they're feeble-minded," Treat said.

Morgan pointed out a green Plymouth and they all stopped talking long enough to see that it wasn't Mac.

Treat continued. "So the guy actually got a little weepy during role-playing."

A gust of jealousy caught Morgan off guard. She pressed her feet into the floorboard, refusing to be swept away. "You're kidding,"

"Nope."

"How about Buck?" Please, please, please say that Marvelous Marky couldn't budge the cabrón of all cabróns.

Treat drummed her fingers on the steering wheel. "The dick kept sneaking out for cigarettes."

Morgan felt her muscles relax.

"Best forklift operator I've got, stacks pallets neat as pancakes, but I'm going to have to fire his ass if he doesn't wake up and smell the future."

John Boy was being awfully quiet in the backseat. Did he realize he was being used? That he was Morgan's pawn in this game of everything-is-fine-I'm-above-being-jealous?

Treat shrugged. "Ah, well. Day's not over yet."

You can say that again, Morgan thought.

They sat quietly for a while, the three of them in their own worlds, no longer pointing out green cars but quietly racing ahead or slowing down to check on them. They were on the outskirts of Gilroy, passing through the patchwork quilt of tree and flower nurseries, the trees root-bound in their boxy wooden planters, the flowers glorious in their rolling geometric beds. Morgan thought about the bouquet of flowers her dad presented to her mom every single Friday of their marriage. There was always that moment when he gave her the flowers. Young Morgan used it to gauge how well they were getting along. If he tossed them into the sink, they were fighting—the longer they stayed in the sink, the bigger the disagreement. If he revealed them from behind his back and she acted surprised, they were getting along. But there was always that moment, the one that forced her to acknowledge that her parents had loved each other first.

Over time, she grew to appreciate their devotion, marveling at her dad's ability to put up with her mom: he was so patient, so accommodating, so forgiving of her mom's razor-sharp Scorpio sting. And her mom, well, she never left the flowers in the sink long enough to totally wilt.

Treat's phone chimed, startling Morgan from her thoughts.

"Hello?" Treat said, using the new hands-free voice-activated car phone system that one of her nephews had installed.

"Oh good. You picked up," a velvety voice said.

Alarms clanged in Morgan's brain. Enemy invasion! Enemy invasion! Secure all perimeters! Man the cannons! Marky Gottlieb has breeched the bulwarks!

"I'm with Morgan," Treat said.

Damn right, you're with me, Morgan thought.

"...and I've got you on the speaker phone."

There was a pause on the line and you could hear a lot of thumping and banging. "Oh...hi, Morgan."

Morgan pulled at a thread from the hem of her blouse and watched it unravel. "Hi." Clothes were so cheaply made these days.

"A staff member from the Villa is also with us," Treat said, her voice strained. "We're still looking for my father-in-law."

"I'm sorry."

I'll bet you are, Morgan thought.

"So, what's up?" Treat said.

"Well...I know I shouldn't have let him get to me, but..." More thumping and banging, and the sound of Marky blowing her nose. Was she crying?

Treat rolled her head around on her neck as if it was too heavy to hold up. "What did Buck do now?"

"He refused to do the Pipeline exercise for one thing. Says he woke up with a bad knee."

Treat groaned. "And?"

"They're in with Shilo now, doing the drum circle? And he's going out of his way to screw up the rhythm. He's whacking his djembe like an angry child. And the other guys..." A bit of heaving. She *was* crying. "...they're laughing—like the whole thing is a big joke!"

So the invulnerable Marky Gottlieb wasn't invulnerable after all. Damn. Treat was a sucker for damsels in distress. Morgan watched for her reaction, but Treat kept her face neutral, her eyes on the road.

"Talk to Santiago, my head foreman. He'll talk some sense into the guys. They respect him. As for Buck..." Treat thought for a moment. "Make sure you don't condescend to him. It will only make him worse."

Another pause, then in a pouty voice, "Treat. I hope you don't think my presentations have been in any way condescending."

Treat glanced at Morgan apologetically. "I'm not saying that." She looked like she wanted to twist out of her own body. "It's just, well…" A short exhale, then in a quieter voice, "Remember what we talked about?" Another glance at Morgan, and a smile, a hand reaching out to Morgan's thigh.

Morgan ooched away. Oh no, you don't. You made this bed…

"Of *course* I remember," Marky said in a petulant voice.

Morgan watched the needle on the speedometer climb from 60 to 65 to 70.

It was tempting to feel sorry for Treat—she looked so miserable trying to untangle herself from The Big Whatever—but Morgan was too damn mad. What had Treat been thinking? Throwing twenty good years of loving under the bus just because things had gotten a little rough. Being tempted was understandable. Morgan herself had been tempted. The dyke who worked at the hardware store was always giving her suggestive looks, she could've taken that somewhere…but didn't. Or that gal in accounting…

"Look," Treat said. 75…80…85…"There's really not much I can do from here. Talk to Santiago."

Marky sighed one of those weight-of-the-world sighs, obviously wanting Treat to feel bad for abandoning her. "I just hope it works. The drumming is the culmination of all they've experienced. It's where the men come together as their—"

"New more sensitive selves," Treat said. "I know."

More sensitive selves? Morgan choked back a laugh.

"So, I'll check in again later," Treat said to Marky.

"Fine," Marky said. "It would just be so much easier if you were here."

"Yeah, well…"

"I know. Talk to you later."

Morgan flipped down the visor mirror to see if John Boy was picking up on the tension, but he was gazing out the window through squinted eyes. He had his own worries. They all had their own worries.

Hell, worries were shooting around the car like pinballs, banking off the seats and windows and floorboards. She needed fresh air, even if it was boiling hot. She cracked her window.

"Whew!" John Boy said. "That garlic stinks."

Morgan pulled a nail file from her purse and filed a jagged nail. "Sounds like Harmony Systems isn't working out the way you'd hoped."

"You could say that," Treat said.

"Why people don't just use garlic salt is beyond me," John Boy said. "It's so much easier. Makes killer garlic toast. Throw on a little butter and douse with garlic salt."

Morgan's single friends all said they never bothered to cook for themselves. She pictured herself coming home after a long day at work to a little apartment—one chair, one mug, one bowl, one spoon—would she really forgo sifting through the garlic basket for the plumpest most pungent bulb, forgo tearing off the generous outer cloves and crushing them with the back of a knife to make the peeling of the papery skin easier, forgo mincing the aromatic chunks and dropping them into sizzling butter which, when sautéed to perfection, would be brushed onto the fluffy white flesh of a freshly baked baguette then placed under the broiler just long enough to turn golden? Would she instead coat a piece of toast with butter and sprinkle on garlic salt? The thought made her shudder.

"I like mine fresh," she said. "So fresh it makes your eyes water."

Chapter Twenty-seven

"M an, I love to drive!" Tawn said.

Cora noted that once again he didn't signal. She was sitting behind Sonia and Nell, making it difficult to oversee his driving, but she'd already identified his erratic signaling pattern, using his blinker to change lanes only when he felt like it, or thought it necessary, as if laws were open to interpretation. He was also driving slightly above the speed limit. Probably not enough to get pulled over, but he was pushing it. Another Gabriel Myers, she thought—the kid on her school bus route who everyone thought was such a little angel. But a school bus driver often witnessed the dark side of children—through mirrors, of course. Oh, the things she saw through those mirrors! Goody-two-shoes Gabriel with his blond locks and winning smile tormenting the less popular kids, taking up two seats daring them to ask him to move; forcing a boy half his age out of his seat so he himself could sit next to one of the cooler kids. Nothing atrocious. Just mean.

Tawn hadn't shown that tendency yet, but she'd keep her eye on him. Oh, yes. Keep your enemies close. Just like that gritty lawman in the Western Hubert loved so much. Then again, she was an outlaw. Still, it applied. Outlaws abided by the code of distrust; it's what kept them alive.

She leaned forward to whisper to Sonia and Nell. "I'm going to ask him to stop in Gilroy. I need a restroom."

"Thank God," Sonia said. "I've got to piss like a racehorse."

"Gilroy…" Nell wiggled her fingers in front of her face. "Where vampires dare not tread." She chortled at her own joke.

Sonia patted her hair. "Too bad. I've always thought it would be fun to tangle with a sexy vampire."

Tawn glanced in the rearview mirror. Cora waited for him to return his attention to the road then whispered, "Girls! We've got to figure this out. What are we going to do with Tawn?"

"Oh. Right." Sonia folded her hands in mock obedience.

"Why do we have to do anything with him?" Nell whispered back.

Sonia elbowed her. "He might squeal."

"Exactly." Cora scrutinized Tawn's profile, that mop of hair—Since when did men wear kerchiefs?—his broad, tan shoulders, his lean, muscular arm. "One of us needs to be with him at all times."

Nell raised her hand and whispered, "Me! Me! I'll play the feeble old grandma that needs to hang on his arm."

"Perfect."

Tawn pulled into the fast lane to pass, no blinker. "Hate to interrupt your scheming, ladies, but would you mind if we stopped in Gilroy? A little caffeine would be the dope."

Cora shot Sonia a look. Dope? What was he talking about?

"We were just talking about that," Sonia said smoothly. "Keep your eyes open for a gas station."

"Not a gas station," Cora said. "We'll be too conspicuous. We need someplace with more people, where we can blend in."

"One of those garlic stores," Nell said. "We can pick up some treats."

"You got it," Tawn said, taking the on-ramp to 101.

Cora leaned back in her seat. "Honestly, Nell, you are a bottomless pit."

Minutes later, they were pulling into the parking lot of Garlic World. A banner about an upcoming Garlic Festival hung from the roof.

Cora reminded Tawn to set the emergency brake.

"I was gonna do it," he said.

She watched him search for the hand brake. Sure he was.

After finally finding it and cranking it, he leapt out of the van to open the door for them. Only Sonia had already done it. He took her hand to help with the last, large step, then Nell's then Cora's. "I'll be needing the keys," Cora said, once her feet were firmly on the ground.

Tawn made a pouty face. "Still think I'm a bad guy?"

Sonia stepped in close and spoke in a threatening tone. "Just hand over the keys so I can go pee."

"It will be safer for everyone," Cora said.

He dropped the keys in her open palm like a sacked jailer who loved his job of keeping people locked up. Another sign they were doing the right thing. Cora glanced at Nell and almost laughed. Stooped over and trembling, she looked a hundred and ten years old. "Give me your arm, would you, Sonny?" she said.

Tawn lifted his arm, seemingly unaware that Nell had previously been walking around just fine.

The parking lot was about half full. They meandered through the sweltering heat past the produce bins: *Yellow Onions 25¢! Hass Avocados 5 for a $1!!!! Locally Grown! Strawberries by the basket or flat!!!!* Cora held the door open for them.

Nell, clinging to Tawn's arm like a barnacle, winked surreptitiously at Cora as they passed.

"I'd like to see him break that grip," Sonia whispered to Cora.

Cora searched the store for the restroom. The place was crammed with people. Each one of them a potential threat: the young Asian man at the register, a squabble of children by the candy, a young mother with her two teenage sons. Cora spotted a sign for restrooms and grabbed Sonia's hand. "This way."

"Don't act so jumpy," Sonia said. "You'll draw attention to us."

Cora glanced over her shoulder at Tawn and Nell heading for the drinks case. They looked innocent enough. "I haven't made my mind up about him."

"Me either. But we've got the keys. If need be we'll grab Nell and make a run for it."

Cora began negotiating her way through the maze of garlic braids, specialty sauces, spices, rubs, jellies, and people to a small utility closet with the added amenities of toilet and sink, a one-holer.

"You first," Sonia said. "And splash some water on your face. You're pale as a glass of milk. But hurry. My bladder's about to bust."

Cora left her standing by a collection of novelty ball caps.

It was difficult to lock the door with her shuddering hands. Difficult to unzip her slacks. How was this all going to end? Driving over a cliff like Thelma and Louise? On a more practical note, where were they going to sleep tonight? Sure, they could rent a motel room, but couldn't their credit cards be traced?

The warm stream of pee came quickly—a blessing. Still, she just sat there. *Until either we can't or don't want to.* Had she reached her limit? Did she want to turn herself in? Now that Sonia and Nell had a driver, she could give herself up without compromising their fun. But of course it would. She would be questioned, grilled. Who knew how long she could hold out? She had a very low tolerance for pain.

Sonia knocked on the door. "Everything all right in there?"

"Fine!"

"Well, hurry the hell up or they're going to need a cleanup in aisle nine."

Cora stood on wobbly knees to fasten her slacks then walked to the sink to wash her hands and splash water on her face. Sonia was right; she was pale. Her hair needed combing too, but she couldn't very well make Sonia wait forever. She took a deep breath and unlocked the door.

"Didn't mean to rush you," Sonia said, returning a cap sprouting garlics to the bin.

"It's fine."

"But I'm about to wet my new Eileen Fishers."

If Sonia had sniffed out her cowardice she didn't let on; she just pushed past her into the restroom.

Cora strolled over to a nearby rack of postcards, coaching herself to look relaxed. She picked one up: a garlic head wearing a cowboy hat with *Greetings From Gilroy!*

"Excuse me," a male voice behind her said softly. "We need to talk to you."

Her heart, already banging in her chest, flew into double time. The jig was up! The end of the adventure was now. She turned to face the man, making every effort to appear nonchalant. "Y-yes?"

Dapper, though quite short, the man was easily in his eighties, and was standing next to a petite, gray-haired woman Cora assumed was his wife.

The doll-like woman glanced warily over her shoulder then said, "We recognized you from the TV."

The man cupped his hand around his mouth, leaned toward Cora, and whispered, "The Runaway Grannies."

Cora screwed her expression into one she hoped looked confused. "You must be mistaken. I'm...I'm here with my son." Why on earth had she said that? They could see she wasn't with anyone. She searched the store for Tawn. Why hadn't she said grandson?

"We saw you come in," the man said. "The three of you with that young fella. A good move, by the way, to have a fella with you."

"Don't worry," the woman said. "Your secret's safe with us."

"But our granddaughter is another story."

"She's out in the car changing our great-granddaughter's diapers."

"She wants to alert the authorities."

"Thinks you're a danger to yourselves." The woman let out a disgusted breath. "And..." She made quote marks with her fingers. "Others."

"We tried to throw her off the scent," the man said. "Told her you didn't look like the women on the TV to us, and that you had a driver, but she's a stubborn one."

The woman took Cora's hand. "We think it's wonderful what you're doing—for all of us."

"Do you need any money?" the man said.

The passion with which the woman gripped her hand, the earnestness of the man's offer, sent a wave of guilt through Cora. How could she have considered backing out? Elderly people everywhere were counting on her. She had an image to uphold—a mission. "No. We don't need any money, but thank you."

The restroom door swung open. Sonia eyed the couple suspiciously. "What's going on?"

Cora released her hand from the woman's grip. "We've been spotted, and these kind people have been thoughtful enough to alert us."

"Christ! Where's Nell?"

Cora scanned the store. "She and Tawn are over by the registers."

"Let's grab them and get out of here."

"Right." Cora brought her attention back to the couple. "Thank you."

"Our pleasure," the man said. "And we'll do what we can to keep our granddaughter from calling it in."

"God bless! And take this little charm with you." The woman pressed a small green stone into Cora's hand. "For luck."

"I couldn't," Cora said.

"She's got a pocket full of them," the man said. "Hands them out as needed."

"Thank you," Cora said, rushing off after Sonia.

She rounded a display of pickled garlic products, gripping the stone, which despite how the man had played it down felt precious to her. How lucky that couple was to still have each other! If only she had Hubert to talk to. Then again, Hubert would tell her to turn herself in. For that matter, if he were alive, she wouldn't even be here making a getaway, which in its own lawless way was pretty wonderful too.

CHAPTER TWENTY-EIGHT

Mac steered into a pullout to let the long line of cars behind him pass. He knew he was driving well below the forty-five mph speed limit, but he could barely see. The towering canopy of redwoods flanking the twisty two lanes of Hecker Pass was blocking out what little light was left of the day. The whole situation made him damn nervous.

Effie, suddenly outside the car, yelled, "Where's the fire?" to the passing cars, her hand raised like a traffic cop, then, just as quickly, she was back inside.

"Would you stop doing that?"

"What?"

"That." He gestured to outside the car.

"People just make me so mad—think they're so important." Oddly enough, she'd been in her gardening outfit for the last fifteen or so minutes: khaki shorts, tattered straw hat, and those silly kneepads she claimed to need for her "old knees." A blush of dirt dusted her cheek.

Mac flicked on his blinker and pulled back onto the road. "This is people's commute. You can't blame them for wanting to get home."

Effie chewed on this a few seconds then came out with, "Nobody on their death bed wishes they'd spent more time at the office. Trust me."

Mac had no idea how this applied to the conversation so he focused on the soft beam his headlights cast on the road. He kept his head twisted to the left so he could use the peripheral vision of his right eye, the clearest. It was like driving through a damn Grimm's Fairy Tale—the twisting road, the dark forest—all it needed was Little Red Riding Hood to come skipping out from behind one of the giant ferns. Another car was already on his tail, damn it. He flicked on his high beams. To hell with oncoming traffic. He needed to see.

"I love these ferns," Effie said. "They're a bit dusty looking, but once the rain comes, they'll drink it right up and turn the most brilliant green. The Celts believed that the trees were the earth's thoughts. Did I ever tell you that?"

Mac nodded. Lots of times. But it was fine with him if she wanted to tell him about it again. Anything to keep her in the car.

"These ferns seem like thoughts, too," she said. "Soft thoughts. Or maybe they're the earth's emotions…or one of them. Gentleness, that's what they are. The earth's gentleness."

Her patter relaxed him, even if he was only half listening. "What would that make cactuses?" He shifted into a lower gear to take the curve. Negotiating shadows.

"Cactuses. Hmmm. They'd be the earth's fear."

Now two cars were on his tail, the one directly behind him climbing up his bumper. The second one swerved briefly into the left lane to see if it could pass—a risky move on a curvy road like this. "Fruit-bearing plants?" he asked, perspiration sprouting from his forehead.

"That's easy. The earth's passion. Cherries are sweet kisses: peaches, sexual desire; and watermelons, a mother's love…" She went on, eventually forsaking fruit-bearing plants for vegetables, "Potatoes, steadfastness; beans, aspiration" then moved on to geological formations, "Mountains have got to be the earth's ultimatums. Some giant platelet gets tired of pushing against another giant platelet and throws up a wall—*I will not budge one more inch or else*—and voila! You get the Rockies. Oh, and sand is the earth's patience…"

Mac stretched out his face to stay awake. The cars behind him were multiplying. He searched for a place to pull over, but it was all trees and ferns, trees and ferns, trees and ferns…

"Did you know our California redwood forests are actually cloud forests?" Effie asked, startling Mac awake.

He swerved to keep on the road. "Huh?"

"California redwood forests are cloud forests. Did you know this?"

"Um...Yes. No. I don't know."

"Are you all right?"

"I'm fine. Now what's this about cloud forests?"

"You went to sleep, didn't you?"

"No. I just thought I saw something in the road."

"Did not."

"Just tell me about the damn cloud forests!"

From the edge of his vision, he watched Effie cross her arms as if deciding whether to tell him or not. "The trees actually rain," she said finally. "They collect the fog and somehow turn it into drops of water. Isn't that amazing? Of course, there's no fog now, but in the winter I've seen it where the only place it's raining is under the trees."

"So redwood trees create the earth's tears?"

She thought about this for a second. "That's a very profound thought, Mac."

"One plus one equals two," he said, trying to sound light and capable and like he wasn't worried about steering them into the gully. But wait. What was that up ahead? It was the inn! They'd reached the summit. Sure enough, a patch of light was up ahead. Out of the redwoods at last! And there was a pullout to boot. He maneuvered the car over and cut the engine. He needed to get his bearings and let his eyes adjust to the light.

"There she is," Effie whispered. "My beautiful ocean."

The overlook towered above the sweep of Watsonville's agriculture fields to the distant glistening turquoise expanse of the Monterey Bay. The sun hung low over the water. Only about an hour of daylight left.

Once again, Effie was out of the car in a blink, only this time she was holding her arms open wide as if trying to hug the view. He watched a small breeze ruffle the soft wisps of snow-white hair peeking out beneath her ratty hat.

He was close to making good on his promise to her. So close. His eyes began to sting. He was just a big old redwood leaking tears.

Chapter Twenty-nine

Morgan stared so hard out the window of the 4Runner that the road outside began to blur into the road of her life: the straightaways, exits, U-turns, sharp turns, near misses, and, her least favorite, dead ends. Westbound traffic was crawling over the pass. Was it time to exit her relationship with Treat? Had they reached a dead end? She stole a peek at her wife who seemed to be lost in her own thoughts. Treat's previous geniality had noticeably fizzled. She was probably wishing like hell she hadn't taken Marky's phone call on speakerphone. God, that had been insulting to listen to! Of all people for Treat to choose, to pick someone so shallow, so egotistical, so surgically enhanced. And the irony! Morgan having been the one to talk her into the in-service to begin with, the one who'd personally culled through the zillions of pamphlets and handpicked Harmony Systems. She might as well have handed Treat and Marky a gift certificate to a fucking hotel.

She flipped down her visor mirror to check on John Boy. He could at least offer a diversion from her hamster wheel of self-hatred. But the kid was out cold.

"Pack's moving slow today," Treat said as if she were apologizing.

Morgan didn't know what Treat had to feel sorry about. Traffic over Hecker Pass was often sluggish. All it took was one slow-moving vehicle, or an accident to—God, what if it was her dad? Morgan plunked her head against the window and squinted at the redwood forest creeping past.

Her mom had loved these primeval trees. Every Santa Cruz visit included a walk through the loop of monster-sized, old growth trees at Henry Cowell Park. Once, when Morgan was what...eight? nine?... they were standing in a fairy ring of trees surrounded by the hush of the forest. The late afternoon light, streaming through the canopy, danced in dappled patterns on the soft duff beneath them. But Morgan had had enough of the trees and wanted back to the visitor center to spend some of her birthday money. They had stickers that would look cool on her school notebook—now tattered thanks to some mean girls who'd strewn the contents of her backpack all over the schoolyard. There was no rushing her mom, though. She'd brought Morgan here for some reason besides the natural beauty, Young Morgan could feel it in her gut.

"These living beings are over two thousand years old," her mom finally whispered. "Think they worry about being popular at school?" Morgan wanted to kill her. Earlier in the week, she'd confided in her mother about the mean pack of girls. She'd been hoping for a little comfort, a hug maybe. Not a trip to Santa Cruz to walk in the forest.

Morgan reached for the Twix bar in her purse.

A choppy gasp erupted from the backseat. Morgan twisted around. The kid's head was tipped back, his mouth gaping open. That's one way to deal with stress, she thought.

"I kissed her," Treat said quietly.

Morgan froze. "What?"

Treat glanced over her shoulder at John Boy. Morgan did too, even though she'd just done it.

"I kissed Marky," Treat repeated, as if the reason Morgan had said "what" was because she hadn't heard.

Morgan tried to think of an appropriate response, the obvious one being: *How dare you tell me this now!* But her mind wouldn't—or couldn't—send the signal to her vocal cords. It was too busy fighting off visions of Marky's collagen lips devouring Treat's mouth. Did their tongues touch? Were they sitting? Standing? Hell, a kiss could mean anything from a peck on the cheek to Marky splayed out on a conference room table with Treat's face between her legs.

She offered the Twix bar. "Chocolate?"

Treat shot her an incredulous look. "What?"

"Do you want some chocolate?"

Treat shook her head, making it clear she couldn't believe the way Morgan was responding.

"Well, what do you want me to say?" Morgan whispered. "Good? How dare you?" She fumbled with the candy bar's wrapper. Damn! She thought she'd steeled herself against being hurt, that all her rationalizing about The Big Whatever would protect her. Hands trembling, she flung the unopened bar back in her purse. "I mean, why tell me this now? Why—" She caught her voice rising and took a deep breath.

Treat's phone rang. *This* time she glanced at the caller ID on the console before picking up.

"It's Ignacio. You know, my nephew the cop."

"Well, answer it."

Treat punched the speakerphone. "Whassup, Officer Nacho?"

"Hey, Tía Treat, just wanted to let you know, there's been a report of a stolen green car near that rest home you were talking about. It's a ninety-six Jetta. Stolen out of a Taco Bell parking lot. Stick shift," Ignacio said. "Could Morgan's old man drive a stick shift?"

Treat glanced at Morgan to see if she wanted to answer. Morgan responded with an icy stare.

"Mac could drive anything," Treat said. "I've seen him back a huge Winnebago between two horse trailers—in the pouring rain."

"Before his eyes went bad," Morgan said.

"Hey, Morgan," Ignacio said. "Don't you worry too much; we'll find him. He probably just needed to get away. My wife's abuelita is always threatening to run. And man, I wouldn't put it past her. She's wily. My kids would probably help her too. They're sick of having to sleep in the laundry room. And she's always telling me and Martha we're too easy on them. Says we should use a switch, teach them some respect—"

"You and Martha are doing a great job with those kids," Treat said.

"Thanks, Tía. We think so."

Morgan pressed her thumbs into her temples until it hurt. Here she'd stuck her dad in a home while Ignacio and his family were going out of their way—

"So, the car," Treat said. "Mac hotwired it or what?"

"Naw. The owner said he left his keys on the floorboard..." Ignacio went on with the details, the officer who took the call, the location of the Taco Bell, and other stuff that seemed hardly relevant. Morgan could barely make sense of his words. Her dad had stolen a car! And her wife—

"Wow!" John Boy said, "Mac is like treading in some dangerous territory." He was leaning forward, his head not a foot from hers.

Had he heard about the kiss?

"So keep us posted," Treat said to Ignacio.

"Will do, Tía."

Treat clicked off the phone. "Macky, Macky, Macky, what are you up to?"

Morgan glared out at a hill covered with prehistoric-looking ferns.

"Maybe you should try calling him again," John Boy said.

Morgan snatched up her phone and hit redial.

Dude. This is Dirk's phone. But not Dirk...

She hung up and tried again.

Dude. This is...

And again.

Dude...

"Damn you, Dad!"

"You don't mean that," Treat said.

"Don't tell me what I do and don't mean."

Morgan stretched out the shoulder strap of her seat belt to give herself some room. She hated that John Boy was in the car with them, hated that perhaps he'd heard their conversation about Marky, hated that she was now officially the cuckoldee while Treat got to be the cuckolder. There was nothing to feel for a cuckoldee but pity, while there were any number of emotions to feel about the cockolder, all of them infinitely more interesting than pity. Of course, it *was* only a kiss—provided a kiss meant just that, a kiss—and Treat clearly regretted it. Morgan should feel relieved. But she didn't. She felt pissed. And fat. And ugly.

The SUV crested the summit to that first glimpse of the Monterey Bay, one of her favorite moments in the drive, but today she barely saw it. The two people she loved most in the world were getting away.

"Ever tried surfing?" Treat asked John Boy. She was clearly trying to lighten the mood.

"Once. It's not as easy as it looks. Got my butt whipped."

Morgan was burning up. She snatched the Smart Start Guide from the glove box and began frantically waving it at her face.

"Hot flash?" Treat said.

"What do you think?"

Treat gave her a look that was undoubtedly supposed to express compassion.

Morgan ignored her.

"Your dad must have really wanted to get to Santa Cruz," John Boy said. "I mean, to steal a car. That's serious need."

Morgan punched on the CD player. Catie Curtis started in on a song debunking the myth that love could solve everything, calling it the cruelest lie. The appropriateness was almost funny.

CHAPTER THIRTY

W hat's the rush?" Nell asked, as they pulled out of Garlic World's parking lot. Tawn was once again at the wheel, which Cora found regretful but necessary under the circumstances. No getting around it, three old ladies shepherding themselves around in a big white van looked suspicious.

"We were spotted," she said.

"And recognized," Sonia added.

Nell clapped her hands together. "How thrilling!"

"Yehaw!" Tawn said. "I'm driving the getaway van!"

Cora twisted around to see past Nell sitting in the backseat. "I don't know what there is to celebrate. If that couple's daughter calls this in, it could put an end to our adventure." There was nothing behind them but lazy Gilroy traffic. "Slow down!" she barked at Tawn. "The last thing we need is to get stopped for something stupid like a speeding ticket."

Tawn immediately let up on the accelerator, but her words remained hanging in the air like a schoolteacher's pent-up outburst. Sonia and Nell wouldn't even look at her while Tawn was acting every bit the chastised child. She didn't give a hoot. Someone had to be the adult. She stiffened her posture and stared straight ahead so as not to give away how frustrated she felt. And betrayed. Sonia and Nell turning her into the evil witch. Were they on his side now? Was that it?

Nell leaned forward and squeezed Cora's shoulders. "I think our Cora Bird is scared."

Sonia's warm hand rested on her thigh. "I'll call Ginny. See if there's any news from the Villa."

Cora felt like shrugging them both off, patronizing her like this. If it hadn't been for her willingness to drive, they wouldn't even be on this adventure.

"You ladies are like total rock stars," Tawn said. "Seriously. Most grandmas do nothing but sit around and knit."

Cora bit back saying she didn't know a single old lady who knitted. Which wasn't quite true. There was a small knitting klatch at the Villa, but she steered clear of them—and their gossip.

A nursery of potted trees flew past the window, then several patches of flowers. They were coming up on Hecker Pass. That would slow him down.

"Ginny," Sonia said into the phone. "It's me. What's the latest?"

"Ask her if she's seen the news," Nell said.

Sonia shushed her. "Uh huh…Uh huh…Uh huh…" She pressed the phone to her chest. "Most of the residents at the Villa are totally behind us."

"'Most?'" Cora said.

"Yes. What *do* you mean most?" Sonia said into the phone. She listened for a moment. "Apparently, a few members of our fair community have turned against us. Say we're taking things *too far*."

"Oh, for heaven's sake," Cora said.

"Those would be the knitters," Tawn said.

"Or those stuffy men who do nothing but sit in the dayroom reading newspapers and grumbling about the world going to wrack and ruin," Nell said.

Sonia returned to Ginny and listened intently. She laughed then said, "Gwen Evans hung a paper towel banner in the rec room that says God Bless the Runaway Grannies."

"Good old Gwen!" Nell said.

"Is she the one who always wears that hot pink tracksuit?" Cora said.

"I have no idea," Nell said. "But I like her."

Sonia held up a finger to quiet them. "Oh dear….Oh no…"

Cora felt like snatching the phone from her. "What?"

Sonia put her hand over the phone. "There's a rumor we've added a young male driver."

"Don't confirm it," Cora whispered.

"The less you know the safer you'll be!" Nell yelled.

"Well, all right then," Sonia went on. "Please keep us posted if there's any news. What? Oh. I'm sorry to hear that." She turned to Cora and Nell. "John's getting sacked."

"Oh, no," Cora said.

"Bastards!" Nell said.

"All right then…" Sonia said into the phone. "All right…You too…Oh, wait, say that again so the girls can hear." She held the phone out for a tinny sounding: *Viva the Runaway Grannies!* Then brought it back to her ear. "Thanks, Gin. We'll be in touch."

She clicked off the phone and lifted it into the air. "To us!"

Nell lifted a fist in the air. "To life!"

"I hope she didn't say that where anyone could hear her," Cora said.

"She was in the kitchen with the Mexicans. Those that *can* understand probably don't give a good goddamn about what happens to us."

Sonia was right about that. They were just privileged old white ladies to the Mexican kitchen staff. Cora raised her fist into the air. "To not being afraid! No more Cautious Cora!"

"Cautious Cora?"

"My mother's nickname for me. I always hated it."

"Then let it go," Tawn said. "It's a new-ew-ew day!"

Sonia and Cora ignored him. "Feeling better then?" Sonia said.

"I like that," Nell said. "A new day."

Cora nodded. "Yes. Thanks. I keep getting these waves of nerves."

"Me too," Sonia said. "But I'm determined not to let them stop me."

"You don't show it."

"And I never will." Sonia turned her attention to Tawn. "We need to get off the main road."

"My thoughts exactly," he said.

"The pass is the only route to Santa Cruz," Cora said.

"We could pull off at Gilroy Gardens Theme Park," Nell said. "Get someone to take pictures of us on one of the rides and post it on that Facebook thingy."

"Nell," Sonia said, sternly. "We're trying to lay *low*."

"Yes," Cora said. "We've got to disappear for a while."

Sonia rested her head on the window and gazed wistfully at a passing vineyard. "Besides, if we stop anywhere it should be for a little wine tasting."

Cora followed her gaze. "When did all these wineries crop up? This used to be all orchards."

Tawn snapped his fingers. "Ladies, ladies. Tawn the Man has the perfect plan."

They waited for what he had to say, but of course he had to make a big deal out of it. "Drum roll, please."

Nell, of course, obliged him, whapping her fingers on the seat.

"Come to the retreat center with me!" he said. "It's right at the top of the pass, and way-ay-ay remote."

"Won't there be lots of people there?" Cora said.

"Some. But if we park the van outside the property and walk in, they'll have no reason to suspect anything. You'll be just three old ladies reinventing yourselves."

"Reinventing ourselves..." Sonia said. Cora was sure she hated Tawn calling her old.

"That's why people go there—that and classes—personal and spiritual growth."

Is that what we're doing? Cora wondered. The whole business had started so spontaneously, and altruistically. Going after Mac. But they hadn't mentioned Mac in over an hour. So why *were* they doing it? And for whom? The fans? The world? She stared out the window at a well-maintained split rail fence. A "for sale" sign advertised forty acres. Why did her actions always have to be for someone else?

She slipped the little green stone out of her pocket and began caressing it like a worry stone. The woman had called it a charm. A charm! The third of the three graces! Cora bit back a grin. What were the chances? She considered mentioning the coincidence to Sonia and Nell, but it felt so tender, so hers, that she decided to keep it to herself.

"You can at least eat dinner there," Tawn said. "But I'll see if I can fix you up an overnighter. My friend Sharla works in registration, and she's way cool, and would definitely be into you ladies."

She looked at the back of his head, that silly kerchief. Could they trust him? Could they trust this Sharla?

"I say we go for it," Nell said. "Dinner and a nice soft bed sounds wonderful."

"Do they serve alcohol?" Sonia asked.

"Nope. And it's all vegetarian."

She groaned. "Tell me there are at least a few hunky massage therapists."

Tawn laughed. "You might find one or two of those."

"Then count me in. I could use a little manhandling. And I'd love a chance to get out of these shoes. My bunions are killing me."

Cora gripped the little stone in the palm of her hand; it felt warm, smooth. "I'm in too," she said. Cautious Cora be damned.

❖

The dirt road into the Retreat Center came none too soon, cutting through a dense forest of live oak, madrone, and bay trees—definitely off the grid. It was just after seven thirty.

Tawn switched off the air conditioner and opened the windows. A warm breeze blew into the van. Blue jays squawked. Squirrels skittered through the dappled light. Cora felt her heart rate slowing, her breath deepening. They came upon the Mount Madonna Center sign and drove a little farther.

"You said we'd park off the property and walk in," she said.

"I did," he said, "but it's kind of a long walk, probably more than you ladies want to do. So here's the new plan. I'll drop you off then stash the van."

Cora wasn't sure what to feel about this new plan. She was thankful they weren't being subjected to a lengthy walk—it had been a long day and she was tired—but she wasn't wild about giving up control of the van. She also didn't like the way Tawn kept assuming things about them, and how he kept referring to them as "you ladies" for the sole purpose of herding them, as if they were three old heifers that didn't have the sense to find their way to the feed trough. She kept her mouth shut, though. She was done being the voice of reason.

"We're not leaving you with the van," Sonia said.

"Yeah," Nell said. "We might need to make a quick getaway."

Cora took a satisfied breath of pine-scented air. How could she have doubted her friends?

"You *still* don't trust me?" Tawn said.

Sonia pulled out a small mirror to check her hair. "It's not that, *Tawn…*"

"We three have to stick together," Nell said. "Come hell or high water."

Tawn blew air through his lips as if this would somehow aid his thinking. "Here's what we'll do. It'll be dark soon. We'll leave the van in overflow parking where it'll be less conspicuous. Then first thing in the morning we can reconvene and move the van."

"Actually," Cora said. "Once we check in, your obligation to us is done."

"That doesn't mean you can go blurting our whereabouts to everybody," Sonia added.

"You better not!" Nell said. "Or you'll be swimming with the fishies."

"Don't you ladies worry," he said over his shoulder. "Your secret's good with me. And I can speak for Sharla too. She's gonna love you guys."

So it wasn't just them he felt confident making decisions for. Apparently, he felt comfortable herding this Sharla as well.

He pulled up next to a cluster of small outbuildings. "Shall we do this thing?"

Cora didn't wait for him to come around and help her out; she slid the door open and climbed out on her own. Once Sonia and Nell were out, she made him hand over the keys.

Again, he was reluctant to hand them over, but did. Then he walked around to the back of the van and hefted out his backpack. "Do I at least get my phone back?"

"Sure." Sonia patted her bag. "In the morning."

He shook his head and laughed. "You ladies are all that—and then some." He slammed the van door shut.

The hike in was enough to convince Cora she was glad they hadn't parked off site. She was exhausted, and hungry, and in need of washing up. A change of clothes was obviously out of the question, which was regrettable; the heat of the day had turned her clothes damp and aromatic. But there was no time to worry about that. If they did get a room, she'd rinse out her panties in the sink, a trick she learned while traveling through Europe with Hubert.

The dirt road in was flanked by Mediterranean landscaping, climbing a hillside to their right and showcasing a magnificent view of the valley and bay to their left. Tucked into the hillside was a spectacular ceramic lion's face gushing water, as well as several very exotic sculptures: a man with an elephant head and four arms, a seated boy with blue skin, a pair of monkey-faced men. An ornate red and gold staircase climbing up the sloping property looked like it led to some kind of temple. *What is this place?* Cora wondered, conscious of the crunching of her sandals against the packed earth. It was so quiet, like they were walking through an enormous whisper. Up ahead was a tasteful conference center and registration building, which put her at ease. The building looked quite modern and featured a giant deck for gazing at the view. A line of dusty cars was parked out front.

"Let me go in first," Tawn said. "I'll scope things out."

"And if they don't have any rooms?" Cora asked.

"Don't worry about me," Sonia said, "I'll bunk with those hunky massage therapists."

"I'll take that deck," Nell said.

"Maybe Sharla will let you camp out on her floor," Tawn said.

Cora hoped it wouldn't come to that. "We can always sleep in the van."

They approached the glass doors of the registration building.

"Here goes nothing," Tawn said and disappeared inside. Moments later, he poked his head back out. "*Don't* go anywhere."

Cora followed Sonia and Nell over to the deck. The sun was hanging low over the bay.

"It's making a giant exclamation point," Nell said, pointing to the fiery ball. "Only upside down. See? The sun is the dot and its reflection on the water the line. And it's pointing right at me."

Sonia opened up her arms to the sky, which was starting to pink up. "Nuh-uh. It's pointing at me."

Cora laughed. "It's pointing at all of us."

They stood there quietly, soaking up the feeling of being at the top of the exclamation point. Cora imagined the rays pointing to every single person in the world, people in India and Europe, Mexico and China, and felt a deep connection to every one of them. It was the same feeling she'd had watching the windsurfers, this feeling of connection—of being one of a zillion blades of grass, each of them arching up toward the sun, the center of life. Only now there was this talk about the sun getting too hot and scorching them all to death. Her generation and the ones before had had no idea what they were doing, introducing all these conveniences: cars, refrigerators, dishwashers. One got thrust onto the little blue planet with so little information. And her time was almost up. She felt the pull of the ocean calling. The part of her that was water, that eighty percent they were always talking about, was straining to return.

Not yet, she told it, I feel another chapter coming on.

She reflected on one of the ladies at the Villa, a devout Christian, who worried her deceased husband would think she hadn't made it into heaven because she was taking so long. Cora didn't believe in heaven, but she did have a sense that Hubert was out there somewhere drumming his fingers. Don't worry, she said to him silently, I'll be there soon enough.

She turned away from the ocean. There'd be plenty of time to contemplate these grand thoughts. For now she had to focus on practical things. What was this place? She scanned the property. Mostly deserted, save for a couple of young women walking arm in arm toward what she assumed was the dining hall. They had flowers laced through their hair and spoke softly. A man stood at the top of the opulent red and gold stairway, his back to the temple, and gazed out at the bay. The rest of the people—and judging by the cars there were quite a few—were likely eating dinner.

"No matter what happens," Sonia said. "We can't go back to the Villa."

The simple mention of Sunset Villa caused Cora to panic. She glanced at Nell leaning on the rail and gazing out at the bay. Had she even heard what Sonia said? About not going back? It was huge thought, a line in the sand. Then again, Nell never seemed to give the future the least bit of consideration, so what did it matter? But it did matter. It meant the end of a significant chapter in her life. "I know," she said quietly. Then was flooded with a whole new crop of anxieties. If not the Villa, what? Prison? But surely, the Villa wouldn't prosecute, not after the buckets of money the three of them had sunk into the place. Nor would she foist herself on Donald and his wife. They'd just sent the last of the kids to college and were reveling in their empty nest. Of course, she could rent a condo or an apartment, set up a new life for herself, but she'd never lived alone and didn't fancy starting now.

Then she had a marvelous idea, but Tawn stuck his head out of the building and dangled a set of keys at them, saying, "I scored you a cabin for the night," robbing her of the chance to try it out on Sonia and Nell.

CHAPTER THIRTY-ONE

The possibility of making good on his promise to Effie was giving Mac a second wind. As he drove Highway 52 past the agriculture fields of Watsonville—apples, berries, artichokes, Brussels sprouts—he thought to himself, this is what life is about. Working the land! Feeding the world! He flicked on his blinker for the fruit stand up ahead.

"Oh no, you don't," Effie said.

"Come on, you love strawberries."

She looked at him like he was a complete moron. "If we're going to make sunset at the beach in Santa Cruz, we've got to get a wiggle on."

Mac flicked his blinker off. She was a hard woman to please. Always had been.

"Stop sulking," she said. "We're almost there."

Mac focused on the road coiling trickily through the historic section of town. Too many of its early 1900s storefronts were boarded up or housed second-rate businesses. Just like Fresno, the big boys—Target, Office Max, Ross, and the like—had taken down the town. He kept his eyes peeled for signs pointing to Route 1.

"I can almost smell the ocean," Effie said.

The air did feel moister. Cooler too. It was that coastal fog she was always going on about. He took a deep breath and felt his lungs fluff up, his skin too.

After a second wrong turn, he finally found the on-ramp for Route 1. From here it was a straight shot to Santa Cruz. And traffic was light. They could make it in twenty, twenty-five minutes. A vista opened up on their left: the bay glistening in the late afternoon sun. The sky was already getting rosy. "Maybe we should pull over and watch the sunset from here," he said.

Effie crossed her arms. "No way, José. I want to be sitting at my favorite beach on West Cliff when that big old ball drops behind the sea."

Mac pressed on, the accelerator rising: 55, 60, 65, 70. "Let's hope there's no tourist traffic." He was actually starting to feel quite pleased with himself. His lady had asked him to take her to Santa Cruz, and voila! Her wish was granted. Almost. He glanced at her. She was eighteen and cute as a button in her white wide-legged slacks and pale blue sleeveless blouse, her curly hair clipped back on the side with a sparkly barrette. An outfit he would never forget. He returned his attention to the road.

It had been a day much like this one, miserably hot in Fresno, and he and a few of his buddies made a mad dash for the coast. One of their parents had a bungalow on the cliffs above the beach, and they'd gotten the okay to spend the night. Of course they went straight to the Boardwalk to cruise for girls, and girls there were aplenty, all over the beach in racy two-piece bathing suits. But how to connect with them? By evening, the boys had screwed up their courage. They were at a little dance club on the wharf and managed to work their way over to a table of local girls who turned out to be a witty bunch, making the Fresno boys feel like hicks. But the four-piece jazz band was hopping, the dancing lively, and pretty soon, none of them cared. There was one redhead in particular who caught Mac's eye. A real knockout. The way she dragged on her cigarette with those crimson lips made you feel like she'd seen it all. Mac stepped outside for a smoke with the intention of building up the nerve to talk to her and found one of the other girls already out there smoking. Elbows on the rail, the petite brunette was looking out at the waves slapping against the shore. She was cute as a button and Mac couldn't believe he hadn't noticed her before.

"Just a warning," she said, without looking at him. "That girl in there, the one you've got your eye on, is a one-way mirror. You see her, but she doesn't see you. Only her own reflection in your eyes."

So this puckish beauty had been watching him. He curled his hand around his shiny new Zippo lighter and touched its blue flame to the tip of his Lucky Strike. "Good to know. And you are?"

"Effie," she said, reaching out a hand. "And when we go back in there, you're going to ask me to dance."

This brought him up short. Boy, did it! The whole of his dancing experience consisted of a prissy ballroom dance class his mother insisted he take, and the only thing that had stuck after those five grueling lessons was the one-two-three rhythm of the waltz, which would be *so* out of place among all the swinging and jitterbugging. He decided his best move was to confess his shortcoming. "I don't dance," he said. "Unless you're talking waltzing. Then I can really cut a rug."

She laughed this adorably bubbly laugh. He was off the hook! Or so he thought until she said, "Then waltz it will have to be."

And waltz they did. After going back into the bar, she took him by the hand and dragged him onto the dance floor where they waltzed and waltzed, at first to his embarrassment, but soon to his sheer delight, through and around the swingers and jitterbuggers, the two of them swirling-whirling, cutting an offbeat trail that was theirs alone.

But as the night wore on, he began to panic. What would happen when it was over? Would he ever see her again? He knew nothing about her. The noisy club didn't allow for much real talking, and he couldn't very well invite her back to the beach house where he and the guys were all packed in. And just as he was trying to figure out some kind of strategy, she said, "What do you say we blow this joint and find somebody's abandoned beach fire?"

Mac flicked on his blinker. They'd reached the off-ramp to Ocean Street.

He owed her this.

"I told you we could make sunset," Effie said.

The touristy corridor to the beach, crowded with its restaurants and motels, had a fair amount of traffic, but it was moving. They crossed the river and dropped down to the boardwalk—hub of the congestion—then cruised past the municipal wharf, which, like everything else, had changed so much. Parking kiosks now guarded the entrance and long poles with colorful flags lined the rails.

"I wonder if that little dance club is still there," he said.

"Not for a while," she said.

Sighing, he forged on up the small hill and past the landmark Dream Inn, the only high-rise along the Santa Cruz coast, where the traffic finally began to lighten up. From here on there was nothing to obstruct the view of the bay. Down below, waves crashed against the rocky cliffs sheltering the chain of small, sandy coves. It was shaping into a glorious sunset, the sky laced with feathery clouds. Another lungful of fluffy salt air, and just like that, he was back to that night.

They were strolling along the path above the bay searching the coves for unattended fires. She'd taken his hand. "You're a good one. I can tell." He'd felt so proud—exceptional! This beautiful woman could have chosen any of the guys, and she'd chosen him. Him! He gripped her small hand, his heart swelling in his chest. The moon cast a dreamlike glow over the water, making the wave break seem phosphorescent.

"It's a red tide," she'd said, and went on to explain something about an algae bloom that caused the dazzling glimmer. He'd only half-heartedly listened, instead hearing the swish of her wide-legged pants and feeling the warmth of her palm in his, the pounding of his heart. "There!" she'd said, pointing a slender finger down to a sheltered cove where a small abandoned fire blazed.

Mac drove slowly, searching for their spot. It all looked so different now. The beach bungalows that once lined the inland side of the drive had been replaced by fancy two-story homes. Even the coastline seemed changed. But then it would. It had been years since he'd been here. The sandy cliffs battered by water and wind were constantly being whittled away.

He glanced over at Effie, who'd grown quiet. Her hands were pressed to her cheeks and her eyes were tearing up. She loved her ocean. Told him that night years ago that she'd never leave it. And then she did. For him.

She pointed to an overlook. "There!"

He swung into a parking space facing the ocean. Was this their spot? He sat for a minute studying the contour of the cliff. Up and down the coast, small groups of people were gathering along the cliff edges to watch the sun go down. Was it?

Effie, already outside, waved him toward a bench on the promontory. "Come on! We can watch the sun set from here." Her wide-legged pants flapped in the light breeze.

He opened the car door in time to see a long line of pelicans wheeling past. Using his cane, he hoisted himself from the car—oh, his knees and hips were stiff!—and negotiated his way down the dirt path, cutting through a carpet of thick-fingered ice plant. The air was crisp and clean and delicious to breathe. He followed the path past a bench to six or so feet from the cliff's edge. He didn't want to get too close. The cliffs were unstable. Or so said the sign. He believed it too. Beneath his feet was nothing but soft, sandy dirt. Get too close and the sixty-foot cliff would crumble and send you tumbling.

"You might want to step back," he said to Effie a few feet in front of him.

She pointed to a line of white foam stretching from the shore out to sea. "Riptide."

He nodded. Those things could yank you out quick.

"Oh! And an otter! Do you see it?"

Even using the side of his eye, he couldn't make it out. "I'll have to trust you on that one."

"I told you, I'll be your eyes from now on."

He was satisfied with what he could see: the sky. It was on fire.

CHAPTER THIRTY-TWO

The Catie Curtis CD started in on the second round. Morgan flicked it off. Outside, one of Watsonville's many artichoke farms flew past, the scraggly plants barely registering on her radar. She'd drawn into herself, balled her suffering into a tight fist and shoved it deep inside. She knew her victimized feelings were more or less self-imposed; Treat was clearly sorry she'd "kissed" Marky and was doing everything possible to patch the hole she'd punched into their relationship—as much as was possible with John Boy hunkered down in the backseat texting his little heart out—but that wasn't the point. Treat had crossed the sacred line, had failed to honor the "or worse" portion of the marriage oath. That hurt.

Morgan picked up her water bottle from the floor and took a swallow.

Marriage. Maybe that was the problem. They'd been tricked into believing that that one big commitment was what it was all about, had forgotten it was the thousand little ones that came after, the choosing to be with one another *every day* that really mattered.

She thought of two friends who'd recently lost spouses, one to a sudden death, the other to a sleazy affair. Both women, upon being left alone, were totally incapable of taking care of themselves, barraging Morgan and anyone else who'd listen with needy phone calls. They'd lost themselves in their marriages, compromised themselves into oblivion.

Time to take stock. If she and Treat were to break up now, today, where would that leave her? An image from one of their vacations floated into her mind: snorkeling Jamaica's coral reef with its pretty little fishes and urchins, then drifting out too far, finding herself in a dark, dangerous, unfathomable sea.

She took another sip of tepid water, the Keep Calm And Carry On air freshener dangling from the dashboard mocking her.

She'd never find another woman like Treat. Treat was the remedy for being Morgan. She was grounded in ways Morgan could never be, maintaining a solid hold on the physical world: home insurance, car tune-ups, rototilling the yard. And what a lover! Morgan would never be able to find another woman so perfectly fitted to her—*if* she could even get herself to jump back into the dating world. Which seemed impossible. After Treat, there was only celibacy. Celibacy and her right hand.

"Mac must have been feeling pretty desperate to steal a car," Treat said.

Morgan had the sudden, ridiculous urge to unhook her seat belt and thrust her body between her wife and the steering wheel, grab her by the shoulders, and scream, WHY ARE YOU DOING THIS TO US? but instead said simply, "If I could just figure out where he was going."

"Try thinking like your mother," John Boy said, not even bothering to look up from texting. His tune had sure changed over the last half hour. Apparently, he'd finally come to terms with the reality of being stuck in a car with two middle-aged lesbians, his only lifeline to the outside world his smartphone.

"She's dead," she said, sounding curt, even to herself—probably due to the tons of unresolved feelings floating around after her mom's death. Not that they'd ended on a bad note. No, that would be too movie-of-the-week, too cliché, for them. *Their* last visit had been easy. Fun. Morgan had stopped by with a homemade strawberry rhubarb pie, her dad's favorite. But since he was off playing golf, she'd joined her mom shelling peas on the back porch. They'd talked so easily, no head trips, no hidden meanings, and by the time Morgan left, she'd been full of hope for their relationship, had actually believed she might finally be mature enough to appreciate the wonderful mother everyone said she had.

"Didn't you say she was the reason he was going to Santa Cruz?" John Boy said, obvious from his tone that he was multitasking her.

Did she? Morgan couldn't remember. "Yeah." What was to be done with this lingering hope? This feeling that if her mom had lived a little longer they'd have achieved some kind of mother/daughter nirvana? Or at least a relationship where they could talk without setting each other off.

"So," Treat said, "figure out where *he'd* think *she'd* want him to go."

Outside, some guy in a white pickup bumped along a dirt service road checking the irrigation system. He was probably having a perfectly fine day. No worries. No stress.

"It's worth a try," Treat continued.

Easy for her to say, Morgan thought. She hadn't spent her entire life trying, and failing, to read the inscrutable Effie's mind. A Netflix subscription for her birthday! Wouldn't that be perfect? Ha! What a bust. Her mom tossed the gift card onto the table, saying, "Give up the corner video store? The owners just had a baby." Take a day off from work so she and her mom could do a museum day? Another bust. Her mom canceled at the last minute due to some urgent political meeting that had just "come up." It was always the same. Clueless Morgan and her impossible-to-read mom.

Once again, she considered calling her brother, Mike. He deserved to know his dad was on the lam. But what could he do down there in L.A.? Besides, he'd probably put his wife, Nancy, on the phone. Like when their mom died, only then he hadn't put Nancy on the phone, the shit had sent her in his place so he could finish some real estate deal. Morgan had spent the most horrible day of her life with Nancy of the matching purse and shoes; Nancy, whose emotional expression ranged from little coughs and sideways glances to reciting Hallmark jingles; Nancy, whose reaction to Effie's death had been to start pawing through her mother-in-law's jewelry and clothes to see if there was "anything worth keeping." It was insulting. Infuriating. No. It was all on Morgan. As usual.

But that wasn't quite true. Treat was helping. Like she always did. And there was John Boy the Mormon Cowboy too.

She sighed. "Okay. I'll give it a shot. But no guarantees. Reading my mom's unpredictable mind via my dad's addled one doesn't exactly sound like a winning combination."

"It's all we've got," Treat said.

Morgan closed her eyes to concentrate. The image of Treat running her fingers through Marky's thick black hair flashed across her eyelids. So much for *that* strategy. She glared out at a passing strawberry field. Clusters of migrant workers huddled over the raised rows of delicate plants growing through what always looked to her like black plastic wrap. Nice to know the cash crop was protected from the moist earth, but what was protecting the workers? Their backs must be killing them. Not to mention their fingertips. Morgan kneaded the base of her neck. She had knots the size of walnuts. Think, she told herself. Think.

Someplace in nature, either the ocean or the redwoods, came to her first. Then one of the funky open-air coffee shops along the garden mall in Santa Cruz. Her mom was always going on about how fun it was to sip coffee and watch the street musicians and hippies. Bookshop Santa Cruz was also in the running. Her mom would return from her Santa Cruz trips with a sack of books she'd swear could only be gotten at the independently owned bookstore. But would her dad remember that? There was also the yacht harbor with its—

"Any ideas?" Treat asked.

Morgan loosened her seat belt. "Too many." The damn retractable belts were like boa constrictors, taking up the slack every time you inhaled.

Treat released air through her lips making a blown tire sound. John Boy groaned.

"Hey, I tried. Okay?"

"It's not that," John Boy said.

"What?" Morgan said. "There's more bad than I realized?"

"My girlfriend is all mad at me. She thinks I created this whole mess to 'sabotage' our relationship." He was glowering at his smartphone like it had betrayed him.

"Now, that just plain doesn't make sense," she said.

"She thinks I don't want to move in with her," he said, speaking slowly, like Morgan was mentally challenged. "Thinks that's why I screwed up. So I'd get fired and not be able to move out from my parents." He punched the seat next to his leg. "Guh!"

"Isn't that against some Mormon law? Moving in together before you're married?"

"You're Mormon?" Treat said.

"More or less," Morgan said.

"How can a person be—?"

"Would you quit?" he said. "This is a disaster."

"Seriously," Morgan said. "I would think it's against your religion to—"

"It is, okay? But Kira's not Mormon. And my parents don't know. So I would appreciate it if—"

"Got it," Morgan said. "Mum's the word."

"Ditto," Treat said. "But good luck with that." Treat's seat was reclined lowrider style, which meant her hip was bothering her. "She cute?"

"Yeah," he said glumly.

Treat patted Morgan's thigh. "The cute ones don't come easy, dude. You gotta treat 'em right."

Damn her! Treat was pulling out all the stops.

"Mac running away was not my fault," he said. "Everybody keeps forgetting that little factoid."

Treat raised her eyebrows as if to say, *O-kaaaay.*

A long, sulky pause swelled in the backseat. Then John Boy said sheepishly, "But I know what you mean. It's just…hard."

"You gotta step up," Treat said.

Morgan couldn't believe what she was hearing: Treat was giving him the Nephew Speech, the coming-of-age lecture she gave to all her sisters' boys—and their friends if they would listen—the one about how to treat a woman. Which Morgan usually thought was sweet. Most of the boys had terrible role models, abusive and adulterous. Treat was the surrogate father they never had. They loved her, respected her. But now? Really? After Treat had—

Treat took her focus off the road to look Morgan right in the eye. "You fuck up, she might not give you a second chance. And then you gotta live with that the rest of your life."

Morgan held her gaze. *You got that right.*

"But—" John Boy said.

"No buts, dude." Treat glanced back at the road then returned her gaze to Morgan. "A good woman will change your life. But you got to treat her right."

John Boy let out a little huff of air, then said, "Yes, ma'am."

"And keep your fingernails clean. Shows respect. And women like it."

Morgan didn't know what to say. Treat obviously wanted forgiveness. But did Morgan have it to give? "Mind if I plug in my iTunes?" she said.

"Go for it," Treat said, doing her best to sound nonchalant.

Morgan flipped through her playlists for something appropriate, but didn't have one for My-Dad-Busted-Out-Of-The-Rest-Home-And-My-Wife-Kissed-Another-Woman-And-Now-The-Cowboy-In-The-Backseat-Is-Heartbroken-Too. Even her country-western playlist wasn't that pathetic. She settled on Yo Yo Ma.

"If you don't mind me asking," John Boy said. "How did *you* two meet?"

Is he kidding, Morgan thought. Now? She glanced at Treat. God, this was going to be painful, to recount the well-worn story of their meeting—today of all days. There had to be a way to get out of—

"We met at a poker party," Treat said.

Morgan bit down on her lip. Treat was going for it. Morgan either had to let her go it alone or pick up her usual part about her friend who thought she should "get out more" and how she'd gone mostly to shut her friend up. But she couldn't make herself take up the story. She just couldn't.

Treat coaxed her on. "Ms. Morgan here had never played."

Morgan felt herself begin to flush. All those jokes about *taking it easy on the virgin* and *popping her cherry.*

"She didn't come from a 'card-playing family,'" Treat said, filling in Morgan's traditional part of the story. "But you wouldn't have known it that night. She beat the pants off all of us."

"Just luck," she said. "I haven't won a game since."

"Tell him what you got dealt in your opening hand."

Morgan stared at her sandals. When had her feet gotten so pudgy? "Four queens."

Treat slapped the steering wheel. "Four queens! Can you believe it? My baby gets four queens. Later on, she gets a full house: three sevens, two Jacks. I've never seen anything like it."

Next up: the part where Morgan always said she was lucky in more ways than one that night. And she was. That night changed her life. After the game, she and Treat walked all over Fresno's trendy Tower District with its art deco architecture and bustling nightlife, talking late into the night about every little thing. The following day, Treat dropped a card off at her work with the words "To one Lucky Lady" on the envelope and a laminated four-leaf clover inside. Six months later, they were living together. But Morgan couldn't make herself say it. Not without crying. And she'd be damned if she was going to let John Boy see her sob.

Treat laid a hand on her thigh. "But I was the lucky one that night. Found me the love of my life."

Morgan looked down at the hand on her thigh, the warm, capable hand that she loved so much. Would it be possible to forgive Treat just for today? Could she do it? It would make things so much easier.

She took a deep breath.

Just one day, she told herself. She could commit to that, a kind of short-term amnesty. She'd deal with tomorrow tomorrow.

"I'm a pretty good poker player myself," John Boy said. "Been told I have a face of steel."

God. The kid was almost as clueless as her sister-in-law. She wrapped her fingers around Treat's.

As if sensing Morgan's resolve, Treat gave her hand a grateful little squeeze. "Being good's only part of it. Without luck, you're nothing."

"Wait!" Morgan said. "I know where Mom is taking Dad!"

"What? Where?" Treat said.

"To the legendary beach of the beach fire."

"Huh?"

"The night they met! It's the place! I know it! The only problem is..." She released Treat's hand to rap herself on the forehead. "I'm not quite sure where it is. Hang on. It's along...you know, that road that runs right next to the beach? Past the lighthouse."

"West Cliff?" Treat said.

"Yeah. That's it. But which beach? Which beach? There are tons of little coves along there."

"She never took you there?"

"I won't remember it—Oh! Oh! Oh! She said something the last time she went to Santa Cruz about how some nudists had taken over their special cove."

"Nudists?" John Boy said. "As in naked nudists?"

Treat laughed. "Great. I can just see it now. Mac hanging out with a bunch of bare-assed hippies!"

Morgan slapped Treat's leg. "Would you stop? This is serious." But God, forgiveness felt good!

"I know, chica. But you've got to admit, it's got its comic elements."

"Is it legal?" John Boy said. "To strut your junk in public?"

Treat shook her head. "Santa Cruz is a world unto itself."

Morgan rested her head on the back of the seat. Yo Yo Ma launched into his amazing "Here and Heaven." Now, if they could just get there before her dad did something stupid.

CHAPTER THIRTY-THREE

"This is a first," Sonia said. "Taking shoes off to eat."

The anteroom outside the Mount Madonna dining hall had a shelf of shucked shoes and sandals. Cora sat between Nell and Sonia on a wooden bench. The plan was to eat before checking into their cabin. Dinner was about to be shut down. Cora bent over to slip off her sandals. "I thought you said your feet were killing you."

Sonia stretched out a leg and wiggled her crimson toenails. "I didn't say I didn't like it."

"I was born to be an outlaw," Nell said, unlacing a track shoe. "Living by my wits, on the periphery of society..."

The walls of the small anteroom were decorated with beautiful photos of beautiful people in impossible poses. Yoga, Cora supposed. Each picture featured a natural setting, strikingly lit and edged in some kind of Middle Eastern-looking writing. A carved table by the door to the dining hall held a small figurine, a woman with many arms, who looked like she was from India or thereabouts. All in all, the place was what her conservative sister would call "communist." The perfect hideout.

Now if she could just find a moment to tell Sonia and Nell the idea that had been bubbling around inside her. Since there was no going back to the Villa, why not—

Tawn stepped into the room. "Everything okay?"

Nell mimed a fat stogy and spoke in a gangster accent. "Who wants ta know?"

Three strapping fellows dressed in cotton drawstring pants and T-shirts strolled piously through the door, slid off their Zories, and disappeared into the dining hall without saying a word.

"Vow of silence," Tawn whispered.

"Gorgeous men who keep their mouths shut," Sonia said. "I'll take two."

Tawn laughed. "They've probably also taken a vow of celibacy."

"Such a waste!"

"They're here for Baba Hari Dass."

"Hari who?" Cora asked.

"A monk who hasn't spoken since 1952. He more or less inspired the place. Got a lot of followers."

"Is that what you aspire to do, Tawn?" Nell asked earnestly. "Learn what it's like to be silent and go without sex?"

Tawn squatted on the floor across from them. "That's not really my thing." Resting his buttocks on his heels, he propped his elbows on his knees—a position Cora could not have accomplished even in her youth. "But I respect it. I think there are demons that can only be dealt with in silence. Anyway, that's what Baba Hari Dass teaches. Kind of a mental Kung Fu."

Wise, Cora thought, for one so young. And not at all bad looking—even with the kerchief and beaded bracelets, accessories she generally considered effeminate. Somehow they made him seem even more virile. His lack of deodorant was a whole other story.

"So, I should give you the lay of the land," he said. "Once you're in the dining room there are three areas: the main room, a silent room, and an outdoor deck."

Cora set her sandals on the shelf. The anteroom was so small she was starting to feel a bit claustrophobic. "We should probably go for the silent room, so no one asks us any questions."

"Where's the fun in that?" Sonia asked.

"Yeah," Nell said. "How would we get to practice our cover stories?"

Cora plopped back down. "Cover stories?"

Tawn deferred to Nell. "If you don't mind…"

Nell nodded for him to go ahead.

"Tell people you're on personal retreat."

"What exactly does that mean?" Cora asked.

"That you're not signed up for any class. Just here to get away. Tell them you're from Carmel or Monterey."

"But won't we stick out?" Cora asked. "Being so old?"

Sonia crossed her legs and brandished a sexy smile. "Speak for yourself."

Cora noticed a blush creep up Tawn's cheeks. Sonia, of course, noticed it too and winked at Cora. Oh, she was proud of herself.

"A lot of people who come here are..." Tawn glanced shyly at Sonia. "...on the oldish side. They're the ones who can afford it. The rest of us have to work for our tuition doing the YSC program."

"Let me guess," Sonia said. "Young, saintly, and—"

"Yoga, Service, and Community. We do everything from landscaping to housekeeping. This is my second time."

He's gone to such lengths to help us, Cora thought, and not once have I thought to ask about his life. "So, we tell people we're on personal retreat, three women traveling together..."

"Long lost sisters," Nell said wistfully.

"Too complicated," Sonia said. "We'd have to plan a whole backstory about where we were born and who Daddy liked best."

"I agree," Cora said. "I vote for old friends."

"Who travel once a year, always trying something new," Sonia said.

"Last year was a safari in Tasmania," Nell said.

"The year before Sante Fe," Sonia said.

Cora sighed. "You sure you don't want to just eat in the silent room?"

"Not a chance," Sonia said.

Tawn stood. "Well, you're on your own from here on."

"You won't be joining us for dinner?" Nell asked, sounding genuinely disappointed.

"I told Sharla I'd wait for her."

Sonia raised her eyebrows suggestively. "You like her."

Another blush. "Yeah."

Cora reached out for a sort of hug/shoulder squeeze. "You've been marvelous. Thank you, Tawn."

Nell and Sonia hugged him too.

"Does this mean I get my phone back?"

"Sorry," Sonia said. "Not 'til morning."

"You can never be too careful," Nell said in her gangster accent. Then she nodded toward the door. "So do we do dis ting, or what?"

❖

Cora led the way into the dining hall. She felt self-conscious about her unbridled breasts, but there was nothing to be done about them now. Her bra was presumably still hanging on that bush by the reservoir—if some raccoon hadn't run off with it.

The yummy-looking buffet triggered a hunger she hadn't been aware of feeling. There were two main entrées to choose from: stuffed eggplant and something called curried tempeh. Nothing like the bland menu at the Villa! Even after Sonia's victory in getting them to offer a menu for those not allergic to spices, the entrées were dull dull dull, their most exciting offering being something they called curry, a concoction of ground beef and rice smothered in a tasteless green sauce.

Nell pointed to the tempeh and spoke loud enough that anyone around them might hear. "That one reminds me of a dish I had when we were traveling in Tasmania."

"Yes," Cora said, feeling daring. "Only it was made with fish, wasn't it?"

Sonia made a beeline to the salad bar where the three silent men in drawstring pants were filling up their plates. Cora scooped up a stuffed eggplant and joined her. "Let's take that table by the window. I have something I want to discuss."

"Can't it wait?" she whispered. "The view here is spectacular."

"These guys are too repressed for you." Sonia's new flat-chested profile just about broke her heart. She plopped a dollop of cottage cheese on her plate. "Come on."

Sonia took one last look at the men and heaved a dramatic sigh. "You're probably right." She scooped up a spoonful of pasta salad and tossed a couple of cantaloupe slices on her plate. "And so it goes."

The dining room was fairly empty, but those who were there all looked so interesting, a mixture of old and young, mingling together, table-hopping, engaged in what looked to be stimulating conversations. A welcome change from the Villa where the only young people were the occasional visitor and the ever-perky staff. It always demoralized Cora to feel people had to be paid to talk to her.

A large window looked out onto a deck where an absolutely lovely woman with a mane of white, waist-length hair held court to a table of six or so admirers. She reminded Cora of who Isadora Duncan might have grown into if she hadn't died so young in that horrible accident. The woman seemed impervious to the heat, a whisper-thin, lavender scarf tossed casually about her neck, her long fingers covered in silver rings and gesturing so gracefully when she spoke, as if language were a medium to be danced. No doubt one of the workshop leaders, Cora thought.

"So what is this you want to talk about?" Sonia placed her plate opposite Cora. "Or should we wait for Nell?"

A sudden insecurity settled into Cora's belly. What seemed like such a good idea moments ago now seemed to carry a lot of presumptions. Yes, they'd said they couldn't go back to the Villa, but that didn't mean Sonia would want to live with her. Sonia had three daughters—not that she'd move in with them. More like, she'd find a place of her own so she could hook up with some dashing widower. She certainly had the means to live on her own, and the courage. And what about Nell? Cora hadn't a clue what her situation was. But she couldn't imagine living with just Nell. No, if Sonia wasn't game, Cora would drop the whole idea. She cut into her eggplant with the nerves of someone stepping onto a high wire. At least Sonia wouldn't try to cushion a rejection. That would be awful. Embarrassing—

"Out with it," Sonia said, elbow on the table and head resting on her fist. "Before you talk yourself out of it."

Cora laughed. How well Sonia knew her! She took a deep breath for courage then came out with it. "What if…the three of us rented or bought a place together?"

Sonia arched one of her perfectly plucked eyebrows.

"It just came to me," Cora rambled on, "when we were on the deck looking out at the bay. I mean, we get along, we're reasonably healthy…" But there was no use going further. Sonia had started poking at her pasta salad, refusing to make eye contact, making Cora feel every bit the Plain Jane, the girl standing friendless in the schoolyard. She shoved a bite of eggplant into her mouth.

"I guess she hasn't told you then," Sonia said.

Cora swallowed the eggplant in one gulp, barely tasting it. "Told me what? Who?"

Sonia put her fork down. "Nell. She's got some kind of aneurism. By her brain. Inoperable."

Cora was taken aback. "Nell? But she seems so—"

"From what I understand, that's how these things play out. It could burst at any moment. And she's not completely without symptoms. At times, she has terrible headaches. You just wouldn't know, because, well, she's Nell."

Cora shifted her focus to Nell chatting with one of the employees by the salad bar, her plate piled high with what looked like a bit of everything. "How long has she known?"

"A few months. And don't be put out because she hasn't told you. She hasn't told anyone. The only reason I know is because I took her to the doc. Which reminds me. We need to talk about meds."

"Yes, I thought of that. I'm going to need to get some Lipitor and my water pills. I can skip a day or two, no problem. But Nell..."

"She's on some kind of blood thinner. We need to ask her what it is and make sure we get our hands on some first thing tomorrow."

"That's going to be tricky if it's prescription."

Sonia nodded.

Cora took another bite of eggplant. Was Nell's ailment a deal breaker?

"Of course, Nell could outlive us all," Sonia said. "One never knows at our age. But her diagnosis is rather dramatic. Worse comes to worse, would we be up for caring for her?"

Well, it certainly changed Cora's vision, no doubt about that. She pictured the two of them struggling to lift Nell from a tub, the floor, into a car. "How about hiring someone to look in on us from time to time? Maybe John from the Villa. He'll be without a job."

Sonia loaded her fork with pasta salad. "That could work." She pointed the loaded fork at Cora. "But I'm going to add this caveat: if we do move in together, and you lose your mind, I'm sticking you back in the Villa post haste. I will not go through that again, ever."

Cora returned the fork gesture. "Same goes for you." But inside she was fizzy with excitement.

Sonia laughed. "Good. Now, we've just got to talk Nell into it."

Nell set her brimming plate on the table. "Oh good, what now?"

CHAPTER THIRTY-FOUR

M ac took a moment to read the dedication on the back of the cliffside bench: *In Loving Memory Roland M. Forster 1918–2000*. Was this all that remained of a man's life? A bench? The tin containing Effie's ashes was still sitting on his dresser. She'd asked to be scattered out at sea, but he could never make himself do it. He'd intended to, at least those first few years after her death, but the longer he let that little star-shaped tin sit there, the more Effie's ashes became part of his universe. Morgan had suggested they scatter them when he moved to the Villa. He'd stubbornly refused. Told her he needed them now more than ever.

He kicked a bottle cap into the ice plant. Using his dear wife's ashes to make his daughter feel guilty, what kind of man was he?

"Would you quit worrying about those damn ashes and look at the sunset?" Effie said. She was his soft, wrinkly Effie again, in her corduroy slacks and green cardigan, the way he liked her best.

"I never made good on my promise."

"Mac, the only reason I asked you to bring my ashes to the ocean was so you'd have to come out here and think of me."

"I should have given you a bench, like my friend Roland here." He patted the back of the bench. It was set in the center of the patch of yellow-blooming ice plant. Footpaths cut from the paved walkway behind him through the surrounding sunny flowers like spider webs, each path ending at an overlook or a steep, crumbling descent to the ocean below. "I bet *his* ashes are now one with the sea."

"Oh, for heaven's sake. Did you even hear what I said?"

"What?"

"My wish has already been granted. You're here, back in our favorite spot, thinking of me."

"But I should have had the whole family come, done a ceremony, people reading poems, sharing memories, and then a final dramatic flinging of your ashes into the sea."

"The only other people I care about are our kids, and one of them is looking for you right now, and the other is surely on his way."

Mac scowled at her. "Did you plan this?"

"Maybe I did." She wiggled her eyebrows. "Maybe I didn't."

"You little scamp, you."

He looked out at the foreverness of the ocean. The sky was glorious, all golds and pinks, the water shimmering, the distant blue hump of Monterey and whatever that other hump was. And the air was so fresh—and cool! God, it was good to get out of the inland heat. But wait. Was that a dolphin? It was! And there was another. And another. A school—no, *pod* of dolphins. He watched them mosey their way along the coast until they were out of sight—or out of his measly sight. The sound of the waves gently slapping the cliffs below soothed his nerves. He'd done it. He'd brought his Effie home. He turned to look at her, expecting that she would be gazing at the ocean too, her eyes filled with tears of gratitude, her soul finally at peace. But she was looking right at him, and clearly had something on her mind. "What now?"

"Call Morgan. Tell her where you are."

A line of pelicans crested a wave. "Can't I just enjoy this for a few more seconds?"

"You stole a *car*, Mac. She and Mike must be out of their minds with worry."

Mac stared at her in disbelief. "Lest we forget, dear, you were the one who put that idea in my head."

"There you go again, blaming li'l old dead me."

This brought him up short. It sure did. He placed his palm flat against the bench. Real. Kicked the dirt beneath his feet. Real.

"What was the last thing you said to Morgan?" Effie said, sounding realer than ever. "That you stole a car? Think of what she and Mike are going through. I'm sure they're worried sick. You *know* the Villa contacted the police. There's probably an all-points bulletin out about you right now. And think of poor John driving the bus. He's probably out a job."

The woman was impossible! More so in death than she'd been in life. "Just give me one minute."

Below, on the sheltered beach, small groups of people were packing up for the day and starting the trek across the sand to go home.

Home.

He had no home. Not since the house on Wilson Avenue where he and Effie had raised Morgan. Sometimes at the Villa, when he couldn't sleep, he'd lie in bed recalling every corner of that house: the cozy kitchen with its dining nook overlooking Effie's garden— the perfect place to enjoy a soft-boiled egg, slice of buttered toast, and cup of steaming hot coffee; the generous living room with its old corduroy sofa that just begged you to take a nap. How good it would feel to fall into that sofa right now! He'd just lay his tired bones down and drift off into its home-sweet-homeness. He'd fallen asleep there many times in the evening after settling down with the paper or a good TV show. When Effie was ready to go to bed, she'd wake him, sometimes with a sweet kiss, sometimes with an exasperated thwack to the leg, but always, always, with the words, *Get up, Pops, time for beddy bye.* He'd grumble as if put out and continue grumbling as he padded upstairs to the bedroom, but he'd have been disappointed if she'd let him sleep the night away on the couch. Waking with Effie started a day out right.

And there was his shop in the garage, the smell of sawdust and grease, the pegboard where his tools hung, the metal cabinets full of nails, screws, hinges and drill bits, the old lard bucket where he kept his dad's collection of antique hammers. He'd sit out there for hours doing the million little projects life required: fixing a broken toaster, rigging a wire on a picture, regluing a woogity leg on a chair. At the Villa, he didn't even have a screwdriver. It wasn't considered safe.

A group of young people passed behind him on the walkway, laughing. So much like the scene sixty-two years ago when he and Effie strolled along the same path, not a care in the world, the waves breaking below, the stars twinkling above, her soft hand in his, the swish of those wide-legged pants—

"So if you're not going to call your daughter, what are you planning to do? Sleep in that *stolen* car?" Effie asked.

He blinked a couple of times trying to place this unfamiliar, and rather terse, old woman sitting next to him. "I said I'd call her. I just needed a minute."

Effie made a harrumphing sound.

He was exhausted, hungry. The phone was all the way back in the car. So was that apple he'd picked up at Casa de Fruta. He heaved himself up from the bench, his knees complaining something awful, and picked his way back down the narrow dirt path toward the pavement. He was thankful for the newly acquired cane, plunked it right down in the ice plant to steady each uneven step. When he reached the walkway, some kids on skateboards barreled past nearly knocking him over. "Sorry, dude!" the last of them yelled over her shoulder.

Mac took a moment to calm himself, looked both ways, then headed across the pavement to the parked car. But where had he put the keys? He fished around in his pockets. Nothing. Could he have left them in the car? Had he been that careless? He tried the car door and was appalled to see that not only had he left it unlocked but he'd also left the phone just sitting on the seat for anyone to steal. And sure enough, the keys were dangling from the ignition. What a dunce! He snatched them out along with the phone and the apple, locked the car, and retraced his steps back to the bench.

For a few seconds, he couldn't remember Morgan's number, which was ridiculous. He'd dialed it thousands of times. When he finally did remember it, his fingers felt too big and clumsy for the tiny buttons. It took him four tries. Listening to it ring, he watched the sun threaten to drop behind the bay. He could just make out a white sail on the horizon. *Surrender!* it seemed to call out to him. *Surrender, old man!*

CHAPTER THIRTY-FIVE

T urn in there." Morgan pointed to the Dream Inn parking lot up ahead. "One of the employees is bound to know where the nude beach is."

Treat flicked on her blinker. "Roger that."

The monstrous luxury hotel stood alone, tall and boxy, right on the water's edge, a monolith of tacky sixties architecture. Morgan wondered who slept with whom to get it approved. It was so out of place in Santa Cruz, land of quaint beach bungalows and bayside bed and breakfasts.

Treat pulled up to the hotel entrance. People in various versions of beach attire were coming and going through two glass doors leading to the lobby. The smell of coconut oil was strong. Morgan turned to John Boy. "Would you—"

"No way." He held his arms in front of his face as if she were trying to physically assault him. "They'll think I'm some kinda perv going in there and asking for the naked beach."

Morgan sighed. Fine. She'd do it herself.

"Now just hang on one cotton pickin' minute, pardner," Treat said, giving equal emphasis to each word—her Johnny Cash imitation. She cut the engine. "The little lady asked a favor of you and I think it only right you oblige her." She ran her fingers around an imaginary hat brim. "It's a helluva long walk back to Fresno." She winked. "If you catch my meaning."

Morgan almost laughed—until it worked.

"Okay. Okay," John Boy said. He was like a puppy being shooed outside. He dragged his feet up to the glass doors, stopping briefly to glance pleadingly, and ineffectively, over his shoulder, then made the plunge.

"Well done," Morgan said.

Treat dropped the impersonation. "I told you about the kiss because it's never going to happen again."

Really, Morgan thought, you're going to bring that up now? "Hon, this isn't the time—"

"It was a total cabróna thing to do. But I swear, the moment my lips touched hers—and it was only for a few seconds—it felt so... wrong. Like...I don't know...She wears *lipstick*. That shit tastes horrible—"

"TMI. TMI. TMI!"

"But worse than that, her lips weren't...yours. So I told her I couldn't do whatever it was we were doing, didn't *want* to." Treat gripped the steering wheel so tightly it looked like she was trying to rip it from the dashboard. "Bonita, believe me, the kiss broke the spell. Forever. You're the only one I want, the only one I'll *ever* want."

This had to be difficult for Treat, begging forgiveness. She was a proud woman.

Still.

Morgan stared past her to John Boy who was talking to a bellhop outside the building. The bellhop peered around John Boy to the SUV, an amused expression on his suntanned face.

Treat shot a look over her shoulder then said to Morgan. "What are you looking at?"

"That bellhop thinks we are two very kinky ladies."

Treat set the emergency brake, unbuckled her seat belt, and faced Morgan head on. "Have you even heard what I said?"

Morgan looked into her eyes. Treat's hairline crow's feet were taut with worry, her eyebrows lifted expectantly. "I don't know what to do with this information."

"You could start by forgiving me."

Morgan rested her back against the car door, the seat belt cutting into her neck, the car door's armrest jutting into her lower back. "I already have." She added quickly, "But just for today. Tomorrow when I wake up mad and hurt, I get to be mad and hurt."

"Bring it on," Treat said.

"I hope you mean that, because I'm going to be really really mad and really really hurt."

They sat quietly for a few seconds, Morgan treasuring the gold flecks in Treat's irises, the little mole by her left brow. She hadn't been able to see these for years. What else had she been missing? She thought about the package sitting in the trunk of her car back at Casa de Fruta. "I bought myself some new sexy pajamas today."

"*Real*-ly," Treat said, eyes flashing mischief. "That sounds fun."

"If you're good."

John Boy swung open the back door, slid into the 4Runner, and slammed the door. "Follow West Cliff until you see a triangular sculpture. He says you can't miss it. The beach below is secluded."

Treat fired up the engine.

"Oh. And you're welcome," John Boy said.

Morgan and Treat exchanged amused looks. What were they, his parents now?

"I mean it. That guy looked at me like I was a fa—" He stopped himself so abruptly you could hear the skid marks.

"Like a what?" Morgan said, goading him.

"Nothing," he mumbled.

"All right." Treat put the SUV into gear. "We're burning daylight."

The road curved along the rocky coastline. To the right was an unlikely mix of vintage beach bungalows and huge gaudy mansions; to the left people strolled or rode bikes on a cliffside walkway overlooking a bracelet of small coves. Occasional pullouts for parking were mostly filled.

"Check out the hippies," John Boy said, using his phone to snap a photo of some tie-dyed, dreadlocked teenagers and their mangy dog. "I am so texting this to Krista. She loves hippies."

"Your girlfriend?" Morgan asked.

"Yeah."

Morgan wondered if his sending the photo was a ploy to appease Krista or if he'd already texted his way to forgiveness.

A guy wearing a wetsuit jogged down the path, surfboard tucked under his arm. Approaching the lighthouse, they began to see more and more surfers—some riding the sizable swell, others hanging out on the cliffs or standing by their cars stripping off their wetsuits, towels tied modestly around their hips, their hair dripping wet.

Morgan scanned the coastline for the sculpture. "Did the guy say how far?"

"A ways," John Boy said.

Morgan tried to keep her mind off the uneasy question: What if her dad wasn't there? What then?

"Ohhhh yeah." Treat pointed to a classic woody in one of the pullouts. "Right there, my friends, is my dream car."

The red Corolla in front of them was crawling along, the driver probably looking for someplace to park. Morgan took a few deep breaths. *Stay calm, girl. Stay calm. Worry never helps anything.* But what if—

Her phone rang. If it was Dick Deetz again he was just going to have to...She checked caller ID.

"Dad!"

"Morgan?"

"Where are you? Are you all right?"

"I'm ready for you to come get me."

It was so good to hear his voice! Even if he did sound scared and...so old. But it was no time to get emotional. "That's what I'm trying to do. Where are you?"

"Overlooking our favorite beach—"

"Where you and Mom met."

"Ha!" Treat said.

"Is that Treat?" he said.

"Yes. She's with me and we're almost there."

"How did you know where I'd be?"

"Who knows? Anyway. We just got directions to the nude beach—"

"Nude beach?"

"Yeah, Mom told me once they turned your beach into a nude beach." There was a pause on his end. "Dad?...Dad!"

"Well, I'll be damned."

Morgan smiled even though her throat was battling with a whole host of emotions threatening to be set free. "Just stay where you are."

She kept on the phone with him as they drove along. It was difficult to think of things to talk about so she just gushed about how happy she was that he was safe and how close they were to being with him, occasionally interrupting her own monologue with: "Dad? Are you still there?"

The Corolla in front of them finally found a parking spot, which opened up her view, and like magic, there it was. The sculpture. Silhouetted by the sun and in the shape of a huge gnomon on a sundial, it looked like some prehistoric monument honoring the setting sun. But where was her dad?

Treat made the curve. John Boy sat forward in the seat and pointed ahead to one of the pull-ins. "Green Jetta."

Morgan searched the cliffs. *Come on, Dad. Come on...* And then she saw him: sitting on a bench and looking out to the ocean, a cell phone to his ear. "I see you, Dad! I see you!" He stood up and waved.

Treat swung into a parking spot next to the Jetta. "There he be, m'lady, safe and sound."

Morgan flung the car door open and rushed over the bike path and down the narrow dirt trail, stumbling over a bit of ice plant. "Dad!" She took him by the shoulders. "Are you all right?" She didn't wait for him to answer, just threw her arms around him and hugged him close. "I'm so sorry, Daddy. So sorry."

His trembling frame folded around hers. "It's me that should be sorry, pumpkin."

"But I..."

Treat's strong arms circled them both. "Nobody needs to be sorry. Everybody's safe."

Morgan let herself indulge in the feeling of being sandwiched between her dad and her partner, the two people she loved most in the world, only dimly aware that John Boy had walked over to the cliff's edge to gawk at a group of frolicking naked people on the beach below.

"Daddy, you had me so scared." The salty tears stung her chapped lips. She held him for what seemed like minutes, waiting for cues that he was ready to be let go—that *she* was. They never came.

But they couldn't very well stand there forever so she forced herself to step back, breaking up the group hug.

She held her dad at arm's length. His favorite blue hat, horribly rumpled, was pulled down past his eyebrows and his eyes were watery and there was something…milk?…dried on his chin. She licked her finger and wiped it off. "Don't ever do this again, you hear me?" It felt strange to treat her dad like he was a child—her dad, the guy who could fix anything.

John Boy cleared his throat. Apparently, he'd had his fill of naked people and wanted to be included. Morgan felt a surprising tenderness for him. The cowboy had stuck it out, and been damn helpful too. Even if he was a little shit.

"Dad, do you remember—"

"John?" her dad said. "What the heck are you doing here?"

Morgan felt an absurd amount of relief, as if this small identification meant her dad wasn't as far gone as she feared.

John Boy lifted his chin. "Hey, Mr. Ronzio."

"He's been a big help finding you."

"Tell that to Miss Wright," John Boy said glumly.

"Lost your job?" Mac said.

John Boy shrugged.

"Son, I never meant for that to happen."

John Boy rubbed a boot on his pant leg. "Yeah, well…"

"Maybe you can find something at the Home Depot."

"Maybe."

Morgan knew how much it hurt her dad to even say the words Home Depot, let alone suggest John Boy apply for a job there. How did this happen? How did a man go from being a successful business owner, a man people came to for his opinions, a man of integrity and distinction to this: a doddering wisp of skin and bones living somewhere between the past and present.

"It's good to see you, old man," Treat said. She was balancing on a small rise of earth making her look taller than she was. "You scared the bejesus out of us."

"Well, Effie wanted…" Mac looked around confused.

Morgan felt her heart begin to cave in on itself.

"I'm sure Effie appreciates it," Treat said. "But right now, I think your daughter would like a few moments with you. You warm enough?"

He nodded

"Sure? I've got a blanket in the car."

"I'm fine."

Morgan mouthed *Get the blanket.*

"Hey, cowboy," Treat said. "What do you say we call the Villa and tell that prissy Miss Wright that you found Mac."

"Seriously?" he said. "You'll tell her I did it?"

Morgan took her dad's arm and sat him on the bench.

The golden pancake of the sun was just slipping behind a bank of incoming fog, and the air was cooling, not air-conditioner cool but fresh cool, real cool. She followed her dad's gaze to the rolling water, wrapping a protective arm over his shoulder. He patted her knee affectionately, the same pat he'd been patting as long as she could remember.

What were they going to do with him? There was no sending him back to the Villa. Not after this. She could always move him back in with her and Treat...Treat would be okay with it. But would their relationship? But there'd be time to deal with all this later. Just be here now, she told herself. Me and Dad. Safe. I'll deal with tomorrow tomorrow.

The sea lions stopped barking as the last of the sun dropped behind the low-lying fog. She rested her head on his shoulder and said tenderly, "So, you want to tell me what this was all about?"

Chapter Thirty-six

Bellies full, Cora, Sonia, and Nell strolled arm in arm like schoolgirls down the dirt road toward one of Mount Madonna's cabins, Nell tucked in the middle, Cora clutching the little bag of toothbrushes and other sundries that Tawn had thoughtfully scrounged up for their night's stay. The other guests seemed to be in workshops, or so Cora assumed, and they had the place pretty much to themselves. Dusk had settled, and unseen critters were beginning to rustle beneath the shrubs; the heady scent of lavender and pine hung in the evening air. They spoke in whispers.

"We can plant a garden," Nell said. "Grow pansies. Daisies. And stay up late eating chocolate ice cream."

Cora gave her newfound friend's arm a squeeze. Over dinner, they'd discussed her diagnosis, the ins and outs of sharing a home together, and what they were to do if Nell's aneurism suddenly exploded. "It'll take me out quick," she'd told them. "You'll barely miss a mah-jong move." Cora was aware it might not be that easy, but she and Sonia had vowed to see her through it.

Down the road, a bunny was startled and hopped off into a thicket of grass.

"I just hope that overnight guests will be tolerated," Sonia said.

Nell chuckled. "Just no thumping headboards keeping us all awake."

Cora bit back a smile, afraid to feel too happy lest she jinx it. But how could she not feel happy? She was starting a new chapter. With housemates. She hadn't had roommates since college. Of course, there were a few minor details to get ironed out. She needed to call Donald, for one thing. He'd be worried out of his gourd by now. She'd call Adrian too. He'd be all right so long as he knew she was safe. "Do you suppose the Villa will press charges?" she asked.

"Bitch Wright wouldn't dare," Sonia said. "She's going to want to sweep this whole incident under the rug. Trust me. The woman has an unnatural fear of lawsuits."

She had a point.

Nell halted abruptly and pointed to a clearing where a mangy coyote was looking back at them.

"Well, I'll be damned," Sonia whispered. "I haven't seen one of those since my years on the ranch."

The coyote stood stock-still, scrutinizing them, its lean torso all ribs, its scruffy tail hanging low. You could almost smell the wildness of it, the hunger. Then, with a single swish of its tail, it did an about-face and trotted into the darkening woods—minus, Cora now noticed, a part of its hind leg, which dangled from its haunch, a useless appendage. It didn't seem bothered by the loss at all, save for trotting a bit lopsided.

"Well, we gave him something to think about," Nell said.

But Cora wondered. It seemed to her they'd been forgotten the moment he turned around.

They resumed walking, quietly, steadily, without the slightest idea of what their future held. In no time, they'd reached the stairway leading to the temple. It was lit up with lanterns. "Isn't it magical?" Nell said. Neither Sonia nor Cora answered, but Nell was right, it looked like a passage to another world.

"Let's see what's at the top," Nell said.

"There must be more than fifty steps," Sonia whined.

"Or more," Cora said. "We can do it in the morning—when we've rested."

But Nell freed herself from their hold. "We might not get the chance." She started up the stairs, gripping the railing as she went. She looked like a little tractor.

"I swear," Sonia said. "She's determined to trigger that aneurism."

"We have to go after her."

Sonia grumbled something unintelligible but began climbing. Cora took up the rear. What did one do for an aneurism victim? CPR? Mouth-to-mouth? Five steps up and she had to stop for breath. Five more, another breath. Sonia, meanwhile, seemed to be propelling herself up with obscenities. "Damn you, Nell," Cora heard her mutter, and, "Sonofabitch, my feet are killing me," and, "Hell, I don't know what she has to gain by killing me. She's not in my will." Cora forged on. Thirteen, fourteen, fifteen. Breathe. Sixteen, seventeen, eighteen. Breathe. It was exhausting; her thighs were burning, and she wasn't even halfway. Twenty-two, twenty-three, twenty-four. Not even close. Twenty-five, twenty-six, twenty seven. Maybe living together wasn't such a good idea. Nell was too impulsive, too—

"Isn't it glorious?"

Cora looked up to see Nell standing on a step midway to the top, Sonia on the step below her. They had their backs to the temple and were gazing out at the night.

Relieved for the break, Cora caught up and turned around as well. The separation between land and sky was almost swallowed up in darkness, save for the lights of Monterey twinkling across the bay. The first star flickered to life. "Star light, star bright," Cora said softly.

"What are you wishing for?" Sonia asked.

"I'm not sure. To make it to the top of the stairs, I suppose."

"You need a better wish than that," Nell said.

"I'm too tired to be creative."

"A-*men*," Sonia said.

"But it's the first star!" Nell said. "We have to make a wish. I know. We'll do it at the top of the stairs. That way we'll each have time to pick the perfect wish. But we can't tell each other. We'll just say *one two three* then cast our wishes to the Universe."

"For Christ's sake, Nell," Sonia said. "Isn't it enough we're climbing this damn mountain?"

"Suit yourselves," Nell said. "But when I get to the top of this hill I'm going to have one perfect wish." She began tractoring back up the stairs.

Sonia groaned and started after her.

Cora clung to the railing. Twenty-eight, twenty-nine, thirty. Suppose she did have the opportunity for a wish to come true? Just one, like in the fairytales—though they usually came in threes, managing to cancel each other out. But suppose she got just one. What would it be? Health? Happiness? Too vague. And safe. Like Miss America contestants wishing for world peace. The perfect house? Too materialistic. To be less judgmental?

Before she knew it, she was standing in front of the temple with Sonia and Nell. She'd been so preoccupied with choosing a wish she'd forgotten how hard the climb was. She was breathing heavily, certainly—they all were—but the oxygen flowing in and out felt good. Alive! She chuckled to herself. As long as she didn't think about the climb, it was easy.

"Isn't it beautiful?" Nell said. "Like a church..."

"Only not," Sonia said.

"Exactly," Nell said.

The large temple, although empty of people, was lit up with white Christmas lights and looked like something you might see in a Bollywood movie, beautiful and gaudy and rustic all at once. Underneath the billowing canopy, folding wooden chairs and meditation cushions were scattered casually around an ornate altar featuring another strange sculpture—this one half-man, half-monkey. He had one of those mesmerizing faces that looked as if he understood living and dying, joy and pain; his expression one of fierce, fearless, love, which Cora found quite alluring, also a little disturbing seeing as he was a monkey.

"Hanuman," Sonia said. "The monkey deity of the Hindus."

"Isn't he something?" Nell said.

Offerings were laid at his feet: coins and flowers, tattered photographs and fruit. Lush red and silver fabric was draped around the altar, the little mirrors sewn into the material throwing around coins of light. So exotic and wonderful and part of this magical day's adventure. Cora glanced over her shoulder at the entrance. They had no idea if they were even allowed to be here.

Nell plucked a small folded piece of paper from the altar and unfolded it to read, which Cora found tacky and irreverent, until Nell, after reading it, closed her eyes and held it to her heart, then kissed it and returned it to the altar.

"A prayer for someone's daughter," Nell said. "She has cancer."

Cora sighed. There was so much sadness in the world. She knew this, and felt it deeply, but at the same time didn't feel sad at all. It was extraordinary, this paradox, and new to her. How complex humans were. She'd been living with herself for eighty-one years and never had a feeling quite like this one. She stepped away from the altar and took in a lungful of the cool, pine-scented air. It was a glorious night. And somewhere a woman's daughter was fighting cancer. It was all part of it. All perfect.

She heard footfalls climbing the stairs. "Someone's coming!" she whispered.

Sonia and Nell spun around. Were they going to get in trouble?

A bearded young man in drawstring pants and an open vest with no shirt stepped into the temple. Cora acted like she was leaving. Sonia and Nell followed her lead. But the young man didn't seem to have the slightest interest in them. He just began straightening chairs.

They walked down enough steps to be out of his sight then paused looking out over the vast world before them. Cora's mind whirled with thoughts she'd never thought before. One in particular niggled its way forward. But how to articulate the new thought into something she could understand—and remember?

It had to do with the second half of the climb up to the temple, and that three-legged coyote, and the daughter with cancer. And Nell. There were difficult things in life, sure, but a person only made them more difficult by dwelling on how difficult they were. It was like there was the suffering and then the suffering over the suffering, which made the original suffering so much worse. On the first half of the climb up the stairs she'd been thinking how hard it was—and that made it harder—while the second half, when her mind was occupied elsewhere, was effortless. And that coyote wasn't suffering over a lost foot, wasn't going around saying *Poor me. Only three feet. Poor, poor me....* He was just living. And then there was Nell, who didn't seem to be suffering one bit over her aneurism. She too was just living.

Cora gazed out on the sky, now a rich, glowing indigo. A few more twinkling stars had joined the first. If she could just learn this little trick...

"Well, I've got my wish," she whispered.

"Me too," Nell said.

"Me three," Sonia said

Nell made a fist, holding her wish like a pair of dice. "One... two...three..." Cora and Sonia gripped their wishes too. "Go!" they all three whispered together and flung their wishes out to the universe. Then they stood there quietly as if waiting to hear the wishes land. Below them, a bat flew figure eights—swoop, dive, ascend, swoop, dive, ascend—casting an infinite spell. Cora felt Nell's warm, calloused hand slip into hers then Sonia's smooth, manicured one.

"I have a backup plan in case my wish doesn't come true," Nell said, tightening her hold on Cora's hand. Cora was about to say: *Telling will break the spell*. But Nell went on, "If for some reason I don't go quickly, I have a small bottle of pills..."

Pills, Cora thought. To relieve the pain? Then she understood, and the understanding made her stop breathing for a few seconds. Was she strong enough for this journey? Would she be able to do what Nell might ask? She noticed her pulse quickening, the muscles in her body tensing. How eager she was to jump into suffering! And about something that might never happen. Or might. Either way, why let it rob her of this moment, standing here with these two beautiful women, her friends?

"I wonder what Mac's doing right now?" Sonia said.

Mac. He'd totally slipped Cora's mind. "Wherever he is, I'm thankful to him."

"Me too," Nell said.

"Me three," Sonia said.

Cora focused on the soles of her feet pressed to the step, the warmth of her friends' palms in hers. She would be strong enough. *Was* strong enough.

An owl hooted in the distance.

Chapter Thirty-seven

The sea lions were barking up a storm. Mac studied the evening sky, its first timid stars peeping through. He could feel the warmth of his daughter sitting next to him, her patiently waiting for him to respond to her question. What was all this about, she wanted to know. Why had he made this crazy dash for the ocean? Her arm wrapped around his shoulder felt comforting—and disconcerting. She was his child; he was supposed to take care of her. Why, just yesterday she'd been so...he stopped himself. What an old man thought: just yesterday, just yesterday...Morgan was fifty-five years old. Or was it fifty-six? The years since Effie's death had all blurred into one big ball of time. Not that he was ever very good at keeping track of his kids' ages. That had been Effie's job. She'd hand him a birthday card to sign or a present to assemble. Sometimes she'd just sign his name and tell him about it later.

It was starting to get chilly. Where had Treat and John gone off to? They were with Morgan a moment ago, weren't they? He rubbed his eyes. It had been such a long day. Long and complicated.

"Daddy?"

She was probably afraid he hadn't heard her—or afraid he was so far gone he didn't understand that he'd stolen a car and gone for a joyride. Surely, that's how she saw it, an old man having his last hurrah. He glanced around for Effie. She was nowhere to be found. Typical. She was never around for the hard stuff. How different she and Morgan were, and how much the same. Both stubborn, both smart, but Morgan so cautious.

"Daddy, I would have driven you here if you'd asked."

"I know, pumpkin."

"Is it because you hate the Villa? Is that it? Because you're not going back there."

Mac took her hand in his. She was trying so hard to get it right. Just like when she was little. Such a good girl, always coloring inside the lines, raising her hand in class. Even in second grade when she threw up on her desk. The teacher told them that Morgan had just sat there, hand raised, her sweater and desk covered in puke, waiting to be called on. It drove Effie crazy. "How could we have raised such a meek child?" she'd say. But Mac had never seen Morgan as meek. She just wanted to know where the lines were. Once inside them, her colors were bold, daring.

Now, though, there was no "right" to get. Men weren't supposed to get this old. "I did it for your mother."

"Dad, she's—"

"I promised we'd retire here."

"But she—"

"I should have made it happen."

Her body next to him contracted and expanded as she breathed, her hand plump and soft and so full of life. Those first months after her birth, he'd been so afraid her tiny lungs would give out. She'd seemed so fragile, so quiet. Nothing like her brother who'd stormed onto the scene wailing and kicking. He'd stand over her crib, watching her chest expanding, contracting, expanding, contracting, sometimes her breath so light he'd have to place a finger in front of her mouth to check. Then his hands would be too calloused to feel the faint in-and-out of it so he'd shake her lightly, just enough to elicit a yawn. A couple of times, he'd been too rough and she'd started crying. Oh, Effie had given him hell then.

He gave her hand a squeeze. "I didn't mean to scare you."

"I know, Daddy."

But he had scared her, and certainly not for the first time. It was never intentional. She was just that kind of kid. When she was eight he'd taken her and Mike hunting, thought they'd enjoy it. He was after wild turkey, but on the way, a gas station attendant spoke vividly of herds of boar roaming the hills, which had thrilled Mike. Not so with Morgan. Oh, she'd soldiered on throughout the day, never once letting on that she was scared, and fortunately, the boars never materialized, but for the next month, she'd wake up terrified, her little heart pounding in her chest, crying about the scary pigs in her dreams. "What were you thinking?" Effie'd said. "Taking her out hunting." Morgan rushed to his defense. "But, Mama, it's not *those* pigs I was dreaming about." Boy, had that line lived on. Whenever Mike or Mac got in trouble with Effie, they'd say, *It's not those pigs!* and six times out of ten, she'd laugh. Still, he'd never forgiven himself.

"Sorry I took you hunting."

Morgan shifted on the bench to face him. "I'm not quite following you."

He let out a long stream of air. How to explain that he hadn't lost his marbles when he wasn't all that sure that he hadn't? But he needed to stay strong. For her. "We should call the kid whose car I stole. He's probably pretty upset."

"Treat will take care of it. Her nephew is a cop. Remember him? Ignacio?"

Mac didn't. Treat had dozens of nieces and nephews. "That Treat, she's all right."

"Dad. You're shivering."

"Am I?"

She glanced over her shoulder to the car. "Maybe we should head back."

After all he'd been through? That was it? Head back? "I'm not done yet."

She looked at him suspiciously. "Meaning?"

He looked out at what was left of the horizon. What *did* he mean? "I just want to say good-bye to your mother. Nothing dramatic."

"Then I'm going to get that blanket. And tell Treat what's going on." She got up and circled behind the bench where she wrapped her arms around his chest, bringing her head next to his. "I love you."

He could feel her breath on his cheek, in out, in out. "I love you too, pumpkin. More than you know."

"I'll be right back."

"I'll be here."

The crunching sound of her retreat was swallowed up by the rhythmic moan of the waves. He searched the shadows for Effie, knowing good and well he would never see her again. He'd brought her home. Finally. "Good-bye, love," he whispered to the salty air. A sea lion barked a response.

He tipped his head back. If only he could see! He was sure the sky was filling with stars. What was to become of him? He'd grown too old to be of use to anyone—all customer service with no product. He chuckled. Effie would have liked that line. But there was no more Effie. Never would be. Now that he'd brought her home.

Suddenly, he was bristling with impatience. Like he'd felt so many years ago when he and his buddies hung out on the beach waiting for something, anything, to swoop in and transform their lives. Who would have guessed "the thing" for him would come in the form of Effie, his pistol of a girl.

He turned to see what was keeping Morgan, but something brushed the periphery of his vision. He looked back, blinking a few times. It was Effie! Just as she was that first night, dancing. Her wide-legged pants rippled in the breeze, while loose strands of hair blew across her freckled cheeks. He could hear the band too—playing their song, "Swinging on a Star." He reached for her, but she twirled coyly out of his grasp with a flirtatious smile. He stood, helping himself up with the back of the bench. Reached again, this time with both hands. Again, she playfully inched away. "What do you say you give this girl a dance?" she said, her voice full of mischief. He was lurching through the ice plant now, his feet unsteady but determined, reaching, reaching, just missing. Far away, someone was yelling. Probably one of his pals wondering where he'd disappeared to. "Don't wait up," he yelled back. Then he lunged, whole-body, for his crazy beautiful girl.

"Effie."

She took him in her arms and together they were airborne, spinning, twirling. Radiant.

The End

About the Author

Baffled by reality, Clifford Henderson has fashioned a life where she can spend most of her time in make-believe. Her previous four novels have garnered many awards including ForeWord Magazine Book of the Year, Independent Publisher, Rainbow Readers, Golden Crown and Lesbian Fiction Reader's Choice awards. When not writing, Clifford and her partner run the Fun Institute in Santa Cruz, California, a school of improv and solo performance where they teach the art of collective pretending.

Contact Clifford at www.cliffordhenderson.net. She is always delighted to hear from readers.

Books Available from Bold Strokes Books

Let the Lover Be by Sheree Greer. Kiana Lewis, a functional alcoholic on the verge of destruction, finally faces the demons of her past while finding love and earning redemption in New Orleans. (978-1-62639-077-5)

Blindsided by Karis Walsh. Blindsided by love, guide dog trainer Lenae McIntyre and media personality Cara Bradley learn to trust what they see with their hearts. (978-1-62639-078-2)

About Face by VK Powell. Forensic artist Macy Sheridan and Detective Leigh Monroe work on a case that has troubled them both for years, but they're hampered by the past and their unlikely yet undeniable attraction. (978-1-62639-079-9)

Blackstone by Shea Godfrey. For Darry and Jessa, their chance at a life of freedom is stolen by the arrival of war and an ancient prophecy that just might destroy their love. (978-1-62639-080-5)

Out of This World by Maggie Morton. Iris decided to cross an ocean to get over her ex. But instead, she ends up traveling much farther, all the way to another world. Once there, only a mysterious, sexy, and magical woman can help her return home. (978-1-62639-083-6)

Kiss The Girl by Melissa Brayden. Sleeping with the enemy has never been so complicated. Brooklyn Campbell and Jessica Lennox face off in love and advertising in fast-paced New York City. (978-1-62639-071-3)

Taking Fire: A First Responders Novel by Radclyffe. Hunted by extremists and under siege by nature's most virulent weapons, Navy medic Max de Milles and Red Cross worker Rachel Winslow join forces to survive and discover something far more lasting. (978-1-62639-072-0)

First Tango in Paris by Shelley Thrasher. When French law student Eva Laroche meets American call girl Brigitte Green in 1970s Paris, they have no idea how their pasts and futures will intersect. (978-1-62639-073-7)

The War Within by Yolanda Wallace. Army nurse Meredith Moser went to Vietnam in 1967 looking to help those in need; she didn't expect to meet the love of her life along the way. (978-1-62639-074-4)

Escapades by MJ Williamz. Two women, afraid to love again, must overcome their fears to find the happiness that awaits them. (978-1-62639-182-6)

Desire at Dawn by Fiona Zedde. For Kylie, love had always come armed with sharp teeth and claws. But with the human, Olivia, she bares her vampire heart for the very first time, sharing passion, lust, and a tenderness she'd never dared dream of before. (978-1-62639-064-5)

Visions by Larkin Rose. Sometimes the mysteries of love reveal themselves when you least expect it. Other times they hide behind a black satin mask. Can Paige unveil her masked stranger this time? (978-1-62639-065-2)

All In by Nell Stark. Internet poker champion Annie Navarro loses everything when the Feds shut down online gambling, and she turns to experienced casino host Vesper Blake for advice—but can Nova convince Vesper to take a gamble on romance? (978-1-62639-066-9)

Vermilion Justice by Sheri Lewis Wohl. What's a vampire to do when Dracula is no longer just a character in a novel? (978-1-62639-067-6)

Switchblade by Carsen Taite. Lines were meant to be crossed. Third in the Luca Bennett Bounty Hunter Series. (978-1-62639-058-4)

Nightingale by Andrea Bramhall. Culture, faith, and duty conspire to tear two young lovers apart, yet fate seems to have different plans for them both. (978-1-62639-059-1)

No Boundaries by Donna K. Ford. A chance meeting and a nightmare from the past threaten more than Andi Massey's solitude as she and Gwen Palmer struggle to understand the complexity of love without boundaries. (978-1-62639-060-7)

Timeless by Rachel Spangler. When Stevie Geller returns to her hometown, will she do things differently the second time around or will she be in such a hurry to leave her past that she misses out on a better future? (978-1-62639-050-8)

Second to None by L.T. Marie. Can a physical therapist and a custom motorcycle designer conquer their pasts and build a future with one another? (978-1-62639-051-5)

Seneca Falls by Jesse Thoma. Together, two women discover love truly can conquer all evil. (978-1-62639-052-2)

A Kingdom Lost by Barbara Ann Wright. Without knowing each other's fates, Princess Katya and her consort Starbride seek to reclaim their kingdom from the magic-wielding madman who seized the throne and is murdering their people. (978-1-62639-053-9)

Season of the Wolf by Robin Summers. Two women running from their pasts are thrust together by an unimaginable evil. Can they overcome the horrors that haunt them in time to save each other? (978-1-62639-043-0)

The Heat of Angels by Lisa Girolami. Fires burn in more than one place in Los Angeles. (978-1-62639-042-3)

Desperate Measures by P. J. Trebelhorn. Homicide detective Kay Griffith and contractor Brenda Jansen meet amidst turmoil neither of them is aware of until murder suspect Tommy Rayne makes his move to exact revenge on Kay. (978-1-62639-044-7)

The Magic Hunt by L.L. Raand. With her Pack being hunted by human extremists and beset by enemies masquerading as friends, can Sylvan protect them and her mate, or will she succumb to the feral rage that threatens to turn her rogue, destroying them all? A Midnight Hunters novel. (978-1-62639-045-4)

Wingspan by Karis Walsh. Wildlife biologist Bailey Chase is content to live at the wild bird sanctuary she has created on Washington's Olympic Peninsula until she is lured beyond the safety of isolation by architect Kendall Pearson. (978-1-60282-983-1)

Windigo Thrall by Cate Culpepper. Six women trapped in a mountain cabin by a blizzard, stalked by an ancient cannibal demon bent on stealing their sanity—and their lives. (978-1-60282-950-3)

The Blush Factor by Gun Brooke. Ice-cold business tycoon Eleanor Ashcroft only cares about the three Ps—Power, Profit, and Prosperity—until young Addison Garr makes her doubt both that and the state of her frostbitten heart. (978-1-60282-985-5)

Slash and Burn by Valerie Bronwen. The murder of a roundly despised author at an LGBT writers' conference in New Orleans turns Winter Lovelace's relaxing weekend hobnobbing with her peers into a nightmare of suspense—especially when her ex turns up. (978-1-60282-986-2)

The Quickening: A Sisters of Spirits Novel by Yvonne Heidt. Ghosts, visions, and demons are all in a day's work for Tiffany. But when Kat asks for help on a serial killer case, life takes on another dimension altogether. (978-1-60282-975-6)

Smoke and Fire by Julie Cannon. Oil and water, passion and desire, a combustible combination. Can two women fight the fire that draws them together and threatens to keep them apart? (978-1-60282-977-0)

Love and Devotion by Jove Belle. KC Hall trips her way through life, stumbling into an affair with a married bombshell twice her age. Thankfully, her best friend, Emma Reynolds, is there to show her the true meaning of Love and Devotion. (978-1-60282-965-7)

The Shoal of Time by J.M. Redmann. It sounded too easy. Micky Knight is reluctant to take the case because the easy ones often turn into the hard ones, and the hard ones turn into the dangerous ones. In this one, easy turns hard without warning. (978-1-60282-967-1)